Tempted by Her Wolves
Hungry for Her Wolves, Book Four
A Reverse-Harem Paranormal Romance
Tara West

Used to her independence, Dr. Eilea Johnson represses her sexual desires and avoids the four wolf shifters claiming she's their mate. When a virus sweeps through the Alaska reservation, threatening to wipe out the entire shifter population, Eilea is their last hope for survival. As she races against time to find a cure, a demonic spirit threatening her life may force her to give in to the temptation she's been resisting but secretly craving.

1

Dedications

TO THEO, GOD OF GRAMMAR, blessed by the Ancients, and tasked to save my ass with your red pen of shame. Thank you, thank you, thank you.

To Ginelle, thanks for always coming through with your solid feedback.

To Sheri, I appreciate your eye, especially catching those name oopsies.

Laura, your medical advice prevented me from looking like a complete idiot. Thank you!

Chapter One

EILEA READ HER LETTER of resignation for at least the tenth time. Swallowing a lump of sorrow, she finally folded and sealed it, addressing it to her uncle. Writing that letter had been one of the hardest things she'd ever done, but the Amaroki tribe didn't need a medical doctor when they had Amara Thunderfoot. Eilea had seen the shifter cure her uncle's stage-four cancer simply by laying hands on him. What use did the Amaroki have for a human doctor when one of their own could cure the sick in minutes?

Since opening her clinic over a year ago, she'd had fewer than a dozen patients, all feds who'd worked for her uncle. She also vaccinated and did physicals for the shifters used as trackers, a secret elite team of Army soldiers able to spy in wolf form. Other than the trackers, who were always healthy, none of the reservation shifters had set foot in her clinic asking for medical care. Before she came along, the trackers were seen at the military hospital, so they certainly didn't need her.

She didn't know why she'd stayed around this long, though somewhere deep in the recesses of her soul, she suspected it was because she'd been waiting on the four Romanian shifter brothers, who'd once tried to claim her as their mate. It had been over a year since she'd seen them. She wondered if they'd ever return to Alaska. Perhaps they were still mourning the loss of their first mate. Not that it mattered to her. She wasn't going to mate with them, no matter how hot and bothered they made her.

She shoved the letter in her pocket when she heard the clinic door open. Most likely Uncle Joe was back to check on her. Over the past few weeks, his visits had become more frequent, as if he suspected she wasn't going to renew her contract. Much to her surprise, it was the tribal chieftain, Tor Thunderfoot, along with his retired tracker brother, Van, and their pretty mate, Mihaela. Behind them was their twenty-year-old daughter, Tatiana, who had her mother's pert nose and slender frame, and her Native fathers' dark complexion and black hair.

It had taken Eilea a long time to get accustomed to Tor and other alpha shifters, like his sons Drasko and Hakon. Not only could they turn into wolves, they could also transform into ten-foot-tall, hulking ape-like beasts, able to uproot trees from the ground and flip over trucks. Though Tor had never been unkind to Eilea, he hadn't been particularly friendly either. He always had such an imposing demeanor, reminding Eilea of the monster lurking inside him.

As always, Tatiana had this look, like a shadow cast a gloom over her soul.

Eilea stood and walked around her desk. "Chieftain Thunderfoot, Van, Mihaela, Tatiana... what an unexpected surprise."

Mihaela lunged forward and grabbed Eilea's hand. "We didn't know where else to turn," she said, her Romanian accent thicker than normal.

She squeezed Mihaela's hand. "Would you like to come into my office?"

Tor and Van made noises that sounded like bears waking from hibernation.

Mihaela said to them with a scowl, "I think it's best if you wait in the lobby."

"She's our daughter, too," Tor grumbled.

When Mihaela's expression darkened, he and Van looked away, all knees and elbows when they folded themselves into the hard chairs lining the wall. Tor was well over six feet tall, and his brother wasn't much shorter, making the chairs look like kid furniture.

"Come on Tatiana," Mihaela said, latching onto her daughter's elbow and dragging her to the exam room at the end of the hall.

Eilea followed, feeling less like the doctor in charge, and shut the door behind her. Tatiana sat on the exam table, staring at her feet. Mihaela hovered beside her like a mother hen watching over an egg.

Maybe she should've pulled her file on Tatiana Thunderfoot. She had inherited medical records for all the shifters. What kind of doctor was she, going into an exam room empty-handed?

"How can I help you?" She hoped the she-wolves didn't notice how nervous she was, but they were part animal and probably smelled her fear.

"She's been like this over a year, doctor." Mihaela glanced at her daughter. "Fourteen months." Her voice cracked like splintered glass. "She refuses to open up to anyone, even her mates. I'm afraid she'll never complete the bond with them."

"You've said enough, Mom." Tatiana groaned.

Mihaela's eyes watered. "I-I'm just worried about you, *fiică*."

"Mom," Tatiana pleaded, "can you wait in the lobby?"

Mihaela flinched, as if she'd been splashed with a bucket of cold water. "But I'm your *mamă*."

Tatiana pulled back her shoulders, remarkably cool and calm. "Please go."

"Fine," Mihaela spat, storming out of the room with all the finesse of a bull trampling a field of daisies.

Eilea looked from Mihaela's retreating backside to Tatiana, who instantly deflated. Eilea rolled her stool over to Tatiana, dropping her voice to a soothing whisper. "What's going on, Tatiana?"

Eilea's breath hitched when she saw the look of despair in the younger woman's eyes. She knew the girl had been dealing with depression, and she inwardly chided herself for not checking on her. It was no secret Tatiana blamed herself for the death of her future mother-in-law, Katarina Lupescu. From what Eilea had heard, it hadn't been her fault. Katarina had chosen to run off after she and Tatiana had a fight, even though the tribe was on lockdown after a corrupt federal agent started hunting them.

"Do you have anything that will help me sleep?" Tatiana asked.

"You're not sleeping enough?" Eilea chewed on the end of her pencil, warily eyeing the girl. Something told her she'd have a difficult time getting an honest answer.

Tatiana vehemently shook her head. "I want to sleep more."

The warning sirens in Eilea's head went off when Tatiana averted her eyes. She was hiding something, and Eilea suspected the sleeping pills masked a more serious problem. Was the girl suicidal? Did she plan on misusing the prescription? Eilea didn't recall any mention of suicidal shifters when reading their history, except in cases where the rest of the pack had perished.

"How long are you sleeping at night?"

Tatiana frowned. "Not enough."

She leaned into the girl, not surprised when she scooted back. "Is it sleeping meds you need or depression medicine?"

Tatiana wrapped her arms around herself. "Something to knock me out cold so I don't have nightmares."

Awww, fuck. This kid was definitely messed up. "What kind of nightmares are you having?"

"I can't talk about them." She hugged herself tighter. "I just need the medication."

"Please tell me what's wrong." Eilea took a chance and rested a hand on her arm, pleased when she didn't pull away. "Let me help you."

"Nobody can help me."

Eilea summoned the courage to find the right words. "Katarina's death wasn't your fault."

"Yes it was!" Tatiana said, burying her face in her hands, "and now I'm paying for it."

Paying for it? Had Tatiana's mates rejected her because of their mother's death? She didn't understand the intricacies of wolf culture. She wanted to help the girl, but this was beyond her expertise. "What do you mean?"

Tatiana dropped her hands, focusing on something in the corner and reminding Eilea of an alley cat preparing to lash out.

"I've said enough," she snapped. "Are you going to give me the medication or not?"

Eilea stood, folding her arms, doing her best to sound stern but not threatening. "I need more from you before I can give you drugs."

Tatiana turned away, but not before Eilea saw the tears in her eyes. "I can't give you more."

Eilea did her best to ignore her constricting heart. Something was seriously wrong with the girl, something that Eilea feared required the intervention of someone more qualified. "Let me examine you."

Tatiana shrugged. "Okay."

Eilea took Tatiana's vitals. None of the readings were good. "Your blood pressure is really high." She wrote down the readings on a notepad, cursing herself again for not grabbing Tatiana's chart. "Are you drinking lots of caffeine?"

"No," Tatiana huffed. "I already told you I'm not sleeping."

Tatiana needed serious help. "I can give you something for anxiety, something to help calm you down."

Tatiana clasped her hands together. "Will it help me sleep?"

"Probably." She reached into the medicine chest and pulled out a small box, handing it to Tatiana. "Here's a sample to get you through until you can fill your prescription in town."

Tatiana turned over the box. "Thank you."

"I'm also going to recommend you go into psychiatric care." She wasn't sure a shrink could help a shifter with anxiety and depression but couldn't think of a better option.

Tatiana's features hardened. "You're going to send me to a shrink in Fairbanks, so they can lock me up when I tell them I'm a shifter?"

Releasing a slow, shaky breath, Eilea did her best to keep her cool. "You have to speak to someone."

"I can speak to you."

Yet Tatiana had been tight-lipped since walking into the clinic. Besides, Eilea wasn't a licensed therapist. She'd graduated top of her surgical residency and excelled in medical school before that. She'd had several successful years as a surgeon in one of the nation's most prestigious hospitals. But at this moment, she felt like a fraud—an imposter with a medical degree. She was totally out of her element and had no idea what to do for a depressed and anxious she-wolf.

"Actually." She bit her bottom lip. "I was about to turn in my resignation."

"What?" Tatiana jumped from the table and latched onto Eilea's arm, a crazed look in her eyes as they shifted from dark brown to a brilliant gold. "Why?"

Eilea ran a shaky hand through her hair, trying not to be unnerved by Tatiana's changing facial features. She was a shifter, after all. "Other than tracker vaccinations, you're my only Amaroki patient since I started here. The Amaroki don't need me."

Tatiana tightened her hold on Eilea. "I need you."

Eilea worked free of Tatiana's grip. "I'm not a psychiatrist. You need someone more qualified to handle this."

"You're the only person I can talk to. Please don't turn in your resignation yet," Tatiana pleaded. "Not until I get better."

Something about the ring of desperation in Tatiana's voice made Eilea want to cave. She couldn't walk away from a patient who needed her. If something happened to Tatiana after Eilea left, she'd never forgive herself. "All right. I'll wait."

Tatiana blew out a long breath. "Thank you."

Eilea hitched a brow. "If you expect me to stay, the least you can do is meet me halfway. Tell me what's wrong. Does it stem from guilt over Katarina's death?"

Tatiana's eyes widened as her gaze darted to the corner of the room again. "Don't talk about her in my presence."

"Who?" Eilea felt compelled to look over her shoulder. "Kat—"

Tatiana jumped up, wildly waving her arms. "Don't say her name!"

Stunned, Eilea stumbled back. "Why?"

Tatiana shrunk into herself like a flower wilting under a heat lamp. "Because she's watching."

That caught Eilea by surprise. Had Tatiana's depression been caused by an imagined ghost? "She's dead."

Tatiana gave her a look that made her goose flesh rise. "I know."

TATIANA ATE IN SILENCE, trying to gauge her alpha father's mood. He'd refused to talk about the prescription in the car, but she needed to fill it before the sample ran out. She loved her family and the Amaroki, but she loathed the patriarchal structure of their culture. She'd read enough human books, and seen enough of their movies, to know human women had far more freedom. How she envied Dr. Johnson, who got to live alone in a house behind the clinic, working independently as a doctor and not expected to meet a baby quota. Dr. Johnson could probably get a prescription whenever she wanted. There were times when Tatiana wished she'd been born human. How could she be expected to mate with the sons of the woman whose spirit had made her life a living nightmare? At this point in her miserable life, she had two options: end her life and break her family's hearts or numb her misery with drugs. If Father wouldn't let her have the drugs, she didn't know how much longer she could stand this bleak existence.

Summoning the courage to face down her father, she cleared her throat, pleased when calmness washed over her. Could that one sample pill be working already? "Father, when can we get my prescription filled?"

Tor glared across the table at her and took a drink of his longneck beer. He'd been drinking more lately, and she suspected it had to do with her.

"Wolves don't take drugs," he declared. "I will take you to Amara tomorrow."

Her anxiety returned, and she clenched her fork in white-knuckled fingers. "I've already seen Amara. She can't fix me."

"Of course she can," he said dismissively.

Her blood boiled and resentment welled in her chest. "Not unless she wants to follow me everywhere."

"I told Johnson it was a bad idea, bringing his niece here." He shook his head. "Human doctors don't understand us."

She glanced to her other fathers and mother for support, but they looked away. A blade of betrayal pierced her heart. "Eilea understands me. I've already taken one pill, and it feels like it's working."

Tor pounded the table so hard, she cringed and her mother gasped.

"Just because the Lupescus caught her scent, that doesn't mean she understands us!" he roared. "Those pills are going in the garbage, and you're not getting that prescription."

She froze. Forget the prescription. She had bigger problems. Her father hadn't spoken about the Lupescus scenting the doctor since the death of their first mate, Katarina. Tatiana had hoped everyone had forgotten.

She refused to turn around at the low wail behind her that reminded her of a dying animal. Her parents couldn't hear Katarina's cries. The spirit had only presented herself to Tatiana. The ghoul had been tormenting her since her death over a year ago.

When a glass shattered, Tor swore and Tatiana's mother screamed.

Her gamma father, Arvid, jumped from his seat. "I'll clean it up."

She was afraid to turn around and see the unholy look in Katarina's eyes. A chill swept over her, and her teeth chattered. Shivering, she stood, pushing back her chair.

Tor arched a brow. "Where are you going? Dinner isn't over."

"I'm not hungry," she lied. Truthfully, she was famished, but she was too nauseous and frightened to eat.

Without waiting for his response, she ran, hurrying upstairs as if the hounds of hell were at her heels. Technically one of them was. For over a year she'd kept the secret that Katarina's mates had scented another, a human. She didn't fear what Katarina would do to her, for she'd already made her life a living hell. There wasn't much more she could do, short of murdering her and her family. She feared what the ghost would do to Dr. Johnson. How would the human defend herself against an evil, vindictive ghost-shifter, whose long claws still had the ability to harm? Tatiana should know, as she bore several deep lacerations from Katarina's numerous tantrums.

She hugged herself tightly as the spirit barged through her door, baring sharp fangs. She whipped Tatiana's hair and clothes, and spun in violent circles around the room. Great Goddess, save Dr. Johnson from this ghost's vengeance.

EILEA BUTTERED HER cornbread. She sat across the table from her uncle, who usually preferred to eat in silence. When she'd first started eating nightly meals with him, she'd been offended by his reticence, but she'd grown accustomed to his introverted personality. Besides, he sure knew how to cook, which made up for his lack of conversation. But tonight he'd have to make an exception. She'd been upset since Tatiana's visit. Had the girl implied a ghost was following her? Eilea hoped she'd misunderstood. Ghosts weren't real. Then again, a few years ago Eilea had thought shifters and magical healers weren't real either.

Setting her cornbread and knife down, she said, "Uncle, what do you know about Amaroki afterlife?"

He shrugged, cutting into his pulled pork. "A little."

"Could you tell me?"

He spooned barbeque sauce onto his plate and gave her a long look. "After an Amaroki dies, they cover the body in henna tattoos and then burn it, releasing the soul into the heavens. They go to their version of heaven, a place called *Valhol*."

That was the most he'd said at the dinner table in a long while. "What if the soul doesn't go to heaven?"

He set his fork down, folding his hands. "Like a tornaq?"

She blinked hard. "A what?"

"A spirit that doesn't go to heaven."

Shit. So ghosts were a real thing to the Amaroki. Though it was selfish of her, she'd been hoping Tatiana was suffering from delusions, something that could be treated with medications and therapy. "What happens to the tornaq?"

"It is my understanding that they stay on earth and haunt people. Why do you ask?"

She clutched the table, trying to quell her shaking limbs. "I can't discuss it. Patient confidentiality."

He lifted a graying brow. "You had an Amaroki patient today?"

She straightened. "I did."

"Excellent. Maybe now more will come." He dropped his gaze to his plate and shoveled food in his mouth, signaling their conversation was over.

Though she feared she wouldn't like his answers, she had many more questions.

For starters, did tornaqs simply haunt or could they inflict physical harm? If so, what were the chances Katarina Lupescu's ghost would find out her mates had scented Eilea and come after her next?

"WHAT ARE YOU DOING?" Tatiana hollered at the ghoul, her pale, distorted features passing in a blur as she flung clothes in the air, shredding them in the process. "Stop that!"

But the ghost ignored her pleas, knocking over lamps, flinging glass frames against the wall, and upturning dressers. She fell to her knees with a wail, burying her face in her hands while a whirlwind of demonic energy circled around her.

She shot up when the smell of smoke tickled her nose, shrieking when she saw her clothes on fire in the corner. She tried to stomp it out while Katarina let out a maniacal laugh. She howled when the flames burned her feet and singed her jeans before racing up the wall.

When a roar sounded outside, Katarina disappeared in a flash of light. A giant fist smashed through Tatiana's door, and it splintered open. Tor stuck his massive, furry head inside, then busted the rest of it apart, making room for Van and Skoll as they raced inside with fire extinguishers, dousing the flames.

The wind rushed from her lungs when Tor slammed her to the ground, smothering her with his big, hairy body and rolling her. It took her a moment to realize he was putting out the fire on her legs. She hadn't even realized her pants were flame until the blistering pain set in.

She gagged and coughed on fumes and the thick, acrid taste of the chemicals from the fire extinguisher. Tor scooped her into his arms and carried her down the stairs.

He laid her on the bearskin rug before clomping back up the stairs. Too stunned to speak, she winced when her mother and Arvid peeled off her jeans.

She gaped at the bloody blisters already forming on her shins. What the fuck? She'd been badly burned.

"Call Amara," her mother whispered, wiping watery eyes with the back of her hand.

Arvid nodded and went to the kitchen phone.

Her fathers tramped around upstairs, then threw piles of charred clothes over the railing and onto the floor below.

She swallowed a sob. All of her beautiful clothes were ruined. A flash of light swirled in the rafters overhead, followed by the echo of Katarina's laughter as she flew through the back window, out into the night air. No doubt she'd be back soon. She never left Tatiana alone for long.

"Why are you doing this to us?" her mother asked, burying her face in her hands.

They thought she'd started the fire? She wanted so badly to tell her mother the truth, but Katarina had threatened to kill her family if she told them about her. She opened her mouth to speak, say something— anything—to make her mother understand, but all that came out was a gasp. The ghoul had returned, hovering over Tatiana's mother, eyes glowing fiery red, like the flames of hell were shining through her soul.

Chapter Two

AMARA STIFLED A YAWN as Drasko helped her out of the truck. Even though she was only a few weeks pregnant with Luc's child, her mates were treating her like a fragile flower. She loved their attention, but the way they babied her sometimes grated on her nerves. Case in point, she'd had to argue with Drasko this morning to get him to bring her to the Strongpaw pack before sunrise. The Strongpaw alpha had called at six in the morning, disoriented, scared, and worried over his sick brother, Albert. Amara had wanted to go to them right away, but her mates insisted she eat breakfast and nurse Alexi first.

The Strongpaws had a small log house nestled on the side of a hill overlooking a quaint stream and valley. From what she remembered, they were a smaller pack, only three brothers, who'd just returned from Africa with their new bride. A man Amara assumed to be the alpha waited for them on the porch, looking as haggard as if he hadn't slept in a week. The Strongpaws were supposedly younger than Amara's mates, but the lines framing the alpha's dark eyes and drawn mouth made him look to be in his mid-thirties. Only the dark Mohawk, with blue tips that descended into a long braid down his back, hinted at his youth.

"Good morning, Loki," Drasko said, holding tightly to Amara's hand and leading her up the stairs.

Loki Strongpaw made an odd grunting sound. "Good morning, Hakon."

Drasko blinked, giving Loki a quizzical look. "I'm Drasko. You should know that."

"Sorry." Loki shook his head like he was trying to drain water from his ears. "I'm still disoriented." He opened the rusty screen door and ushered them inside. "Thank you for coming so early."

"We were asleep when you called," Drasko grumbled. "Our mate is pregnant and nursing."

She squeezed his hand, giving him a warning look. Why must he be so grumpy?

"Sorry," Loki said, gesturing to a man hunched on an old velvet sofa. "We would've come to you, but I'm not fit to drive yet."

"No worries. We're here now." Drasko's nostrils flared as he sniffed the air. "Why can't you drive? You been drinking?"

"No." Loki banged his ear. "Still confused."

She shared a quizzical look with Drasko. *What's wrong with him?*

Drasko shrugged. *Probably smoked too much pot.*

She scented the air, but there was no trace of the skunky smoke smell.

They followed Loki into the small but cozy living room lined with fur rugs. The room was lit only with a few kerosene lamps and a fire in the stone hearth. The newest piece of technology was a pellet stove in one corner, next to an old-fashioned water pump. She realized they were one of the few packs who still lived off the land and didn't use electricity. Yikes. She'd go nuts.

She turned her attention to the man on the sofa, clutching a bucket between his legs. Thick furs were draped over him. He dry-heaved into a bucket while a pretty woman with skin glowing like polished onyx patted his back.

"This is our mate, Nakomi," Loki said. "Nakomi, meet Drasko and his mate, Amara."

She greeted them with all the regality of a queen. "Nice to meet you," she said in a thick accent.

"Nakomi," Drasko asked, thoughtfully rubbing his chin. "You from an African tribe?"

"I am." She sat up straighter. "Ethiopia."

"We've only been mated a month. We would've brought her to the tribal meeting, except we missed it." Loki's tanned cheeks flushed crimson. "We lost track of time."

"It's okay." Drasko chuckled. "I remember our honeymoon phase."

Amara nudged him in the ribs with a wink. "I thought we were still honeymooning."

He scratched the back of his head, flashing a knowing grin. "Are we?"

She rolled her eyes. The reason they were so exhausted this morning was because Drasko and his brothers had pounded her brains out the night before. She was tired, but it had been worth it.

When Albert's dry heaves became more substantial, Drasko swore and looked away. Used to dealing with sick patients, Amara rolled up her sleeves and sat beside him, waiting for him to finish. He finally lay back with a groan, spittle dripping down his smooth chin.

"Albert, let's have a look at you."

She felt his head, which was feverish. His face and neck were covered in little red welts that looked like the human chickenpox. Her breath caught when she pushed up his sleeve and looked at his arm. She recognized those welts.

"Omigod!" She turned to Drasko with wide-eyed alarm. Drasko leaned over Albert, squinting in the low light. "Looks like demon burn."

"It itches like hell." Albert moaned, his head lolling to the other side while he scratched scabs off the pustules, smearing bloody streaks down his arms.

Amara cringed. "Yeah, I remember." She waited for him to stop scratching before placing her hands on him.

"Amara and I both had demon burn from the Hoia Baciu Forest a few years ago. Did you just return from Romania?" Drasko asked Loki.

"No." Loki frowned at his brother. "We were hunting locally when he got sick."

Amara shot up like a bolt of lightning had zinged through her. "I don't understand. There are no haunted forests here."

Loki shrugged, then stumbled and fell against an oak table.

Drasko helped him sit in a stuffed chair beside the fire. "Are you okay?"

"No." He dragged a hand down his face. "We've been disoriented since the hunt."

The door slammed open and what appeared to be a smaller version of Albert crossed the threshold, a bundle of firewood in his arms. "Here's the wood," he said, slurring like a drunk. He dropped the wood on the floor with a *thud* before collapsing into a chair beside Loki.

Amara and Drasko exchanged concerned looks.

Ice cold fear pricked the back of her neck. What the hell was going on?

Hurry, so we can get out of here, Drasko said. *We need to alert my fathers.*

Something strange was going on with the Strongpaws, and the tribal chieftains needed to be made aware.

She laid her hands on Albert's shoulders and channeled her healing magic. Over the past few years, the magic had grown stronger. After she cured Drasko of a zombie virus, and Agent Johnson of stage-four cancer, her healing strength poured through her fingers like they were busted firehoses. There was nothing she couldn't heal. She closed her eyes tight, feeling the magic pulse through her, stunned when her fingers started to ache. She released Albert with a shudder and looked at her swollen hands.

What the hell? That's never happened before.

Her fingers throbbed as if they were water balloons ready to burst. Had the magic pooled in her fingers instead of pouring into Albert? She gazed at Albert's skin with alarm. The hives were still there.

Nakomi's eyes bulged when she looked at Amara's fingers. Then she mumbled something in a foreign language.

"Drasko?" Amara breathed, resting her heavy, trembling hands on her knees.

"What is it?" He stood over her, a sharp edge to his voice.

She looked at her throbbing hands once more, her eyes welling with tears at the pulsing pain. "I can't heal him."

"What do you mean?" he snapped, his harsh tone slicing through her like a blade.

"I mean, my magic isn't working on him." She held up her hands.

Drasko's mouth fell open. "That's impossible."

A tear slipped down her cheek. "The magic pains me. It won't leave my fingers."

"What in Ancient's name?"

Nakomi shut her eyes, rocking back and forth, hugging herself. Her indecipherable chants grew louder.

"What do we do?" Amara asked Drasko in a panic.

"Call Raz."

Amara silently nodded. Raz Spiritcaller was the tribe medicine woman and an elder with knowledge about Amaroki history. If anyone could explain what was going on, she could.

"We've already tried the Spiritcallers," Loki said, rubbing his temples. "Nobody answered."

Drasko's expression hardened, and he latched onto Amara's elbow, pulling her to his side. "Go to the clinic."

Nakomi's eyes flew open. "The human doctor?"

Amara clutched her throat. She wasn't sure, but she thought she saw sparks of red in Nakomi's eyes. She had to have imagined it. Shifters didn't have red eyes. When they changed forms, their irises turned bright silver, gold, or orange.

"Yes." She pressed into Drasko. "Eilea's a good doctor."

Nakomi turned up her nose, shoulders stiffening. "I'd rather take care of him myself."

"He's getting worse." Loki shot to his feet, then groaned and clutched the chair. "We don't have a choice."

"I'm so sorry," Amara couldn't fight the note of panic that had slipped into her voice. "I don't understand what's wrong with me. This has never happened."

Drasko wrapped a possessive arm around her waist. *We should go. You shouldn't be exposed to this. Think of the baby.*

Amara clenched her teeth when she realized she had put not only her health in danger, but her baby's health as well. What if it was contagious? She had touched Albert. What if she brought it back to her family? Her babies?

Drasko tugged her to the door. "I'm really sorry. We have to go now."

Nakomi shot to her feet, hands clenched into fists, red flecks flashing in her eyes again. "You can't just leave him."

Amara, we need to go. Drasko's urgent command was a low rumble in her skull. *Now.*

"I wish we could've done more for you, Strongpaws," she said as she backed out the door. "We will pray for you."

Prayers might not be enough. Drasko dragged her toward the truck.

She stood helplessly by the passenger door. "Can you open the door and buckle me in?" she asked, holding up her fingers.

He wordlessly helped her in, then held her hand to the overhead light.

"I-I think my magic is trapped." She cried when she saw her fingers were even more swollen.

She shrank back when Drasko took out his pocket knife. Was he going to cut her fingers open? But he sliced open his arm with a hiss, blood streaming down to his hand.

Instinctively, she latched onto his arm with both hands, her healing warmth pulsing through her fingers and instantly sealing the wound. She let out a sigh of relief when the throbbing subsided. She turned over her hands, pleased that her fingers had shrunk considerably. She looked up at Drasko. "Why can I heal you but not Albert?"

"I-I don't know." Drasko's face hardened. "But if this virus spreads, we're all fucked."

CHECKING HER REFLECTION in the mirror, Eilea frowned at the fine lines under her eyes. She'd always prided herself on her smooth, mahogany skin. Her grandmother used to say she had the complexion of a doll, though most of the dolls she had growing up were fair-skinned. She did have one dark-skinned handmade doll that looked like her, with large, mocha eyes, high cheekbones, and full lips. Her grandmother had knitted a doctor's lab coat for it, telling Eilea she could be anything she set out to be. Eilea had taken her grandmother's words to heart and completed medical school at the top of her class. Dabbing moisturizer under her eyes, she wondered what the Lupescus would think of her wrinkles. Then she chided herself for caring. She wasn't mating with the tall blond shifters, so it didn't matter.

She emerged from the modest, two-bedroom home she'd shared with Uncle Joe the past year, pulling her jacket tightly around her shoulders and breathing in the frigid air. It was cold enough that Eilea's breath clouded her vision, and it was only fall. Winter was coming, which meant longer nights, short, dreary days, and heavier clothes. She admired the Amaroki and her uncle for braving such an icy, dark climate year after year. Alaskan winters weren't for her, though. As soon as she saw Tatiana had decent care, she would give Uncle Joe her notice.

She climbed the knoll, grass crunching under her boots, and rounded the corner to her clinic, surprised to see an unfamiliar old Army Jeep parked in the gravel drive. Leaning against the Jeep was a thin, dark-skinned woman with large, mocha eyes, full lips, and a neck that stretched for miles. She wore a thick, multi-colored shawl over a long bright dress, reminding her of the beautiful women she'd met during the year she'd worked for a charity hospital in Africa. Though she knew shifters came in many colors, there weren't many African-born among the Alaskan tribe. When Eilea smiled at the woman, she was taken aback when her smile was returned with a scowl. Perhaps the scowl wasn't meant for her. Maybe the woman was upset about the sick man who was bent over beside her, clutching his knees and looking like he was about to retch. Two men hovered nearby, patting his back and giving Eilea helpless looks. Alarm bells went off in Eilea's head at the distinctive white pustules on the sick man's neck and face. Though he wore long sleeves, she suspected the rest of his body was covered in blisters as well.

"Hello. May I help you?" Eilea cautiously approached them, having learned from Uncle Joe that females could sometimes get possessive when other women came near their mates.

The woman gave Eilea an assessing look. "You the doctor?" she said in a thick accent similar to what she'd heard from the African villagers she'd encountered. Eilea squared her shoulders. "I am."

The woman puffed up her chest. "I am Nakomi Strongpaw. My mate is sick."

"Wasn't Amara Thunderfoot available?" Eilea was shocked that the shifters would come to see her when Amara could heal him in seconds.

Nakomi's top lip pulled back in a snarl. "You don't want to see him?"

Eilea blinked hard at Nakomi, thinking her hostility was out of fear for her mate. "I assumed you'd rather see Amara."

"We did see her," Nakomi spat, her tone as venomous as a viper's. "She couldn't heal him."

Amara couldn't heal chickenpox? For Eilea was almost positive that's what she was looking at. Odd, because she knew Amara had healed terminal cancer. Chickenpox should've been a simple fix.

Eilea backed up a step, limbs shaking when Nakomi growled at her. "Bring him inside."

She opened the clinic door and turned off the alarm with a trembling hand, mind reeling. What had she done to anger Nakomi? She ushered the Strongpaws to the waiting room, remembering this time to grab their file.

The pack was grouped under one file. All packs were. Forget patient confidentiality among the Amaroki. Actually, forget all rule of law among them. They lived by an entirely different code.

She quickly scanned their history. They were a smaller pack, with only three brothers and one alpha. Their new mate had recently moved to Alaska from Ethiopia. Odd. That's where Eilea had done her charity work in a run-down third-world hospital. She'd chosen Ethiopia after running a DNA test and learning she was 20 percent Ethiopian, and though she'd hoped to bond with her patients, most of them mistrusted her American background. Eilea wondered if she and Nakomi had ever crossed paths before. Maybe Eilea had accidentally offended her, though none of that mattered at the moment. What mattered was healing her sick patient.

According to their chart, none of them had been vaccinated, save for Rene, the tracker. The sick shifter appeared to be the youngest, Albert Strongpaw, barely twenty-years-old with a broad frame and baby face, like most gammas.

Her innards churned. If Amara couldn't heal Albert, Eilea feared she wouldn't be able to either. She tried to quell the rising tide of fear that gripped her. Wolves could smell fear, and she didn't want to give them another reason to worry.

She led them to an exam room, puzzled when the two older brothers wobbled like drunks. Had they been drinking? She asked them to remove Albert's jacket and shirt. She wasn't surprised to see his torso covered with the same pustules. She slipped a thermometer under his tongue, shocked when her fingers brushed his skin. He was burning up. She looked into his eyes, which were glassy and red. His blood pressure was slightly elevated, and his oxygen reading was too low for her liking. Most alarming was his 103° temperature. Albert needed more than what her small clinic could provide. He needed to be hospitalized.

"What's wrong with him?" Nakomi asked, settling a hand on her mate's forehead.

Eilea attempted to sound calm while she measured fever-reducing medicine into a cup. "He has the chickenpox."

"Impossible." Nakomi snorted, and her other mates grunted their agreement. "Amaroki don't get human diseases."

Eilea set down the medicine and turned to them. "What diseases do you get?"

Nakomi gave her another cold look. "None."

Eilea knew as much after reading Amaroki files, but she'd been hoping she'd overlooked something, maybe a simple and easily curable virus. It did not bode well for Albert Strongpaw if chickenpox was new to his species. He wouldn't have any inherited immunity to the disease.

"Well, I'm sorry." Eilea stared down Nakomi. "But I've seen enough cases of chickenpox to know that's what we're dealing with."

When Nakomi growled at her, the alpha laid a hand on her arm, giving her a warning look. He stepped forward, clutching a woolen skullcap in a white-knuckled grip. Eilea recognized his face from the Strongpaw file: Loki, with piercing gray eyes and a thick Mohawk that hung in a long tail down his back.

"What do we do for him, Doctor?" he asked.

"His temperature is too high." She held up the small cup of medicine. "I need to bring it down right away."

His brothers had to hold Albert down as she practically forced the medicine down his throat. He was becoming more listless by the minute.

"Help me get him to a bed." The room across the hall had almost a dozen hospital beds. "I'll hook him to an IV and get him oxygen."

Ignoring Nakomi's grumbling, Eilea moved them into the other room and prepared an IV. Albert didn't flinch when she stuck him with the needle. He appeared to be drifting in and out of consciousness. She hooked him up to oxygen, hoping to see an improvement in his levels. He should be taken to a hospital along with his family, in case they come down with the virus. Without nurses or other staff, she didn't have the facilities to accommodate them all.

Loki sat by his brother's bed, clasping his hand. "Will he die?"

"Not if I can help it," she said as she checked his temperature once more. She frowned at the thermometer. It hadn't budged.

She looked over the other shifters for signs of the virus. None yet, but they were all wearing long sleeves. She'd have to do full physicals.

"I'll need to examine all of you for signs of chickenpox."

Nakomi crossed her arms. "We're fine."

What was wrong with this woman? Eilea refused to let Nakomi intimidate her, even though she knew the shifter had the power to rip out her throat. Hopefully, Nakomi's mates wouldn't let her kill Eilea.

She gave Nakomi a long look before turning to Loki. "I need to check everyone, and if there are no signs, you will need to get vaccinated before it spreads."

Nakomi threw up her hands. "You must be joking."

"Why would I joke about this?"

The smallest of the brothers stood and faced his pack, wobbling slightly before righting himself. "I've already had the vaccine. It's no big deal."

He had to be the tracker, Rene.

"I don't like needles." Nakomi pouted, crossing her arms.

"You'll be fine." Rene took Nakomi's chin in his hand, gently kissing her forehead. "I don't want you getting this."

When Nakomi sighed and leaned into her mate, Eilea was compelled to look away, a twinge of jealousy stabbing her chest. Seeing this little display of affection kindled a flame of hope she'd snuffed out long ago. The Lupescu men had probably forgotten her by now, not that she'd blame them when she'd so adamantly refused them. She was human, and they were wolves. Though they'd claimed to have scented her, they had to be mistaken. Eilea was a strong, independent woman, and from what she'd seen of the Amaroki society, women were mostly baby machines. No thanks. She wouldn't mind the devotion and attention of four virile, sexy-as-fuck wolf-shifters, but none of the attached strings that came with the relationship appealed to her.

She decided to do her best to put the Lupescus out of her mind as she checked each of their vitals. How strange that the brothers seemed off balance but she didn't detect alcohol on their breath. They were slightly warm, but not feverish. Possibly from the exertion of dragging their bother into the clinic. She did a quick reflex check. They were a little slow.

"Have either of you been drinking?" she asked them.

"No, Doctor," Loki answered. "We've been out of sorts ever since our hunt."

Dehydration had to be the cause. "Did you drink enough while hunting?"

Loki scratched the back of her head. "I don't remember stopping to drink at all."

She gave them each two bottles of electrolytes and made them drink while she prepared the shots. Luckily, she had vaccinations on hand for trackers and federal agents.

She started with the alpha, who seemed to be more alert after drinking electrolytes. She then went to Nakomi, dreading having to touch the angry woman.

Her stomach churned when she met Nakomi's cold, hard stare. She bit her lip to keep from smiling when Nakomi hissed as the needle pierced her skin. Though she was supposed to be objective, she felt gratification as she pressed the needle into the shifter.

When she was finished, she called Uncle Joe, explaining that a sick shifter needed transport to the military hospital in Fairbanks. She then checked on her patient, concerned that his temperature had risen another degree. She examined his pustules again. It had to be chickenpox. She'd seen too many cases to count. Again, she wondered why Amara couldn't heal him, and if it was true shifters didn't catch human diseases, what had caused this, and why was he getting worse?

EILEA WAITED OVER AN hour for the ambulance to arrive, yet nobody came. She called her uncle again, concerned when it went to voicemail. She was about to call the military hospital when a familiar truck barreled into the drive. A red-faced Tor jumped out, followed by the second alpha named Skoll. They pulled Tatiana out of the vehicle and half-carried her toward the clinic. Mihaela followed at their heels, begging for them to be gentle with their daughter.

Well, fuck.

Tor surged ahead while Skoll held onto Tatiana.

Eilea's knees weakened when Tor's eyes glowed a dazzling gold.

He burst into the waiting room, slamming the door so hard against the wall, he cracked the glass window. "What was in those pills you gave her?" he boomed.

"Why? What happened?" She stepped away from the phone and cautiously walked around the counter. Her uncle had worked with Tor for years. He always said Tor was a gentle giant and a fair leader. She sure as hell hoped he was right.

"She set fire to her room." Tor threw a glance over his shoulder as Skoll pulled her into the waiting room. "The whole house damn near burned down. We're at our wit's end with this girl. I don't know what to do."

"She needs a fierce beating," Skoll said through his teeth.

"Skoll, no!" Mihaela cried, falling into a chair.

Tatiana hung her head, a lone tear slipping down her cheek.

Something in Eilea's gut told her Tatiana was not to blame for the fire. She repressed a shudder when a sudden chill swept into the room.

She plastered on a pained smile. "Let me speak to Tatiana alone for a moment." She held out her hand to the girl, her heart sinking when Skoll refused to let go. "Please."

Skoll dug his fingers into Tatiana's arm. "Don't you think you've done enough?"

Sheesh! Amaroki men were way too fucking controlling. Eilea gave herself a mental pat on the back for rejecting the four shifters who'd tried to claim her as their mate.

"Skoll," Mihaela said, rising to her feet and clenching her hands. "Let the doctor talk to her." She let out a low growl, her eyes shifting to a blinding white.

Much to Eilea's amazement, Skoll released Tatiana and backed away. Whoa, and here she'd thought Amaroki women were just doormats.

"No more drugs!" Tor said to Eilea as she took Tatiana into an exam room.

She shut the door on the grumbling shifters and heaved a sigh of relief. Holy shitfire, she didn't realize how badly she was shaking until she released the door handle and looked down at her trembling hands. She shoved them in her lab coat, balling them into fists and willing the tremors to subside.

Tatiana had taken a seat on the table, hanging her head like a dog who'd been scolded for messing on the carpet.

"Do you have a tornaq following you?" Eilea asked.

Tatiana's head shot up, her eyes going wide. "Yes."

Another chill swept up Eilea's spine, and she had the feeling she was being watched. Last year she hadn't believed in ghosts, but that was before she met a species of people who could shift into wolves and hulking beasts. Believing in ghosts wasn't as big a stretch as believing in Bigfoot.

She swallowed back another lump of fear, her mouth going as parched as the Texas panhandle during a dry spell. "Is she here now?"

Tatiana nodded.

Eilea's gut churned as the chill along her spine turned more frigid. "Why don't you tell your parents?"

Tatiana turned her gaze to the frayed end of the old sweater draped over her shoulders. Eilea wasn't used to seeing Tatiana dressed in hand-me-down clothes.

"She will kill them if I say anything," she whispered.

"Tatiana, she tried to burn your house down. She will kill them anyway. Tell them."

The cabinets rattled.

"Look out!" Tatiana screamed.

Eilea ducked and a syringe clattered against the wall behind her. She stumbled toward Tatiana, clutching the girl's hands. The metal cabinet doors flew open, and the contents fell to the floor.

"Katarina knows her mates have scented you, Dr. Johnson," Tatiana spoke with a tremor in her voice. "She heard my parents discussing it last night."

Well, shit.

Eilea held Tatiana, digging her fingers into the girl's back when the scattered medical supplies rose from the floor and spun in a vortex around them. Tatiana let out an ear-piercing scream when a needle flew past her head.

The door burst open and a ten-foot hairy beast Eilea assumed to be Tor stood on the threshold, mouth agape. "What is the meaning of this?" Tor yelled with a deeper than normal voice.

Tatiana and Eilea held each other as the vortex spun faster, creating a din and rattling the walls.

"Tatiana, are you doing this?" Tor demanded.

"No!" Tatiana cried, burying her face in Eilea's shoulder.

"It's Katarina's ghost," Eilea said.

Tor let out such a roar, Eilea swore a freight train was driving through her eardrums.

The vortex stopped, vials and syringes clattering to the floor.

Plastic crunched under Tor's big feet as he crossed to Tatiana. "Is she gone?"

Tatiana looked around the room, a haunted look in her eyes. "I don't see her anymore."

He leaned over his daughter, clutching her shoulder. "You had a tornaq haunting you, and you didn't tell us?"

"She said she would kill you if I told." Tatiana's voice cracked.

"It's okay, sweetheart," he said, scooping the girl into his arms and carrying her out of the room.

Eilea hopped over glass and quickly followed. No way was she being left alone.

The scene in the waiting room made her heart clench, and a twinge of jealousy made her flush. Tatiana's parents took turns holding her while wiping her tears.

The thin scar along Eilea's back itched when she recalled waking up in the hospital when she was a child and having no parents to comfort her. She had been the only survivor after her family was killed by a drunk driver. She'd had her grandmother, but she wanted her mother and father. Besides, her grandmother's idea of comfort was usually some hokey spiritual cleansing. After she'd recovered enough to leave the hospital, Eilea had longed for her parents, crying herself to sleep that first night. Then her father's twin had shown up for the funeral, the elusive uncle her parents had named as Eilea's guardian in their will. He looked a lot like her father, but she didn't see the same love and devotion in his dark eyes. He hadn't even offered Eilea a hug before he was gone, saying his demanding job left him no time to raise a child. Her uncle's rejection had hurt her almost as much as losing her parents and big brother.

Another chill swept into the room, reminding Eilea they were not alone. Tatiana hugged her mother. Tor growled and the chill dissipated. So the ghost was afraid of Tor. Too bad he couldn't be with Eilea at all times, because she suspected the angry spirit would be back.

"Now what?" she asked him.

His eyes shone a blinding gold. "Now we banish her to the afterworld."

A low moan from the back reminded her she had a patient.

Skoll's nostrils flared. "Smells like the Strongpaws are here."

"They are. I need to get back to them."

Tor arched a brow. "Which one of them is sick?"

"Albert," Eilea answered.

His brows drew together. "Why didn't they go to Amara?"

"They did. She couldn't heal him."

"Impossible."

Eilea let out a weary sigh. Fatigue from stress had already hit her, and it was still morning. "That's what they told me."

"What's wrong with him?" Tor asked.

Eilea hesitated. She didn't want to violate patient confidentiality, not that it mattered among shifters. They shared everything, starting with their women. Besides, the chieftain needed to know they could be facing an epidemic. "Looks like chickenpox. I think it would be a good idea if the entire tribe was vaccinated."

He crossed his arms, widening his stance. "We don't get infectious diseases."

"He's very sick," Eilea said, "I've asked my uncle to send for an ambulance. His fever isn't coming down despite fluids and medicine. In fact, it's rising."

"Let me see him."

The knots around Eilea's spine tightened. "Have you had your chickenpox vaccination?"

"Of course not." He let out a laugh. "Only the trackers are vaccinated, and only because our government insists."

Eilea worried her bottom lip. "He may be contagious."

"I am his chieftain." His tone left no room for argument. "I'm seeing him." He bent down and kissed the tops of Tatiana and Mihaela's heads. "Wait here," he whispered to them before turning to Skoll. "If the tornaq returns, holler for me."

Eilea followed him on legs that felt weighted down with bricks. Her heartbeat thudded in her ears. She'd known the life of a doctor was stressful, but none of her schooling had prepared her for jealous ghosts and mysterious shifter illnesses.

Tor paid his respects to the Strongpaws and then stood beside Eilea while she checked Albert's temperature. His temp had gone up another degree, to 105. She hoped the ambulance arrived soon. She added more fluid and fever reducer to Albert's IV.

When a chill tickled the nape of her neck, she looked at Tor. Had a breeze just blown into the room, or was her imagination working overtime? She tried to rub warmth into her gooseflesh, but her skin still tingled.

He gave her a quizzical look. "Is something wrong?"

The chill suddenly vanished, and she shook her head. "Probably just my imagination," she mumbled. Even though she'd witnessed the spirit's rage only moments earlier, she had a hard time believing it existed.

Relief washed through her when she spotted Uncle Joe's black truck pulling into the drive. She excused herself and rushed outside, needing to breathe in the cool morning air rather than the stifling, sick fog inside the clinic.

He jumped out of the truck and gave her a dark look before she had a chance to speak. "We need to talk."

"Where's the ambulance? I have a very sick patient."

Her uncle frowned. "There won't be an ambulance."

Eilea's knees weakened, and she had to lean against the side of the truck for support. "Why?"

"We're on lockdown."

"I don't understand."

"The Amaroki aren't supposed to get infectious diseases," he said.

Eilea threw up her hands. "That's what everyone keeps telling me."

"My higher-ups are concerned it may be contagious." He smoothed a hand over his short, gray hair. "They don't want to risk infecting the human population."

Eilea's veins ran cold. What if she couldn't save Albert Strongpaw? Or worse, what if it was contagious and more shifters became sick? Surely the feds had some sort of contingency plan and didn't expect her to tackle this problem alone. "So now what?"

Uncle Joe shrugged. "Now it's up to you to save him."

EILEA SLUMPED INTO her chair and gulped down coffee. Albert's fever hadn't gone up, but it hadn't come down either. The rest of his family still showed no signs of sickness and had refused to leave Albert's side. Skoll had taken Mihaela and Tatiana home, but Tor stayed behind, following Eilea around like a big, protector bear. Though his presence was a bit stifling, she had to admit she appreciated his concern, especially since she no longer felt that frigid chill racing down the back of her neck. Her uncle had stayed for all of five minutes before he'd gone, but he promised to send backup. She sure as hell hoped so. She wouldn't be able to run the clinic by herself if more Amaroki became infected.

She'd just finished her coffee and a leftover stale bagel when an old rusty truck pulled into the drive. A woman, who had to be older than dirt, and four stooped old men got out. One man used a cane and another relied on a walker. She vaguely remembered they were the Spiritcaller elders. Raz had been the tribal medicine woman until Amara showed up, rendering Raz almost as useless as Eilea. She hoped the old people weren't coming down with the virus. Tor went outside to greet them, and one of the Spiritcaller men handed him what appeared to be a sandbag.

Tor hoisted the sack over his shoulder as if it weighed no more than a bag of feathers before following Raz around the building. Weird. Didn't they want to come inside? She didn't have time to find out what they were doing. She quickly used the restroom and then checked Albert. His temperature was the same, and his breathing sounded more ragged. She kept a straight face while taking his vitals, though she suspected she wasn't fooling anyone. His mate sat on the bed, holding his hand and boring holes through Eilea's skull.

Again, Eilea wondered what she'd done to offend Nakomi. Determined not to let the shifter get to her, she turned up her nose, returning her glare. This was her goddamn clinic. Nakomi could take her attitude somewhere else.

She heard the ring of the front door and looked up to see the Spiritcallers filing inside, Tor following them. The old folks were mumbling something and grabbing fistfuls of what appeared to be sand from Tor's bag and tossing it on the floor.

She left Albert and cautiously approached them. "Excuse me? What are you doing?"

They ignored her, continuing their strange incantations and spreading a line of what Eilea now realized was salt all over Eilea's polished floor.

"Hang on," she said, trying to step in front of them.

One of the bigger Spiritcallers growled at her, his eyes flashing yellow.

She quickly scooted back, throwing up her hands. "Fine. I give up."

"We're laying down salt circles," Tor said with a wink, as if that explained everything.

When he offered no further explanation, she marched back to Albert's room. Images of her grandmother pouring salt in front of their weathered porch every time there was a death in the neighborhood flashed through her mind. The neighbors had laughed and whispered behind their hands. She sure as hell hoped these wolves didn't practice the same crazy voodoo.

Nakomi looked up with her usual glare. "Is this place haunted?"

The fact that Nakomi was talking to Eilea at all caught her off guard. "Maybe. Did you see something?"

Nakomi's nostrils flared as she slowly rose from the bed. "Why didn't you tell us?"

Eilea stepped back when Nakomi jutted a foot toward her.

"It just happened. Did you see something?"

"I saw nothing, but there's only one reason for a salt circle, and I won't have some demon attacking my sick mate." Nakomi's teeth elongated into sharp daggers, and her hands shifted into furry paws. "You need to find out what it wants and get rid of it."

Was she for real? "I'm a doctor, not a ghost whisperer."

"I don't know what kind of doctor you are if you can't bring Albert's fever down." Nakomi snarled.

Her alpha stood, whispering into her ear, but she shook him off.

"Look, I don't know why you dislike me so much, but I don't have the time or energy to fight with you." Eilea planted both hands on her hips. "I have a patient to look after."

Eilea stifled a shriek at a sound behind her, relieved when it was only Raz. There were odd tribal markings on the elderly woman's neck and hands. She imagined that beneath the woman's fleece sweatshirt there were even more tattoos. She had crinkly gray eyes and deep smile lines around her mouth. She affectionately patted Eilea's hand and murmured something unintelligible before walking around the bed to Albert.

Nakomi and her mates bowed to the old woman and backed up, giving her a wide berth.

"Do you think you can help him, Raz?" Nakomi asked.

On the bed beside Albert, Raz shrugged. She pulled a big jar out of her bag and unscrewed the top.

Eilea was immediately hit with the sulfuric smell of rotten eggs as Raz wiped something on Albert's arms.

"What are you putting on him?" Eilea asked, feeling more useless than affronted. Raz should've asked the doctor before treating the patient, but at this point, Eilea would welcome any help.

"A salve for demon burn," the old woman answered. "If it works, then we'll know that's what it is."

Nakomi gasped, falling into a chair while covering her face with her hands. Her mates sat stoically beside her, their mouths and eyes twitching with emotion. "What's demon burn?" Eilea asked.

"That tornaq had to pass through a portal to get here." Raz felt Albert's forehead. "If it was somehow left open, that would explain the burn."

"I'm not following you," Eilea said. Portals and demon burn?

Raz chanted again before pulling what appeared to be a bundle of sage out of her bag and setting it on fire with a match.

Eilea fanned her nose when the room filled with smoke.

What the hell was this lady doing?

Raz handed the sage to one of her mates, and he carried the smoking herb out of the room, filling her clinic with the strong smell. When the smoke detectors started buzzing, Nakomi and her mates covered their ears and howled.

Eilea's heart sank when Loki ripped the nearest smoke alarm off the wall and smashed it on the floor. Were these monsters intent on destroying her clinic? When it continued to buzz, he shifted into protector form and stomped it to pieces.

Seemingly oblivious to the giant, angry protector, Raz took another bundle of sage out and handed it to Nakomi. "Light this if your mate should pass into the afterworld," she said. "You must ward off the demons, so they don't change him."

"Demons?" Eilea clutched her throat, her knees as wobbly as runny jelly. "Change him?" What the hell was this old woman talking about?

Raz gazed at the patient and let out a string of undecipherable words that Eilea assumed was cursing in some other language.

Eilea gaped at Albert. She could hardly believe it. Beneath the thick smear of pungent jelly, the pustules had shrunk. "It's a miracle!" She clasped her hands together, beaming at Raz. "His rash is healing!"

Raz shook her head, the crow's feet around her eyes deepening. "It's no miracle. This only proves he has demon burn. The portal is open. Ancients save us all."

Chapter Three

EILEA DUG THROUGH THE storage bin, looking for large sets of hospital scrubs after Tor and Loki shredded their clothes. She wondered how much shifters spent on clothing every year. She'd have to keep working full-time just to keep her mates in shirts and jeans if she ever bonded with the Lupescus. She inwardly cursed her foolishness. She wasn't bonding with the Lupescus. Why had that thought even crossed her mind?

"Have you found something for my mate?"

Nakomi's cold glare unnerved her. Eilea was trying to save Nakomi's mate. You'd think she'd show the doctor a bit of gratitude.

"Yes."

"Good." Nakomi crossed her arms. "I was wondering what was taking so long."

"I've only been gone a minute." She tossed a set of scrubs to her.

Nakomi held out the shirt. "These are too small."

Eilea bit her lip to keep from speaking her mind. They were too small. Though Loki Strongpaw wasn't as tall as Tor Thunderfoot, he had a barrel chest and thick arms to match. His last name fit him perfectly. He'd have to make do with what was on hand.

"They're the largest I've got," Eilea drawled, pretending to be unaffected by Nakomi's nasty attitude. "Maybe you could run home and get him some of his own things."

Nakomi's scowl deepened. "I don't drive."

"Oh?" That seemed to be a theme among the Amaroki women; act helpless while their mates did all the work. She'd never once seen any of them drive, and when they did go out, they were always accompanied by their protectors. It's like they weren't trusted with the slightest bit of independence. And the Lupescus had expected Eilea to assimilate with their culture?

"Do you think the women in Ethiopia had access to cars and medical schools?" Nakomi snapped, as if she could read Eilea's thoughts.

"I-I didn't say that," Eilea stammered, heat creeping into her chest. It was wrong to judge Amaroki women. It wasn't their fault they were born into a patriarchal culture. "I read you were from Ethiopia. I volunteered at an Ethiopian hospital for a year after medical school."

Nakomi cocked her head, smirking. "Why do I care?"

Eilea let out a frustrated breath. "I was only saying I might have come across your tribe."

"We lived high in the mountains. Unlike the Alaskan Amaroki, we were smart enough to stay far away from humans."

Damn. Eilea jerked as if she'd been slapped. "Not all humans are bad. Some of us just want to help."

Nakomi tossed her head with a laugh. "Says the doctor who just gave my mate and me unnecessary vaccinations."

More heat flamed Eilea's chest and face. "I was unfamiliar with demon burn. This is the first time I'm hearing of it."

"That is because you don't understand us. You're not one of us." Her words came out like hissing arrows. "You don't belong here."

Eilea's heart raced. "I don't understand where your animosity is coming from. I never did anything to make you hate me."

Nakomi turned with an eye roll. "Not yet," she muttered before walking out the door.

TOR PACED, HIS EYES shifting from gold to brown as he rubbed his bearded chin, lost in thought. As comical as he looked in the too-tight scrubs, Eilea was not amused as she observed him from the doorway. Being physically attacked by a ghost and verbally abused by a prejudiced she-wolf with a misplaced grudge had put her in a sour mood. Then there was Albert, whose temperature still hadn't come down. Eilea feared she'd develop an ulcer before she left this cursed clinic. Luckily, Nakomi had gone to the restroom, giving Eilea a reprieve.

"Do you think the portal is by your house?" Tor asked Loki, continuing to pace.

"No, Chieftain." The borrowed scrubs stretched so tautly across his shoulders, the fabric looked ready to tear. "But we did experience something strange when we went hunting."

Tor stopped, giving Loki a long look. "What happened?"

Loki emitted a canine whimper. "We were following the scent of an elk and got lost."

"What do you mean, you got lost?" Tor asked. "You should know your reservation like the back of your paw."

"I know." He scratched his head, sharing a quizzical look with his brother. "I don't understand what happened."

"I do." Raz said, still keeping vigil beside Albert's bed. "They were at the heart of the portal."

"Did you see anything unusual, like a demon or shadows?" Tor asked Loki.

"We saw nothing. It was so peculiar. We didn't even hear a bird."

A foreboding sensation snaked up Eilea's spine as the shifters glanced at each uncertainly. The shifters had superior hearing, so for them to not hear a bird was troubling indeed.

"Do you know how many days you were gone?" Tor asked them.

"Three," Loki answered. "I only know this because I checked my phone when we got back."

"You must be famished," Eilea said, her healing instinct kicking in. Emergency food was stashed in the storage cabinets.

Loki shook his head. "We did nothing but eat and sleep for three straight days. All our winter stores are gone."

Tor flashed a weak smile. "We will help you replenish them."

Loki released a long breath. "Thanks, Chieftain." A bead of sweat rolled down Loki's brow, and his eyes seemed foggy.

"When did you notice Albert was sick?" she asked.

"This morning. He woke up with a fever and started throwing up."

"Then came the blisters on his arms," Rene added, sweat also dripping down his brow.

Eilea made a mental calculation of available beds and medicine. She had enough supplies to treat about a dozen patients for a week, but she was not prepared for an epidemic.

Tor heaved a breath, punctured by a low growl. "Raz, how do we close the portal?"

She shot him a pointed look. "You start by banishing the demon who opened it."

Another shiver stole up Eilea's spine.

"Don't worry." Raz flashed her a lopsided, nearly toothless grin. "She is not here now."

"Do you think it was Katarina?"

"Yes. She somehow escaped passing to the afterlife." Raz clucked her tongue. "She must have sensed the Ancients wouldn't welcome her. The portal will remain open until she passes through it."

"How do we get her to do that?" Tor asked.

"I do not know." Raz paused, rubbing her pointy chin. "We must ask Amara to consult the goddess. I'm not good with spells, and I believe we need a witch to close the portal."

Loki and Rene stiffened at the mention of a witch. Up until that moment, Eilea hadn't even realized the Amaroki had witches among them.

"Raz, there's something else," Loki said.

She narrowed her eyes at him. "What?"

He dragged a hand down his face with a groan. "We were so disoriented, it's like a dream, but I think we passed the Eaglespeaker elders on our hunt. They were lost, too."

"I'll go check on them." Tor pushed off from the wall, flexing his fingers. "If they're not home, I'll organize a search party."

Eilea's heart quickened. "You're leaving us?"

He nodded at the line of salt that ran past the door. "The circles and the sage should keep Katarina from the clinic. We've also salted your house so Katarina can't destroy it." His voice dropped to an ominous rumble. "Do not leave the clinic without a protector, Eilea. And make sure no one breaks the circle, or Katarina can get back in."

She swallowed hard, willing the knot in her chest to go away. "Okay." She wasn't just worried about the ghost. She also feared the chieftain's presence was the only thing preventing Nakomi from unsheathing her claws.

"Don't worry," he said. "I'm sending for reinforcements."

Eilea wasn't sure, but she thought she saw Tor wince when he mentioned reinforcements, as if he dreaded asking for assistance.

"Thank you." She released a slow breath, forcing herself to unclench her hands, but the barbed noose that had tightened around her spine refused to unwind. She had a sinking suspicion the reinforcements would only cause more trouble.

EILEA WAS LIVING A nightmare. Soon after Tor left them, both Loki and Rene fell ill. Loki projectile vomited green goo on the floor and wall. It was like something out of *The Exorcist*. Rene rushed to help his brother, slipped in the vomit, and banged his head on the floor.

Without any nurses to help her, Eilea was stuck with the gruesome task of cleaning up them and the clinic. Fortunately, Nakomi helped, taking on most of the work. In her eight years as a doctor, Eilea had been subjected to all kinds of body fluids, but none as putrid as sick shifter vomit. Eilea tried to help him to bed but ended up getting puked on. After a quick wash and change of scrubs, she found all three shifter brothers tucked in bed, with Nakomi and Raz fussing over them. She was grateful to the shifters for their help but wondered if they'd soon fall ill, too.

"Raz," Eilea said, wanting to lay a hand on her shoulder but thinking better of it. "I thank you for your help, but I'm worried about you being exposed to this." The elderly usually suffered the most during epidemics. She would feel terrible if the old woman died.

"I'm not worried." Raz shrugged a bony shoulder. "If the Ancients call me, it's my time."

Eilea felt totally overwhelmed and out of her element. "But your mates."

"They will follow soon after." Raz cupped Eilea's cheek with a wrinkled, dry hand, her weathered face crinkling like an old map. "I've sent my mates home, and I've been exposed to demon burn before."

"You have?"

She nodded. "When I was a child, visiting relatives in Romania."

"Does this mean you've built up an immunity?"

"Possibly." Raz winked. "We will find out in due time."

Eilea looked at Nakomi, who was smoothing a cool cloth across her alpha's head. "And what about you?"

"You need not concern yourself over me." She didn't meet Eilea's eyes. Could this be a sign she was finally softening?

Eilea strengthened her resolve. "I'm a doctor. It's my job to be concerned."

Nakomi stiffened and let out a low growl.

Raz clucked her tongue, giving Eilea a sympathetic look.

She heaved an exasperated breath, storming out of the room. Fuck! Why had she promised Tatiana she'd stay? She'd never hated a goddamn fucking job so much in her life. She had to find a way out of this shithole before she went insane.

Chapter Four

FUNNY HOW AMARA KNEW her in-laws were on their way before Luc did. She hadn't even scented them, but she just knew, as if she could sense things before they happened. She was only about two weeks pregnant, and already her child's powers were starting to work through her. They'd just sat down to dinner when she felt the pull of their presence and knew they came bearing terrible news. Her appetite soured, and she walked onto the porch without a word, too choked up to speak. Legs weak from fright, she clutched the banister and gazed at the silhouettes of trees just beyond their house. Why did it feel like she was being watched? A chill swept down her arms, and she had a feeling it wasn't due to the cold.

Luc was the first to reach her. He'd been unusually possessive since they'd conceived a child. "Amara," he said, "What are you doing? Come back inside." He gently tugged her elbow. "It's too cold out here, and you need to eat."

She shook off his hand and hugged herself as a frigid breeze blew through her hair, making her shiver. A sudden whirlwind tossed leaves around her feet.

Aaaaamara, the wind whispered in her ear.

Overcome by a wave of dizziness, she leaned against Luc. Had the wind called her name? A clearer vision of her mates' family flashed across her mind: Tor gripping the steering wheel with whitened knuckles, Tatiana in the backseat, crying on her mother's shoulder, the rest of her mates' fathers sitting stoically, looking out the windows as if they expected the forest's shadows to lash out at them.

She turned to Luc, searching his dark eyes. "Your fathers are coming." Her alpha, Hakon, stood in the doorway. "They bring bad news."

"Are you sure?" Hakon asked.

40

She nodded.

He scanned the horizon. He believed her. She'd predicted the Strong-paw's phone call this morning.

Luc's nostrils flared. "I smell them approaching."

The wind whipped Amara's hair again. *Aaamaraaa*. A shiver wracked her. "Did you hear that?"

Luc scrunched his brow. "Hear what?"

She shook her head, trying to clear the sudden fog. "I'm not sure. Some-one is calling my name."

Hakon held out a hand. "Come, Amara. We can wait for them inside."

She followed him on legs that felt like two wet noodles. He pulled her into the house, eyes turning from mahogany to gold.

"I scent something dark," Luc said, trailing them and shutting the door behind him. "Something wicked."

Hakon turned up his nose. "I smell it, too. Reminds me of... never mind. It can't be."

Amara had smelled something, too. Foul, like rotten eggs. She followed her mates to the table, sat, and twirled pasta on her fork, though she wasn't hungry. That rotten egg stench was embedded in her senses, sticking to her tongue like a fine coating of dust.

Luc nudged her. "The baby needs you to eat."

She complied, absently chewing and forcing herself to swallow. Not only did the baby in her womb need nourishment, but she was still breastfeeding another baby and a toddler.

Her youngest son, Alexi, wore most of his food in his hair, his chubby, tanned cheeks stained red while he played with pieces of chopped up pasta. Hrod was trying to twirl his spaghetti on a plastic fork, getting angry with himself and banging the tray when the noodles unraveled. He was still cute, even when upset, with impossibly chubby cheeks and large, playful eyes. He was determined to conquer his dinner, no matter how many twirls it took.

Her mates leapt from their chairs at the sound of their fathers' truck tires peeling into the drive.

Her alphas, Hakon and Drasko, rushed to the front door. Luc held a hand down to her. She glanced at her Gamma, Rone, who stayed behind with the babies, wiping sauce off Alexi's chin and showing Hrod how to capture his noodles. How she loved him for his steadfast kindness and patience with their children. She thought of the sick Strongpaw gamma, and her heart clenched. If anything happened to Rone—if anything happened to any of her family—she'd die from heartbreak.

Amara's legs grew as heavy as concrete as she went with Luc. A sulfuric smell hit her as soon as Hakon opened the front door. She remembered that evil odor from Romania's haunted forest.

"Fathers, what's wrong?" Hakon asked as he went down the porch steps.

Tor helped Mihaela out of the car. "We need you to keep your mother and sister safe." He nodded at Tatiana, who jumped out of the truck, sticking closely to Tor's side.

"Where are you going?" Hakon asked.

Shadows fell across Tor's features. "The Eaglespeakers are missing. We need to find them."

Luc released Amara and stepped forward. "I'll come with you."

She reached for him with a trembling hand. "No, Luc," she breathed.

When Tor held out a staying hand, Amara heaved a shuddering breath of relief.

"Why not, Father?" Luc asked.

Tor threw a glance at the forest behind him. "Because it's too dangerous."

"What do you mean?" Luc asked, then fell silent.

Amara watched with a slackened jaw when Skoll, her second alpha father-in-law, ripped a hole in a bag of salt. He and Van, her tracker father-in-law, each held an end of the bag and poured a line around the porch. Her gamma father-in-law, Arvid, followed behind them with a smoking bushel of sage.

What the hell were they doing?

She thought she heard a whisper on the wind, but it was cut off when the air abruptly stilled.

Tor crossed his arms. "The salt circle and sage are for Katarina."

"Katarina?" The wicked stepmother who had died over a year ago?

Tor wrapped a protective arm around Tatiana. "Her spirit's been haunting your sister."

Tatiana nodded. "I kept it secret out of fear of reprisal."

Tor hugged her tighter, kissing the top of her head.

Amara's knees gave out, and she fell back on the porch step with a *thud*, ignoring the pain shooting up her sore behind.

Luc was at her side in an instant. "Are you okay?"

She nodded as thoughts whirled in her head. That hadn't been the wind calling her name. That had been Katarina. Fuck. She suspected step mommy dearest hadn't returned from the dead to bring her fresh-baked cookies.

"There's more." Tor grimaced. "She's opened a portal to the underworld. That's how the Strongpaws ended up with demon sickness."

Amara swallowed bile. "All of them are sick?"

"All but their mate."

"Great Ancients," Amara breathed. Was this infection contagious? If so, how was she going to cure it?

"The portal entrance causes shifters who go near it to become disoriented," Tor continued. "The Strongpaws wandered the forest for three days before they found their way out. They thought they heard the elder Eaglespeakers in the forest. We just came from their home. It's empty. There's no sign of them."

Fuckity fuck. This was bad.

"And you can't make their sons go after them?" Drasko asked.

"No. They are visiting their mate's family in Romania." Tor gestured to his brothers, who were pouring salt on the other side of the house. "We are the chieftain pack. It's our job to go."

"Father," Luc pleaded, "if anyone can find them, I can."

Sirens went off in Amara's head. He couldn't go.

"No, Luc." Tor vehemently shook his head. "You are not to go into the forest. I won't risk your soul to this beast."

"What if you don't come back?" Hakon asked, standing as still as a statue and staring at Tor as if he was looking at a dead man.

"Then leave us." Nervous-sounding laughter bubbled up in Tor's throat. "And find a way to close the portal from outside the forest."

Hakon urgently threw out his hands. "But you'd all be trapped."

Tor's brothers returned with an empty bag of salt and stump of smoking sage.

"We know," Tor said.

Mihaela cried out, then bit down on her knuckles.

Amara pitied her mother-in-law. She'd probably lose her cool, too, if her mates had to go into a dangerous, cursed forest. She looked at the set, determined jaws of her mates and knew without a doubt that if their fathers didn't come back, they would disobey Tor's orders and go after them.

AMARA HAD A HARD TIME falling asleep, knowing her mates' fathers were out searching for the Eaglespeaker pack. Before he left, Tor had said they would find the missing pack and then close the portal. He'd kissed Mihaela and Tatiana goodbye, leaving them with Amara and her mates. Her mother and sister-in-law were in the spare bedroom. They were probably wide awake, like her.

After checking on her sleeping boys in the crib next to her bed, she laid down between her mates, tossing and turning while trying to get comfortable.

Hakon rubbed her back. "Sleep," he soothed. "Ask the goddess to visit you in your dreams and explain what's happening."

"I will," she breathed. She sent a prayer to the goddess, begging her to come to her. Her tribe needed answers.

AMARA FLOATED TOWARD a familiar silhouette, mist swirling at her feet. Her namesake, the Goddess Amara, waited for her by a raised pool of water.

"Goddess!" She propelled herself faster, her legs unmoving as she leaned forward, letting the wind carry her. "Thank you for seeing me."

The beautiful goddess with the long black hair and porcelain skin stood, holding her hands out to her. "It was the least I could do." Clasping Amara's hands in hers, she pulled her to the stone ledge that circled the mists.

She sat beside the goddess, desperately searching her eyes. "Please tell me what's happening. Tor says Katarina has opened a portal to the underworld."

The goddess solemnly nodded. "Portals to the afterlife open for spirits when they die. They close when those spirits pass through. Katarina fought the pull of the afterlife. She knows she will not be welcomed into heaven."

If Katarina couldn't get into heaven, would she haunt Earth forever? Would the portal never close? "Where will she go?"

The goddess's brows knitted together. "A dark and lonely place."

She bit her lip, twisting her fingers in her lap. "I suppose I don't need to ask why you won't take her." She wanted to beg the goddess to take Katarina into heaven, but she knew her stepmonster wasn't deserving of a rewarding afterlife.

The goddess flashed a smile that appeared forced. "We could not bear her complaints and tantrums for an eternity, especially when her mates bond with another."

"But look at what she's doing to us. Amaroki are getting sick."

"You will have to find a way to force her through the portal. Only then will it close."

"How do I do that?" Amara pleaded.

Her eyes lit up. "Use the witch."

"The witch?" Amara drew back. "Where do I find one?"

"There is one among the Amaroki." The goddess stood, holding out her hands. "She will know what must be done."

Amara took the goddess's hands, letting her help her up. "And if she doesn't?"

Shadows fell across the goddess's luminous eyes. "Then more of your tribe will get sick. Some may even die."

She clung to the goddess as she felt the pull of gravity, dragging her back to the mortal plane. She still had questions that needed answers. "Why can't I cure them?"

"You can't heal them until the portal is closed." She stared at something over Amara's shoulder. "You must hurry before more spirits find their way through. Some worse than Katarina. Demons."

"Demons?" Amara gasped. "What will they do?"

"Once the demons pass through, it may be too late to close the portal." The goddess's voice dropped to an urgent whisper. "They will turn your beloved reservation into a haunted forest like the Hoia Baciu."

"Wait!" Amara cried. "Who is this witch? Where do I find her?"

"I cannot out her. She will reveal herself when she's ready."

Amara panicked. "What if she doesn't? What if everyone gets sick and none of us can close the portal?"

"You will not get sick. If you've already had demon burn, or you have human blood, you are protected from this virus."

So she was immune to the virus? "What of the witch? Is she immune, too?"

A scream died on Amara's lips as she tipped over the edge of the clouds, falling back into the black hole from where she'd come. Great Ancients! Her beloved reservation was about to turn into a haunted forest and she had no idea where to find the witch.

Chapter Five

WHAT IS THIS PLACE? Arvid's thought projected into Tor's mind as he spun a slow circle, his tail tucked between his legs.

Tor scanned the area, his thick protector legs feeling oddly weak. Despite his superior wolf-touched eyesight, he could barely make out the dark trees surrounding them. His vision tunneled on the humming white orb in front of them, stretching into a long shaft of mist spinning like a sideways cyclone. Strange how he heard not a sound in this part of the forest, as if all life had been sucked into the orb. The air was heavier, too, pressing down on him, crushing his lungs as if he was breathing in soup.

I-I don't know. Tor scratched his head with a furry paw. What had his brothers been talking about?

Do you remember what we were doing? Skoll asked Tor, his furry protector face draped in a frown.

I think we were looking for someone, Tor answered. But he didn't remember who. He shook his head to try to clear the fog, but it was no use. That soupy, stifling air had settled in his mind, too.

Van looked at his hind legs. *Why is there a rope tied around my waist?*

Tor followed the length of rope attached to his wolf brother's waist. It disappeared into the trees. *I think it's to show us the way out.*

Van let out a low whimper. *From where?*

I'm not sure.

With a low whine, Arvid took a step toward the orb, which pulsed like a living heartbeat.

Don't touch it, Tor thought to his brother. *I think it's a portal of some sort.*

Arvid whimpered, arching his back like a feral cat and backing away from the orb.

A cry for help cut through the fog in Tor's brain. *Do you hear that?*

Voices, Van said, angling his gray ears toward the sound.

Arvid's whimpers grew louder. *What are they saying?*

Help us! The cry resonated through the small clearing, echoing against the trees.

The echo appeared to be coming from inside the orb. Tor held a hand to one ear. *I recognize their voices.*

They sound like the Eaglespeakers. Van raised his snout. *I can smell them, too.*

Skoll puffed out his hairy chest. *We should go in and help them.*

Tor laid a hand on his brother's shoulder. *No.*

Skoll arched a bushy brow. *Why?*

Tor didn't know why. He just knew, once they went into the portal, they were never coming out.

Over here! Van called.

Tor gave a start. He hadn't realized his brother had left them.

He plodded over to Van, feeling as if he was marching through quicksand with each step. *What is it?*

Van pointed at four lifeless wolves, whose haunted eyes stared up at them, gray tongues falling out of their slackened jaws and their bodies covered in raised welts. *The Eaglespeakers.*

Damn. Though Tor knew he should've had more of a reaction to finding his tribe members dead, he hardly felt any remorse. It was as if he'd lost his empathy. *How did they die?*

Van sniffed their bodies, then shrank back. *I'm not sure.*

They need a proper burial, Skoll said.

A wave of shame washed over Tor for not thinking of it first. What kind of chieftain was he if he didn't care? *They do, but not here.* Tor shook his head, frowning down at the old wolves. *This land is cursed.*

The cry for help was louder this time, and there was no mistaking the alpha Eaglespeaker's voice.

Van looked at Tor with luminous eyes. *How can we hear them if they're dead?*

I don't know. Maybe it's not their voices we hear.

What else could it be? Skoll demanded.

Though Tor's mind was still in a fog, one word projected into his skull. *Demons.*

EILEA WOKE WITH A START and sat up, rubbing the kink in her neck. Morning light was coming through the window. She didn't remember dozing off in her uncomfortable office chair. She'd gone in to call Uncle Joe and ask what the hell happened to her backup.

She checked the time. It was almost nine. Fuck. She'd left Raz and Nakomi alone to take care of the patients for two hours. If Nakomi had hated her before, she loathed her even more now. It wasn't her fault she'd gone soft since agreeing to be the Amaroki clinic doctor. She was losing her stamina after not having any real patients for over a year.

She stumbled into the clinic, alarmed to see four more patients in the ten-bed room. They only had three beds left. Where would she put them if more shifters came down with this virus?

"Nice of you to join us, *Doctor*," Nakomi drawled in her heavy accent. "Hope you enjoyed your nap."

"Go easy on her." Raz draped a cloth over a patient's forehead. "Humans don't have our stamina."

"Yes, I know how weak they are."

Ignoring her, Eilea approached the first bed, her heart hitting the floor when she recognized the old man who'd poured salt on her floors the day before.

Raz hummed softly while gingerly stroking her mate's long, gray hair and then kissing his cheek. She then tended to her other mate.

"Raz," she said. "I'm so sorry."

"Not your fault."

Eilea took their temperatures, alarmed at the readings, which ranged between a 103° and 105°. These old men wouldn't live another day if their fevers didn't break. Surprisingly, all the men were hooked to IVs. She moved to the medicine cabinet.

"I already gave them fever reducer," Raz said to her back.

Eilea was surprised by Raz's calm demeanor. "What else can I do?"

"There's only one thing left to do," Raz said, smiling at her unconscious mate. "Pray to the Ancients."

RAZ'S MATES ALTERNATED between vomiting and sleeping, and their fevers still hadn't come down. If Eilea couldn't bring their temperatures down soon, they'd sustain permanent brain damage or worse. The oldest alpha was nearly eighty. She wasn't sure if he had the strength to pull through. Nakomi's mates had stopped vomiting, but they still had fevers. At some point during the night, they'd started to mumble. Eilea had no idea what they were saying. Neither did Nakomi or Raz, but Raz said she suspected it was an ancient tongue. What the ever-loving fuck?

She heaved a sigh of relief when her uncle's truck pulled in. Hopefully he brought good news. Though the government had refused to transport the sick shifters to a military hospital, the least they could do was send her a team of doctors and nurses. This epidemic would soon be too big for her to handle—not that Raz and Nakomi weren't helpful. Raz had proven to be especially useful.

A man got out of the truck with Uncle Joe. She vaguely remembered the agent from last year, when she'd given him a flu shot. He'd asked her on a date afterward, and she'd flatly refused, watching with disgust as he skulked out of her clinic.

It was Uncle Joe's turn to skulk. She could tell by his posture that the news wasn't good.

She left the sick room and quickly crossed to the front door, opening it and breathing in the cool fall air, relishing the smell of pine needles as opposed to the stench of vomit.

She told both men to jump over the salt circle, as per Tor's orders. No way did she want the vengeful spirit getting back inside.

Uncle Joe came in, sniffed, made a face and swore.

"You think the stench is bad?" she asked with a smirk. "Try cleaning it off your clothes and out of your shoes."

He shuddered. The agent who'd followed him into the clinic was a short, stocky white guy with spiked, dark hair and a tan that had to be spray on.

"Eilea, this is Jimmy Parelli. He's not only one of my agents, he's also a licensed LVN."

Uncle Joe couldn't expect her to work with this loser. She gave the guy a half-hearted nod. "Agent Parelli." She refused to call him by his first name. No way did she want to get on familiar terms with him.

The look in his brown eyes reminded Eilea of a snake getting ready to pounce on a mouse. "Hi, Eilea." He licked his lips and held out a hand.

Gross, and where the fuck did he get off, calling her by her first name? She glared. "Dr. Johnson, please."

He shrugged, flashing a crooked and blindingly white grin. "Of course."

She hated bleached teeth, or at least she hated teeth that were so white, they looked blue. Uncle Joe rocked on his heels, ignoring both of them while checking something on his phone. "Jimmy is going to help you with the clinic," he said with disinterest, tapping his screen.

She groaned. "I need doctors and RNs. I already have people to clean up bed pads. No offense, Agent Parelli."

"None taken." He purposely scraped her shoulder as he brushed past. "I need to change." He wore an expensive suit and shoes.

"Supplies are in the backroom," she said with a resigned sigh. Any kind of help was better than none.

"Thanks, Eil..., err, Dr. Johnson." He headed for the back.

His smug tone grated on Eilea's nerves.

Uncle Joe slipped the phone in his pocket, giving her a pointed look. "I can get you supplies. I can't get you more staff."

"Why not?" She didn't mean to sound so harsh, but fuck, she couldn't be the only doctor on call. She'd need to sleep and eat at some point.

"The clinic and reservation are on lockdown. Nobody is allowed to leave, and Jimmy was the only agent who volunteered."

Panic threatened to split her skull in two. "This is stupid!" She was trapped on this godforsaken reservation?

"Until this virus is contained, the government is not taking any chances." The lines framing his eyes deepened. "We don't know if it can spread to humans yet."

"It can't be transmitted to humans," she insisted.

"How do you know that?"

"Drasko Thunderfoot was by this morning. Amara spoke with their goddess, and humans aren't affected."

"That's what I'm supposed to tell my superiors?" He snorted. "That the Amaroki gods said it's not contagious?"

"Look, I don't have the time or the energy to fight this."

"What supplies do you need?"

"Beds, food, electrolytes...." She threw her hands in the air. "A bigger clinic."

"I can get those," he said and marched out of the clinic.

She stared after him, hurt that he hadn't even asked how she was holding up and feeling too much like that orphaned little girl whose uncle had abandoned her for his career. He had always been reticent, somewhat aloof, but he could've shown her a little compassion. Maybe even thanked her for her sleep-deprived sacrifice.

"How do I look?"

Jimmy had reappeared in tight blue hospital scrubs that stretched across a broad chest, emphasizing muscles so big, he had to have been on hormones or steroids. He winked at her and flexed a bicep.

"They're a little snug, but I'm used to it." He flexed his other arm. "Most everything nowadays is made for puny men."

"Yeah, whatever," she said, averting her eyes and hoping he understood she wasn't impressed. After seeing the Lupescu alphas transform into hulking white beasts easily ten feet in height, all men were puny to her, even this 'roid freak show. "Go see if Raz needs any help," she said brusquely.

He strutted away with his chin held high and chest bowed out like a peacock in a henhouse. She rubbed the dull ache in her temples with a groan. She was going to need to throat-punch someone if she had to put up with Nakomi's scowls and Jimmy's flirting another day.

Chapter Six

AMARA HELPED RONE FEED Hrod and Alexi breakfast while her other mates paced, watching for any sign of their fathers. Her mother and sister-in-law, both with red-rimmed eyes and noses, sat on the sofa and held each other. They hadn't seen or heard from the search party all night. Their phones went to voicemail, and they didn't return Luc's persistent howls. Luc had begged Hakon to let him go after them, but he'd refused, saying they needed to respect Tor's orders. Hakon's resolve was weakening. He and Drasko had finally decided Drasko would go after them if they didn't return by nightfall.

The thought of Drasko alone in a forest that was most likely haunted turned her stomach into knots, even though she knew he was their best hope. After he'd suffered demon burn a few years ago, he was immune to the sudden sickness plaguing their tribe. With Amara's new gift of premonition, she had tried many times, but she couldn't see any signs of them approaching. She asked her toddler, Hrod, who'd been blessed with the gift of sight, if he could see his grandfathers, but whenever he closed his eyes, he saw only darkness. It was as if the forest had swallowed her mates' fathers. Would it swallow Drasko, too? If so, would her other mates risk their lives and go after him?

The disease was spreading, and there was no sign of the witch. Drasko had just returned from the clinic after talking to the tribal medicine woman, Raz, but she denied being a witch. Like the goddess, Raz told Drasko the witch would reveal herself soon enough. Amara sure as hell hoped so. Instinct told her this virus was about to get worse. Raz's mates were already sick, and they hadn't been near the portal, which meant they'd contracted the virus from the Strongpaws.

Suddenly a vision of Tor and his brothers returning in their truck, swerving down the road like drunks, popped into her head. She jumped to her feet. "They're coming." She clutched her chest when she saw another vision of them nearly hitting a tree. "They're sick."

Tatiana and Mihaela ran to the door, neither stopping to grab their jackets.

"Fathers!" Tatiana screamed while throwing open the door.

Luc draped a thick blanket over Amara's shoulders and kissed her hand, his eyes dazzling with something akin to pride. Luc had always been kind and caring, but never like this. How she relished his attention. They followed Amara's alphas, leaving Rone with the babies. She cast Rone an apologetic look, but as always, he didn't seem to mind staying behind with the children.

The frigid fall air hit her like a frying pan to the face. Her nose and cheeks burned with the chill. She breathed in deeply, disturbed by the odd taste on her tongue. The rotten egg stench was far worse than yesterday. "Do you smell that?"

Luc nodded. "It's the smell of evil."

She shuddered, her knees weakening. When he tightened his hold on her hand, she managed a thin smile. If Luc hadn't been lending her his strength, she'd probably pass out from fright. She wasn't afraid for herself; she was terrified for her family, especially her defenseless children. After witnessing the evils of Romania's haunted forest, she feared what would happen if her reservation was taken over by something similar.

They waited far too long for her fathers-in-law.

Tatiana and Mihaela danced around, rubbing their hands together while watching the road for them.

Eventually, Tatiana huffed and puffed at Amara. "I thought you said they were coming."

"They are."

"Should we go after them?" Luc asked.

"No." Hakon frowned. "Father said to wait."

A cool breeze ruffled Amara's hair. *Ammmmara,* the wind whistled.

She looked at Luc, who didn't show any signs of alarm. Was she the only one who could hear the wind?

Drasko went back inside, returning with coats for his mother and sister, and then they waited and waited while Amara swatted the breeze that ruffled her hair. She heard her name a few more times. A demon or ghost was taunting her. She wondered how far the spirit would go before taunts turned into aggression. Just when she thought she'd go insane from the wind's heckling, Tor's truck crawled into the driveway and rolled into a tree. Their doors creaked open, and they stumbled out of the truck.

Drasko's arm shot out, latching onto his mother when she tried to go to them. "Wait." Tor bent over, using his knees for support. "Don't come near us."

"Darlings, what happened to you?" Mihaela begged, falling to her knees in a prayer pose.

Tor slowly straightened. "Stay where you are. We don't want you to get sick. We only came to warn you."

"Warn us of what?" Hakon asked.

Tor rubbed his bloodshot eyes. "I-I don't remember."

His brothers groaned muttered unintelligible noises while leaning against the truck. Van fell on his knees, vomiting into the grass.

Drasko shot Amara a look over his shoulder. *The goddess had better be right.*

She's never failed me before. But she sent a silent prayer to her anyway, that she and Drasko were truly immune to this curse.

"Everyone else back inside the house," Drasko said. "Amara and I will take care of our fathers."

"But, but," Mihaela cried.

"Please do as he says, Mother," Hakon pleaded, jutting a finger at the front door.

Amara's heart broke when Mihaela took Tatiana's hand and went back inside after casting one last woeful glance at her mates.

Luc planted a tender kiss on Amara's forehead. *You mean everything to me. If anything happens to you and our child....*

She nuzzled his neck. *Please don't worry, sweetheart.*

When he released her hand and walked away, she felt as if her world had tipped on its side. She hadn't realized until that moment how much she'd been relying on his strength.

Hakon came to her, lifting her off the ground in a big bear hug. He set her back down and kissed her. *I love you.*

And I love you, she answered back, grateful she could communicate with him through thought, because she was too choked up to speak.

Please give Rone and the babies my love.

I will, Hakon answered.

Drasko took her hand and led her toward his fathers.

"I said to stay away." Tor groaned, hunched over again, his normally tanned skin diaper-doo green. "I'm still your chieftain."

Drasko ignored his father's protests and helped him into the front passenger seat. "Amara and I are immune."

Tor gave him a doubtful look. "How?"

"We've already had demon burn." Drasko buckled Tor's seatbelt. "We can't get this. Plus, Amara's human blood gives her more protection."

She helped Drasko with the others, alarmed when she felt their foreheads. They were feverish and disoriented. Luc's father, Van, was in the worst shape, with raised welts all over his arms. After she sat beside her mate on the bench seat, she prayed nobody vomited on her.

Drasko peeled off down the road, swearing and punching the steering wheel when the truck pulled to the right. "The alignment is fucked up."

"Will we make it to the clinic?" she asked.

"Yeah." He grimaced. "We'll just have to go slower."

She thought about asking Drasko to turn around and take his truck instead, but she didn't want to have to go through the headache of loading her sick fathers-in-law into another vehicle. When Tor slumped beside her, she knew he'd be too weak to stand again.

"Fathers," Drasko asked, "what happened to the Eaglespeakers?"

"The who?" Tor groaned, pressing his cheek against the side window.

"The Eaglespeaker pack." Drasko enunciated each word. "Did you find them?"

His expression went blank, and he let out a blubbery sigh. "They're dead."

Amara's heart slammed against her ribcage, and she sent a silent prayer to the Ancients to protect their spirits in the afterlife.

"And the bodies?" Drasko asked.

Tor moaned into his hands. "We couldn't carry them. We could barely make it out ourselves."

Drasko gave Amara a knowing look. *If we can't stop this virus, we'll be all that's left of the Amaroki.*

"EILEA, WE'RE ALMOST out of electrolytes."

She fought to keep from rolling her eyes at the 'roided meathead. "I've already told you to call me Dr. Johnson."

He shrugged, flashing his stupid ultra-white smile. "Agent Johnson calls you Eilea."

"He's my uncle. You're not."

"Good thing." He chuckled. "That would be weird."

He stretched his arms over his head, no doubt in an attempt to show off biceps that looked like stuffed pillows. There was no way in hell those bulging muscles were real. Just like his teeth and tan, this guy was head-to-toe artificial. She gave him a long, dark look. "Believe me, it's already weird."

"How so?" He leaned against Albert Strongpaw's bed, acting as if the sick man was nonexistent.

Eilea stole a glance at Raz and Nakomi. They alternated between watching Eilea and Jimmy and bathing their mates with cool rags. She was embarrassed by Jimmy's crude behavior. Not that she cared what Nakomi thought of her, but she didn't want the shifter to think she was encouraging him.

"Look, I'm not interested in flirting." She had to work hard to unclench her hands when the pain in her palms became severe. "I have a job to do."

"Maybe after all this is over." He winked, then inclined his head at the back room.

Was this douche for real? "Maybe not," she said clearly.

"Aw, shot down. Good thing I'm no quitter." His laughter was like nails on a chalkboard.

"Listen, *quallu*, she's not interested in you," Nakomi said, eyes gleaming feral gold.

Was the shifter actually defending her?

"This doesn't concern you," Jimmy said with a sneer.

Did this idiot have a death wish? The guy sure was ballsy for someone on steroids.

"Like hell it doesn't." She stood, nose lengthening and voice dropping several octaves. "Get off my mate's foot."

He jumped as if he was standing on electrified wires. "Oh, sorry."

Apparently, his apology wasn't enough, because Nakomi moved toward him like a wolf stalking a baby lamb. She jabbed a slender finger into the hollow of his neck. "If one of my mates is injured, or Ancients forbid, dies due to your negligence, I will rip out your throat." Her eyes glowed an ominous yellow, like twin suns were shining through her skull, and her voice dropped so low, it sounded like Satan himself was speaking through her.

Holy fuck. Eilea sure was glad she wasn't on the receiving end of Nakomi's wrath for once.

Jimmy's cheeks reddened, and a line of sweat formed across his brow. "You don't need to worry about that." He let out a nervous chuckle while flashing Eilea a pleading look.

As if she'd save him.

"It's you who should be worried," she snapped, jabbing him as if she was trying to poke a hole through him. "Focus on your job, you *quallu*."

"Roger that," he said, wiping sweat off his brow with a shaky hand before excusing himself and rushing to the bathroom.

Nakomi returned to her work. Eilea wanted to thank the shifter, but she was too afraid to even look at her. Besides, she didn't think Nakomi had been defending her. Jimmy had been sitting on Albert's foot, after all. One thing for sure, she admired Nakomi's dedication to her mates. She hadn't slept in over twenty-four hours and showed no signs of fatigue while she tirelessly looked after her three sick men. Raz was right. Wolf shifters had more stamina. Eilea was so damn tired, she just wanted to crawl under her desk and sleep for eternity.

She quietly made her rounds, starting with Raz's mates. "What's a quallu?" Eilea whispered to the matronly shifter.

Raz laughed. "Humans call them trolls."

"Sounds about right," she said, warily looking at the bathroom door.

She wondered if he'd pissed his pants or worse. If Eilea had been on the receiving end of Nakomi's dark voice and blinding eyes, there was no telling how many body fluids would squirt out of her. She sure as hell hoped he stayed gone a long time, and that when he returned, he'd leave her alone.

He finally crept out of the restroom, looking at the floor while checking IVs. Nakomi growled at him the whole time, which only made the tremors in his hands worse.

With a resigned sigh, she fished her phone out and walked to her office. She looked outside and not surprised to see the sun had set. Damn. She was going on two days with only two hours sleep. How long could she last? She called her uncle and waited for him to pick up.

After he answered, she spoke in a rush. "Uncle Joe, you have to find someone to replace Jimmy." She could hear the echo of her voice on his Bluetooth but thought nothing of it. He usually traveled alone.

"I can't. He's all I've got right now."

She swore under her breath. "I'll take anyone. No medical experience required. What about Amara Thunderfoot's cousin, Roy?" The kid was about twenty and fairly green, but at least he understood the Amaroki, and she could trust him not to act like a major douche around the shifters.

"He was sent to Texas last week."

"Shit. I can't work with Jimmy."

"Why?" He sounded too casual.

"Because he's a first-rate douche-nozzle," she snapped, then added. "A quallu."

When a chorus of male laughter echoed through the receiver, her whole world came to a grinding halt.

"Tor sent for the Lupescus," he said.

She fell into the chair. "And you're just now telling me?"

"I knew you'd try to get me to send them back," he said. "We'll be there in half an hour."

She heard a click and then a dial tone, and gaped at her phone.

The Lupescus would be at her clinic in thirty minutes! The four virile Romanian shifters who'd lost their minds last year and tried to claim her as their mate?

Un-fucking-believable.

A noxious smell wafted up from her legs, and she remembered she was covered in sick shifter puke. Not exactly the first impression she wanted to make on the Lupescus. Then again, why did she care what they thought of her smell? She wasn't mating with them. No fucking way was she giving up her independence, no matter how hot and bothered they made her.

When the odor of sour onions hit her, she sniffed her armpits and instantly regretted it. She couldn't help sweating while under duress. She hadn't had time to shower, but what she wouldn't give for a fresh bar of soap and new clothes.

She threw down her phone and ran out of the office. "I have to go," she said to Raz. "I'll be back in a few minutes."

Raz adjusted the blanket over her sleeping mate. "They are in good hands."

She raced out of the clinic, remembering to hop over the salt circle. When she ran down the grassy knoll toward the small house she shared with Uncle Joe, she thought she heard the wind whisper her name. Lack of sleep must be making her hallucinate. She ran faster, tripping over the salt circle as she raced across the threshold. She halted and looked behind her. She'd only made a small dent in the circle. Probably not enough to make a difference. Besides, bushels of sage lined the doorway. If one didn't work, the other surely would. She mentally smacked herself in the head. All her years of medical training, and she was counting on voodoo herbs and minerals to keep her safe? Sheesh. She had to get a grip. Besides, she didn't have time to worry.

Her mates were coming.

Correction.

The men claiming to be her mates were coming.

She was a fool for letting vanity prevail over common sense, but she didn't care. She had to smell good for the Lupescus and maybe give herself a quick showerhead orgasm, so she wouldn't be so hot and bothered when she had to again turn down the four tempting men she so desperately wanted to fuck.

EILEA FRANTICALLY SCRUBBED the stench of vomit off her skin. She'd only intended on being in the shower a few minutes, but vanity won over and she was compelled to shave everything and even create a neat little landing strip between her legs. Not that she expected anyone to see it, but just in case a bomb went off in the clinic and burned off all her clothes, she wanted to be presentable. Between each swipe of her razor, she tried to remember the last time she'd actually shaved. Sadly, she couldn't. She thought back to the last time she'd had sex. It had been during her brief stay with her ex-fiancé, Derek. After dating for over a year, they'd moved in together all of six months before his controlling ways had her running for the door.

She'd been an ER surgeon, which meant her hours were nuts. She couldn't exactly clock out after they brought her a motorcycle accident victim with a brain injury. But Derek had expected her home at a certain time. After the breakup he admitted he'd been looking for, as he put it, a "traditional wife," which she decided was a euphemism for obedient doormat. Eilea had lost a lot with that failed relationship, from her deposit on the apartment and her flat-screen TV to her trust in men. He had been so perfect when they'd first met, allowing her the freedom she needed to be an independent woman. He didn't become possessive until after he'd moved in with her. If only she'd known from the start, she wouldn't have wasted two years of her life.

Funny, but when she pulled the showerhead from the cradle and washed between her thighs, it wasn't Derek's face that came to mind. First she saw Boris Lupescu, with his pale blond hair and stunning gray/blue eyes that shone like diamonds. Then there were his brothers, Jovan, Geri, and Marius, all equally handsome. Jovan was as tall and wide as Boris, with a devastatingly sexy smile that made Eilea cream her panties. Geri wasn't as big as his older brothers, but he was the most feral. Eilea's uncle had told her that all beta sons had the best sense of smell and tracking abilities. They led the hunts and then their larger brothers took down their prey. Then there was Marius. He had a different kind of smile, an infectious one with dimples emphasizing his easygoing nature. He was the mate who helped with the children and household duties.

Eilea had once thought about having children, even adopting after two serious relationships didn't work out. But trying to raise a family and balance a career would be too difficult. Perhaps maybe if she had a man like Marius to look after the kids.... She shook her head at the thought. The Lupescu brothers already had five full-grown children. They wouldn't want to start over with a new family, and even if they did, they'd likely be even more possessive than Derek. One controlling asshole had been enough. How would Eilea handle four of them? Not to mention they were a totally different species. No, it would never work, though a part of her secretly wished it could.

A soft moan escaped her, and she looked at the water pulsating between her thighs, surprised she'd been playing with her labia while spraying the water between her swollen folds. All this time she'd been thinking about the Lupescus, she hadn't even realized she was masturbating.

She leaned against the wall and hiked a leg up, resting it on the soap dish. She tickled her labia with the water and imagined Boris was between her legs, pleasuring her with his tongue. She pinched a nipple into a tight peak, pretending Geri was stretching it with his teeth, his sharp canines leaving impressions on her sensitive flesh. How she wished she could fantasize about someone else, but ever since she'd met the Lupescu brothers, only they came to mind when she masturbated.

Usually it took her a while to work up to orgasm, but the thought of the Lupescus so near sent a trill of excitement straight to her sensitive parts. She spread her swollen lips wider as the water pulsed between her legs, building, building, until she was almost over the edge. As she was about to crest, she involuntarily called Boris's name. Suddenly the ground shook, and the walls rattled like a freight train was driving through her house.

Earthquake!

She dropped the showerhead and screamed when the curtain fell on her. The rod banged her head so hard, she was momentarily dizzy. She slumped to the shower floor, the room spinning so hard, she had no idea if the tremors were still shaking her or if she'd suffered a concussion.

Pushing the curtain off her, she saw pink water circling the drain. What the hell? Her period wasn't due for a couple weeks. She wiped the sore spot on her head again, shocked when blood trickled down her arm.

Damn. She needed medical attention.

She got up on her knees, holding onto the grab rail as a shiver wracked her. The water had turned cold. She reached to shut off the water, then jerked back when the hose coiled and then rose, the showerhead nozzle hovering over her like a cobra preparing to strike.

Not an earthquake then. That small break in the salt line had left her open to attack.

When the showerhead lunged for her, she tried to fight it, but fear or shock or both had slowed her reflexes. She screamed when the hose wrapped around her neck like a noose, choking her. She fought the demonic snake, struggling to pry it loose with slippery fingers, then trying to jerk it out of the wall. But the more she fought it, the tighter it wound around her neck. She slipped to the tile floor, a crack resonating through the room while she thrashed, gasping for air.

Was this how her life would end? Murdered by a jealous ghost? She had sick patients who needed her, and she still had so much to accomplish. The faces of her pale-eyed shifters flashed in her mind. Would they mourn the mate they never got to know?

Chapter Seven

AMARA HAD A VISION of her fathers in Agent Johnson's truck. They were headed to the clinic on a different road. "Oh, no!"

"What is it?" Drasko asked.

"My fathers are here." Her heart sank. Why would they risk their lives by coming to a place they knew was infected? Amara had just spoken to them on the phone yesterday. They had to have known it was risky coming here. Then Amara remembered Eilea. Of course, they would risk their lives for the pretty doctor.

She wondered if Eilea knew they were on the way. The human doctor had been fighting her attraction to Amara's fathers since they'd picked up on her scent. She still wondered why the Ancients would pick a human to mate with her fathers, and a strong-willed, independent one at that. She knew from experience that Amaroki men tended to be possessive and a bit controlling. Having known the doctor for over a year, she knew there was no way Eilea would put up with domineering mates.

Joe Johnson pulled into the clinic's gravel parking lot the same time Drasko did. Four broad-shouldered men with familiar blond hair were with the agent.

Marius jumped out of the back of the truck first, holding out his arms and beaming at Amara. "*Dragă mea!*"

Her fathers had been young when she'd been born. Marius, the youngest one, had been tricked into mating with her human mother when he was just a teen. Now Marius was barely forty, with a wonderful smile and sparkle in his eyes, despite the hard life he'd led in Romania.

Ignoring Drasko when he grumbled for her to wait, she got out of the truck and threw herself into Marius's arms.

He held her tight, murmuring words of love in Romanian.

64

She sank into his embrace, soaking in his love, pleased when each of her fathers took turns hugging her. The last time they'd come to Alaska, her fathers had been so consumed with Eilea's scent, they hadn't paid her much attention.

She looked up at her alpha father Boris. "What are you doing here?"

He stroked her cheek with a calloused hand. "Tor sent for us."

He looked thinner than when she'd last seen him. Older, too. Her breath caught when she saw the sparkle in Marius's eyes had gone.

"Fathers, what happened to you?"

"What do you mean?" Boris asked.

She cupped his unshaven cheek. "You don't look well."

"We're fine," he said, but his eyes wearily closed, and he let out a groan when her healing magic sank into his skin.

"You weren't at all fine," she whispered, pulling away. She suspected her healing magic would only be a temporary fix, that whatever had put him in poor health stemmed from a darkness in his soul.

"How do you expect us to look?" He heaved a sigh, clasping her hand. "We've been in mourning."

"I'm so sorry." She placed her healing hands on her second alpha father, Jovan. She didn't know why she had expected their mourning period to be easy. Their mate had made their lives miserable. She'd made everyone's lives miserable.

She suddenly felt selfish for imagining her fathers celebrating Katarina's death. She might have been a vindictive shrew, but her fathers were kind and loving. Besides, Katarina had been the mother of their children, Amara's four brothers. She imagined her fathers had mourned not just the loss of their mate, but the fact that Katarina would never have a chance to change.

Jovan's smile didn't quite reach his eyes. "Our mourning period is over. We're ready to begin our lives again."

"Oh." She blinked, processing what he'd just said. "No. You can't be here." Panic zinged through her at the thought of them getting an incurable virus.

"*Dragă mea,* our minds are clear now," Boris said, sharing a knowing look with his brothers. "We will be on our best behavior. Promise."

"No, no, that's not it." She jerked away from Jovan when he reached for her. "There's a virus I can't seem to cure. I don't want you getting it."

Jovan crossed his arms. "We know about the sick pack."

Panic threatened to split her skull in two. "Three packs are sick now. It might be contagious. You have to go back," she said, desperation ringing in her words.

Agent Johnson stepped forward, palms up. "The Lupescus must stay. No shifters are allowed off the reservation until the virus has been contained."

Amara swore under her breath. "You can't be serious." A deep, angry heat stirred in her belly. "Humans can't get the virus. I've already spoken to the goddess."

Johnson snickered. "You and I both know our government won't believe that."

"We don't care." Boris's eyes changed to a blinding white. "We're not leaving our mate unprotected."

"B-but, you won't be able to protect her if you're sick," Amara stammered.

Jovan frowned, nodding to the copse of trees just beyond the clinic. "Tor believes Katarina's spirit has opened a portal."

She wrung her hands together, her gaze desperately flitting from father to father. "Yes, but—"

"And that she threatens Eilea," Geri added.

"We will make sure she is safe," Boris said and trailed after Drasko.

Her fathers helped Drasko carry in her sick fathers-in-law. She worried that touching them might put their health at risk.

She looked around for Eilea after they entered the clinic, surprised she didn't scent the doctor nearby. Was she hiding from Amara's fathers? Though Amara acknowledged it would be a good idea for Eilea to have protection, she hoped her fathers didn't expect to mate with the human. Amara feared Eilea wouldn't accept the bond.

Raz greeted them, giving directions to Drasko and Amara's fathers. Amara worried when she saw they were short a bed. After Tor said something about giving the beds to his brothers, a familiar-looking male nurse helped Tor onto a narrow cot. This would never do. The clinic was already too crowded. What if more shifters fell ill?

After everyone was settled, Drasko gave Amara's alpha father a pointed look. "You need to leave. We don't want you getting sick."

Boris returned Drasko's glare. "And yet you're here."

Drasko shrugged. "The goddess told Amara we're protected because we've already had demon burn, plus Amara's human blood gives her extra protection."

Her tracker father, Geri, thumbed his chest. "I've been burned, too."

"Then you can guard Eilea," Boris said to his brother, "should we fall ill."

Geri nodded, giving Boris a look so severe, Amara knew they were telepathically speaking.

Boris clutched Drasko's shoulder. "You just worry about protecting our daughter."

Drasko stiffened. "You already know I'll guard her with my life."

Her heart warmed at the thought. Drasko had already sacrificed his life for her once. She knew he'd do anything to protect her again.

Her world suddenly spun, and she cried out, stumbling toward the wall. A pair of strong arms caught her, but she no longer saw the clinic. She was inside a steaming shower with Eilea, who writhed on the floor with a hose wrapped around her neck. She screamed, then the steam evaporated, and she was looking up into Drasko's concerned eyes.

"Are you okay?" he asked.

She nodded, clutching her throat when she was assailed by the memory of Eilea being choked.

She gaped up at Drasko, then at Boris, who hovered beside him, and told them what she'd seen.

"What?" Boris hollered, eyes shifting from blue to blinding white. With a roar, he dashed out of the clinic, shifting into his protector form and bursting through the front door, shattering glass in his wake. He sprinted out of view, his brothers following closely. She hoped they reached Eilea in time.

JUST AS EILEA'S WORLD dimmed, she heard a crash, followed by a thunderous rumble. An unholy shriek rattled her eardrums, then the cord around her neck loosened and she rolled onto her side, painfully trying to suck in air.

She was lifted by warm, furry hands and placed on the bed. Strong hands were on her chest, pumping. She coughed up water, gasping, though she felt only fire in her lungs. Cracked lips pressed into hers, breathing warm air into her mouth. She gasped, and her lungs filled with air.

"Fix the salt circle," a deep voice bellowed. "Get that bitch out of here."

The room spun and shadows blurred before things slowly came into view. She was seized with panic when she saw two white, furry faces with blinding eyes leaning over her. Then she noticed the only human face, the gamma, Marius Lupescu, Amara's birth father. She recognized his sexy dimples and the shallow smile lines around his mouth and eyes. She ran her tongue over her teeth when she saw his wet, cracked lips. He'd been the one to give her mouth-to-mouth, which meant he and his brothers had scared away Katarina's ghost. Well, shit. Now she was obligated to the Lupescus for saving her life.

"Are you okay, *lubirea mea*?" Marius asked, stroking her cheek with calloused knuckles.

"I think so," she ground out, then winced at her scratchy voice. She sounded like a ninety-year-old chain-smoker. And what the hell was a lubirea mea? She sure as hell hoped it wasn't a term of endearment.

"You're safe now." Marius unscrewed the cap off a bottle of water. "Geri is fixing the circle and adding more sage."

After furry hands propped pillows behind her, and Marius wrapped a bandage around her head, she reluctantly let Marius tip the cool water into her mouth. At some point she blinked, and the two furry beasts turned into two naked men. She couldn't help but take in the sight of their virile bodies. Though she'd never seen them naked before, they were thinner than she last remembered, and holy fuck, they were well-endowed.

She swore under her breath and tore her gaze away from their genitals. They smirked at her, a feral look in their eyes that made her shiver. That's when she realized she was naked, too. Oh, this wasn't good. She covered herself with the comforter.

Boris smiled. "You don't need to cover yourself."

"Yes, I do," she snapped, "and so do you."

Boris's smirk widened as he crossed his arms, his heavy appendage swinging with the movement. "We don't need to be ashamed of our bodies."

"Especially not you," Marius said, the blush in his already pink cheeks deepening. "You're beautiful, Eilea."

She wanted to tell Marius to call her Dr. Johnson but didn't, heat flaming her face. She swung her legs over the bed. Dizziness returned, and she thought it had to be from her sudden movements and not due to the fog of lust that had spread through her body like a virus.

"Thanks, but that's not the point." Clutching the comforter, she rubbed her aching temple. "What are you doing here?"

"Amara told us you were in trouble." Boris sat beside her without invitation. Still naked, still hung like a horse, his knee grazing hers like it was the most natural thing in the world.

She had a hard time thinking with the Romanian alpha so near.

"How did she know?" she rasped, then regretted using her vocal cords at the pain speaking caused.

Marius handed her the water, and she took several slow sips. The liquid was cool and refreshing, but she figured her throat would be sore for a long time.

"She's having visions of the future," second alpha Jovan said as he sat on her other side. "Her unborn child is a seer."

The last thing she needed was to be stuck in the middle of this naked stud sandwich. Or maybe she did need it. Maybe she wanted to straddle each of these shifters, slowly fucking them until they begged for release. That would show them who was in charge.

She shook her head at the thought. She had to get in control of her hormones. What were they talking about? Amara's unborn baby somehow enabling her to have visions. She would've asked the Lupescus what they'd been smoking, but she remembered Amara once had her last unborn child's power to create earthquakes.

"I don't understand." She stood, shaking off Geri when he tried to help her. She fell into a nearby chair, facing the shifters and trying not to be perturbed by their hairy, bare balls on her Egyptian cotton sheets. "Why didn't she warn me?"

"She just had the vision," Boris said matter-of-factly.

She brushed a wet strand of hair behind her ear, shivering when water droplets dripped down her back. When Marius draped another blanked across her shoulders, she thanked the thoughtful gamma with a smile and was rewarded with a shit-eating grin. As she got momentarily lost in Marius's eyes, an uncomfortable throb pulsed between her thighs when she recalled she hadn't finished masturbating. How easy it would be to let the Lupescus finish her off. She was sure they'd be more than willing. Fuck. She had to get the hell away from these temptations.

Wrapping the blankets tightly around her shoulders, she quickly stood. Boris and Jovan were at her side in a heartbeat.

"Sit down, Eilea." Jovan latched onto her elbow. "You need rest."

She bristled at his commanding tone and jerked free. "First off, I don't take orders." She glared at all three men, refusing to cower when the alphas glared back. "Second, it's Dr. Johnson, *not* Eilea. Third, since I'm a doctor, I know when I need rest." She spun on her heel, intending to march majestically out the door, but stumbled over her own feet as a wave of dizziness washed over her. She fell against a hard chest and was once again lowered onto the bed.

Damn them!

Jovan was closest, eyes shifting from blue to white as he lowered himself on top of her until the fine hairs on his chest grazed her bare breasts. Holy hairy balls! She'd lost her blanket. She placed her palm against his chest, feeling the steady beat of his heart. "Stop," she cried, though deep down what she really wanted was to spread her legs and let him finish what she'd started in the shower.

His nostrils flared, a wicked grin splitting his face in two, revealing two sharp canines. Holy fuck! That smile made her so damn wet.

His smooth, hard shaft pressed against her thigh. "Were you thinking of us when you were in the shower?"

She wanted to say yes, and let him sate her desire, but instinct told her once she surrendered to these brutes, they would think she belonged to them. She belonged to no man, certainly no wolf-man.

She pushed him hard until he backed away with a grunt. "You need to leave so I can get dressed," she said evenly, proud of herself for remaining calm when her pussy wept with need.

He let out a string of expletives she assumed were Romanian swear words. "You don't expect us to leave you alone after you were almost killed."

"Please go." Once again she sat up, this time covering herself with a body pillow. "I'm fine." She couldn't help gawking at the two naked shifters, whose impressive erections jutted toward her like heat-seeking missiles. Heat flamed her cheeks. "And for the love of all that is holy, find some goddamn pants!"

Boris scowled at her as if she was a wayward child. "You're not fine, Eilea."

Rage threatened to split her skull in two. Forget that they refused to show her medical degree any respect. They treated her like a baby. She pointed at the door. "Out!" she screamed, then instantly regretted it because it made her throat hurt.

The dimwits just stood there blinking at her.

She grabbed a medical journal off the side of the bed and rolled it up like a newspaper. If they wanted to treat her like a helpless child, she'd treat them like dumb mutts. "Shoo!" Jumping up, she clutched the pillow to her and waved the journal in their faces, relieved when she only felt slightly dizzy.

"Very well," Boris said and backed up, "but we will be right outside the door, and I will not hesitate to break it down if I suspect you're in trouble."

She dug her nails into the pillow. "Or you can just leave the door unlocked."

Marius frowned, his bottom lip turning down in the most adorable pout. "If that is what you want?"

No. That wasn't what she wanted. What she wanted was for one of them, or all of them, to relieve the throbbing between her legs with their fingers, tongues, or heaven help her, those glorious cocks. But her wants did not align with her needs. What she needed was for these virile and tempting wolves to return to Romania and never come back, but she didn't think that was going to happen anytime soon.

AFTER EXAMINING THE bloody bump on her head, she changed into a clean pair of jeans and a T-shirt, wincing when the fabric slid past her neck. She checked it in the mirror, not surprised to see a purple ring forming. The reality of her situation hit her. She'd almost died, murdered by a vindictive ghost. She was lucky the Lupescus showed up when they had, but what if they hadn't? What if they weren't around next time? She pushed the dark thoughts into the recesses of her mind, locking them away with all the other depressing thoughts she'd so carefully learned to bottle up and ignore. She'd survived a horrific car accident and the death of her family when she was just a child. She could survive this, too. She had to. Now was not the time to go soft. She had patients who needed her.

She quickly laced up her boots and strode out of her bedroom, marching straight for the front door.

No surprise, Jovan, the big, brooding second alpha, was guarding the door, arms crossed, brows raised, the hum of his low growl reverberating in her bones, reminding her of a sentinel at the gates of hell. She inwardly laughed at the thought. She was living her own personal hell. At least he'd wrapped a towel around his waist.

"Where are you going?" he demanded.

"To the clinic." Jutting a hand on her hip, she impatiently tapped her foot. "Where else?"

His frown deepened, creasing his brow in deep, dark lines. "Next time alert us. You cannot go anywhere without an escort."

She snorted. Was he her keeper now? She jabbed his chest, wincing at the pain in her finger. Damn. Was the guy made from granite? "Now you listen to me. You are not my boss, and you're certainly not my mate. I do what I want when I want." She turned at a familiar heat on her back, like a dragon was breathing fire down her neck. She glared at Boris. "The only person I answer to is myself."

If it was at all possible, his scowl was even darker than Jovan's. "So what you're saying is you want to be choked again, maybe even killed next time?" His pissed off look made him even sexier, especially with a flimsy towel wrapped low around his hips.

"Believe us," Jovan rumbled, "Katarina's tornaq will attack again."

"My patients need me. I'm leaving." Her patients did need her, but more importantly, she needed to get the hell away from these mountains of testosterone before she salivated all over them.

Jovan held the door for her. "This time, jump over the salt circle."

"I did," she spat, angry with him for making her speak when her throat was still sore.

He jerked her back before she could jump. "Wait."

Enraged, she shook off his hand. Boris jumped over the circle and held out his hand. "You will stay between us."

With an exaggerated eye roll, she reluctantly took his hand and hopped over the circle, Jovan following close at her heels.

They'd just begun to walk up the grassy knoll that led to the clinic when Eilea froze at the distinct sound of a bone-jarring snap.

She screamed when she heard deafening roars and a loud crack. Jovan pushed her to the ground, shifting into a furry beast and crouching over her. Dear Lord, if she'd thought his genitals were big before, they were gigantic from this viewpoint, slapping her thigh like swollen water balloons.

She blinked up into blinding white eyes, noting for the first time that two elongated fangs hung over his lower lip and his mouth was so wide, he probably could have swallowed her head whole. Holy shit, he was frightening. Her heart raced, her limbs iced over, and her bladder responded in an embarrassing way. Good thing she'd worn a panty-liner, mostly because being near these studs made her cream her undies, though she didn't think that thin liner had been enough. They'd made her piss her pants.

Jovan straightened, holding down a meaty paw to her. She prayed she hadn't soaked through her jeans. Somehow, she found the courage to slip her small hand in his. He hoisted her to her feet so fast, he nearly pulled her arm out of its socket.

A tree branch had fallen at Boris's feet. It had to be at least sixteen feet long and four feet wide at the base, and it probably hadn't dropped by accident.

"We need to get her inside," Boris grumbled.

Before she could stop him, Jovan swept her into his arms, racing for the clinic in long strides. He hopped over the salt circle and ducked through the entrance, setting her down. Not until she fell into a chair did she breathe a sigh of relief. Holy shit. First, she'd been strangled by her shower, then she'd been nearly crushed by a tree limb.

Jovan hovered over her, grasping her shoulder. "Are you okay?"

"Fine," she mumbled, thoughts jumbled.

Jovan stomped back out the door before Eilea could thank him for saving her. After ducking through the frame of shattered glass that was once the front door, he pounded his chest like an ape and let out an enraged war cry. "Katarina!" He shook his fist at the sky. "I will not let you hurt her!"

Eilea watched with horror as wind swirled around Jovan's body, tossing up leaves while ominous feminine laughter filled the air. He swatted the wind to no avail, getting so angry he finally punched a hole through the wall.

"She will die," the wind hissed.

Eilea struggled to quell her shaking limbs. This ghost was seriously intent on killing her, and she wouldn't stop until she succeeded.

Chapter Eight

AFTER THE WIND HAD died down and Eilea's heart had stopped threatening pound its way out of her chest, she hopped over jagged glass and right into Amara's outstretched arms.

"Eilea!" she squealed. "You're okay."

She clutched Amara's elbows, searching her friend's eyes. "I am because of you. I can't thank you enough for sending your fathers to save me."

She shrugged, blushing. "Anyone blessed with the gift of sight would've done the same thing. I was so worried about you."

"I'm fine, thanks," she croaked, throat still aching.

Still in protector form, Jovan ducked his head inside the door. "Heal her throat," he said to Amara in a rich, deep baritone. He ducked back out, his long arms swinging as he tromped across the parking lot.

Eilea strained to see any signs of his brothers, but she didn't see anyone else. Where had they gone? Though she tried swatting Amara away, the shifter latched onto her throat with a firm yet tender grip, and within seconds the burning was gone. She pulled the bandage off Eilea's head and pressed her hand against the bump. Eilea felt a mild tingling and then the tenderness on her scalp disappeared. She checked her reflection in a mirror hanging on the wall. The bruise circling her neck was gone. Though she'd witnessed the shifter's healing powers before, she'd never experienced them first-hand.

"Th-thank you," she stammered.

Amara shrugged. "No problem. I only wish it worked for...." She wiped watery eyes. "I'm sorry. I'm just worried."

She clutched her shoulder. "As am I, but I promise I'll do whatever it takes to help your people heal."

Drasko Thunderfoot climbed through the shattered door, a tool belt around his waist and several boards under his arm. At least someone was working on fixing the door. Wooden planks would darken the room, but at least they'd keep out the frigid night air.

He laid the boards against a wall. "Dr. Johnson, I'm so glad you're okay."

"Thanks." She acted as if being strangled by a possessed shower hose was no big deal. Then she wondered if Amara had only seen the strangling or if she'd seen her masturbating, too. She hoped not. She flushed at the thought.

When Drasko wrapped his arms around Amara's waist from behind, she felt a twinge of jealousy. Amara leaned into her second alpha with a sigh while Drasko kissed the top of her head. This wasn't the first time she'd been envious of Amara. It wasn't so much that the she-wolf had four big, buff, beautiful mates as that she had men who loved her. Growing up, Eilea had just wanted one man, her uncle, to give her the fatherly love she'd longed for after losing her dad in the car accident.

Unable to watch Amara and Drasko a moment longer, she stumbled into her office and dug out the spare lab coat and stethoscope she kept in the cabinet. The coffee pot was empty. Who the hell drank the last of it without brewing more? Empty creamer and sugar packets were scattered across the counter, and the wastebasket was overflowing with her eaten yogurts and granola bars. She suspected Jimmy was to blame. Swearing, she poured water into the machine and peeled the lid off the can of coffee.

"Eilea," a deep voice rumbled.

She shrieked and spilled coffee grounds down her shirt. Slamming the canister on the counter, she turned, ready to chew out the big, bad wolf that had scared her. It was Boris, naked as a babe, his arms and neck covered in bloody cuts. Damn him. He hadn't even told her he'd injured himself protecting her from that branch.

"You're hurt." She reached for him. "Let me see." Large splinters protruded from his back, stuck deep inside bloody welts, like he was sprouting branches. "Jesus," she hissed. "Come into an exam room. Let's get you fixed up."

"Never mind me. You are not to leave this building without an escort. Do you understand?"

"I'm not leaving the goddamn clinic," she snapped. He winced at her tone. "Look." She heaved a sigh. "I'm sorry I snapped at you. I'm just not used to taking orders."

He cupped her chin in a blood-encrusted hand. "I know you're not, but your life is at stake."

Her resolve to distance herself from this man melted a little at the tenderness in his eyes and in his words. He had to have been in excruciating pain, yet he cared more about her wellbeing than his.

She led him toward a private exam room, passing Jimmy in the hall. The annoying nurse looked at them with bulging eyes, not even offering to help. He lurched forward, rattling a keychain on his hip.

"I locked the exam rooms. Do you need in?"

She stopped, looking at him as if he'd grown a second head. "Why would you lock them?"

He nodded at the small infirmary, where Raz and Nakomi tended to their mates. "That old lady was going through the cabinets."

She squeezed Boris's hand when his low growl rattled her insides. "Maybe she needed something. You don't lock my rooms without my permission." She held out a hand, wagging her fingers impatiently. How did he get her keys in the first place? He had to have gone through her desk. "And stay out of my shit, Nurse Parelli, including my coffee and snacks."

"Sorry." He dropped the keys in her hand. "I thought I was helping."

She rolled her eyes to the ceiling, praying she didn't smack Jimmy's big, boxy head "No. If I need your help I'll ask for it."

He kicked a shard of glass like a petulant child. It had probably been missed when they'd cleaned up from the shattered door.

"Jesus," she snapped, pointing at it. "Pick that up."

Turning ten shades of red, he snatched up the glass and tossed it in a nearby wastebasket.

"Sweep the floors again, and make sure there isn't anymore," she commanded, bracing herself for a mantrum.

He smirked. "Ask one of the women to do it."

When Boris's growls intensified, she knew Jimmy was running out of time. Either Jimmy was too stupid to notice, or he just didn't care. In which case, he wasn't just stupid, he was a certified moron.

Sorely tempted to smack that smug look off his face, she clutched the keys so tight, metal dug into her skin. "That wasn't a request, Nurse Parelli."

Jimmy answered with an eye roll.

Boris moved so fast, she had no time to stop him. One second they were holding hands, and the next Boris had Jimmy pressed up against the wall, his hands around the nurse's throat. Jimmy kicked and gasped, flailing like a fish out of water.

"Boris! Put him down."

"Not until he apologizes," Boris said with a grunt.

She winced at seeing Boris's back. The blood from his wounds flowed faster, as if the movement had caused his injuries to worsen.

"S-s-sorry." Jimmy kicked and gasped, whimpering and letting out an explosive fart.

Boris swore, dropping Jimmy like a rag doll and fanning his face.

She instinctively slapped a hand over her mouth and nose. "You ate those old fiber bars in the back of the cupboard, didn't you?"

He nodded, tears streaming down his face. If anyone should've been crying, it should've been Eilea. His gas smelled worse than a rotting colonoscopy bag. She took Boris into the exam room at the end of the hall, jamming the keys in the door to unlock it and slamming it behind them.

She shared a look with Boris, and they both burst out laughing. She clutched her sides, tears streaming as she laughed harder, her ribs aching. In just a day, her life had gone from incredibly boring, to frightening, to awkward and then even more awkward. Could things get any worse? Probably. She laughed harder.

When Boris sat on the end of the exam table, his garden hose flopping over the side, she yanked a sheet out of the closet and threw it at him.

"Could you at least cover yourself?" she asked, wiping her eyes.

"Sure." He gave her a knowing smirk. "If that's what you want."

"What I want is for me to wake up from this nightmare, but I doubt that will happen anytime soon."

His smirk faded, replaced by frown lines around his mouth. Funny, she didn't remember those lines. She wondered if he'd acquired them while he was in mourning. She also wondered if he'd mourned the loss of Katarina being that she'd never been a good mate to him. She'd heard enough about his late wife from Amara to know Katarina hadn't been kind.

For the briefest of moments, she considered what life would be like mated to Boris and his brothers. Amara had said the Ancients chose Eilea to mate with the Lupescus. Why would they pick her, a human, when she'd probably end up resenting them for their overbearing nature? Their clashing personalities would make everyone miserable.

She fetched tweezers, gauze, and antiseptic from the cabinet, needing to focus on what she was good at, which was being a doctor. There was no way she was mating with four wolf shifters, so why was she even thinking about it? "I'm going to remove the splinters, then ask Amara to heal the cuts. Unless you'd rather I got her first?" Though she admired Amara's magical talents, she was dismayed that her expensive Ivy League medical degree was second-rate compared to the shifter's abilities.

"*Nu*." He settled a big hand on her wrist, his pale fingers a sharp contrast to her dark skin. "Remove the wood first."

When she looked into his silver/blue eyes and saw pain, her breath caught. She hated that he'd been through so much heartache, and that she had to break his heart again. She set to work cleaning his wounds, amazed he didn't flinch when she pulled out the larger pieces.

She was finishing up when there was a soft knock on the door.

Amara slipped inside and looked at her father's bloody back. "Want some help?"

"Sure." Eilea shoved her hands in her pockets and stepped aside. Time to feel useless again.

Eilea watched in awe as Amara laid on hands and each wound magically sealed, leaving nothing behind but dried blood.

Boris jumped off the table and wrapped the sheet around his waist. "Thank you, *fiică*," he said, kissing Amara's cheek.

Eilea's father used to kiss her every night before bed. What she wouldn't give to have him with her now, kissing her and telling her she had the power to accomplish anything she set her mind to. He hadn't been referring to healing cursed shifters or battling demonic ghosts in his little pep talks, though. She shook her head, forcing dark thoughts of her long dead father out of her mind. Her melancholy wouldn't help anyone now.

"I need to get back to my patients," she said, though she knew conventional medicine would do them no good.

WITH BORIS AND AMARA following, Eilea went to the infirmary and looked out the windows to the waiting room. Two Lupescu brothers were outside, adding more salt around the clinic while Geri helped Drasko repair the door. Clearly, they weren't taking any chances, which warmed her heart. While she appreciated their presence, there was no way she would give up her human life and move to Romania. If they stayed too long, they'd wind up getting too attached to her or worse, she'd get attached to them.

She stopped at the door to the infirmary and saw all of the beds had been taken and Tor Thunderfoot was sprawled in a chair, his tanned arms covered with hives. "Goddamn it!" She turned to Amara, raising her voice to carry over the din of Drasko's hammer. "I didn't know the chieftain was sick."

"They went looking for the Eaglespeaker elders and returned like this," Amara said.

Boris straightened. "Did they find the pack?"

"Yes. They were dead." Amara's lower lip quivered.

"Omigod." Her heart pounded so hard, she thought she was having a cardiac episode. "Why in hell would you risk coming here?" She jutted an accusatory finger at Boris. What if this virus killed her mates?

Hang on a second. They weren't her mates. Not yet, not ever.

Boris's features hardened. "We came to keep you safe. No use arguing now that we're on lockdown."

"How do you expect to do that if you're sick?"

"Geri already had demon burn. He won't get sick." Boris gazed at the row of beds. "As for the rest of us...."

She reached for his hand again. "Boris, I don't want anything to happen to you."

He squeezed her hand, eyes crinkling as he smiled. "I'm touched to see you care so much about us."

She jerked away from him. "I don't give a rat's ass about you," she lied. "I'm a doctor. It's my job to limit the spread of infection." She cared about the

Lupescus, despite all her protestations. How could she not when thoughts of them constantly invaded her mind? How many times had she been tempted to call them in Romania and ask if they were okay? How the numerous sleepless nights she'd pined for a call from them? Now they were here, and she wanted nothing more than for them to leave, flee to the safety of their home country.

Boris bridged the distance between them and searched her eyes with such intensity, she could've sworn her insides melted. "We're not going near the portal. We are here only to protect you."

"Raz's mates didn't go near the portal, and they're sick."

He leaned into her, so close her heartrate quickened. "They were feeble and old. Sadly, so were the Eaglespeakers."

She backed away from him. "You're not invincible, you know." Her voice trembled.

"Father, Eilea is right," Amara said. "You shouldn't be around this. Go to my home and wait with Hakon."

She mouthed her thanks to Amara.

Bracing himself, Boris crossed his arms defiantly. "We're not leaving."

She snorted. "Pigheaded, stubborn shifter."

"We could say the same for you." Boris jabbed her collarbone, not hard, though his touch electrified her.

She swatted his hand away. "I'm trying to save you, you ungrateful jerk."

"I should leave you two alone," Amara mumbled and went to join Drasko.

"Wait," Eilea called, but Amara didn't return.

Boris grabbed her wrist, tugging her toward him, and stroked her cheek with calloused knuckles, his wolfish grin sending a zing straight to her unfulfilled and swollen labia.

"You call us names," he purred against her cheek, "yet you deny this attraction between us."

The trickle in her underwear turned into a steady stream. "Stop," she said feebly, pushing against him. No way did she want him to stop. Images of him shoving her into her office, ripping off her clothes, and taking her against the door flashed through her mind. Damn, she so needed to get laid. The showerhead was out, but she still had her vibrator. If only she had time to use it.

Boris pressed into her, his impressive erection stabbing her belly and refueling her desire. "Do you really want me to stop?" he teased, dragging his fingers through her hair.

"No," she breathed, hating that she surrendered so easily. Would it be so bad if she had sex with Boris? Get the lust out of her system so she could think clearly.

Someone loudly clearing their throat behind them brought her back to her senses. Nakomi was leaning against the doorframe, giving them accusatory looks.

"Sorry to interrupt," she hissed like a feral cat. "But my mates will be out of fever medicine soon, and we are short a bed."

When Boris untangled himself from Eilea, her eyes bulged when she saw the massive pole poking out from under his sheet. She should've known his cobra would grow into a python.

"Where can we get more beds?" he asked Eilea.

She forced herself to look at his face, wildfire racing through her cheeks at the mischievous look in his eyes. "I have a folding bed at my house. It's more comfortable than the cot."

"Will you get it?" Nakomi asked Boris.

"Of course, but you'll stay in the clinic."

"Jesus!" Eilea spat. "I'm not going anywhere." How many times was he going to tell her?

He responded with an annoying chuckle as he strutted away. She wanted to get him alone and teach him a lesson, but she bet her plan would backfire, and she'd wind up on her back with her ankles above his ears. The thought of being pinned down by Boris sounded more tempting than frightening.

Nakomi stuck a hand on her hip. "One additional bed is only a temporary solution."

She didn't like the weight of Nakomi's stare, though she refused to break eye contact with the overbearing shifter. She would not be the weaker woman, even if she lacked the ability to grow long fangs and razor-sharp claws. Much to Eilea's relief, Nakomi raced to her alpha's bedside when he moaned.

She returned to the infirmary, making her rounds and not liking that the Spiritcaller alpha's labored breathing had worsened. She hooked him up to one of two ventilators, praying Uncle Joe came through with more supplies soon.

Amara walked over to Eilea. "The tribal meeting lodge has more beds. It's an emergency shelter equipped to hold the entire tribe."

Drakso followed Amara, setting a hand on her shoulder. "We should move the patients there instead of moving beds here. If the virus continues to spread, this clinic can't accommodate everyone."

"I thought the lodge was in the heart of the reservation," Eilea said, recalling the map Uncle Joe had given her. "If we move patients there, we risk infecting more Amaroki."

Drasko frowned. "We won't have a choice if the epidemic grows."

The Spiritcaller gamma and beta were so still, they resembled corpses. "I don't think it's wise to move them. They're too sick."

Drasko rubbed his smooth chin. "Best to move them now while the numbers are small."

"You have a point," Amara agreed.

"I will call Hakon and discuss it with him." Drasko fished his phone out.

"Hang on," Eilea said. "I'm the doctor here. Don't I get a say?"

"No, you don't." Drasko gave her a dark look, one that would've intimidated a lesser human. "Hakon and I are acting chieftains now. We will decide what's best for our people." He marched out, already on the phone.

He'd completely blown off the only doctor among them. Did her extensive years of medical training mean nothing to these people?

"What a brute," Eilea huffed.

"I know." Amara stared after Drasko as if he was a tall scoop of butter pecan ice cream on a scorching summer day. "He's totally turning me on right now."

"Seriously? You like a man who's so controlling?"

Amara tossed her head with a sultry laugh. "I know how to control him, too."

Her heart raced. Maybe Eilea could learn from Amara how to bring the Lupescus to heal.

"You do?" This was the first time Eilea had heard of the female shifters controlling their mates.

Amara eagerly nodded. "There's this thing I do with my tongue that makes him whimper like a puppy."

Eilea couldn't refrain from rolling her eyes. "I didn't need to know that."

"Yes, you do," Amara said matter-of-factly, "if you want to control my fathers."

Was she for real? If a man wanted Eilea to be his queen, she shouldn't have to get on her knees. "I'm not mating with them, so it doesn't matter. I shouldn't have to use sex to control them."

"Why not?" Amara hid a smile behind her hand. "They salivate like dogs whenever you are near."

"You mean they act like idiots?" Eilea fought the urge to smack some sense into Amara with her stethoscope. "That's on them."

"Actually, it's on you." Amara waved at Eilea's crotch. "I can smell you whenever they're close."

"You can?" She crossed one leg over the other. "Oh, God."

"It's nothing to be ashamed of." Amara chuckled.

She gritted her teeth. "Easy for you to say. You're a shifter. I'm human."

"I'm half human, and love is love." Amara flashed a wide grin. "It doesn't matter what you are."

"I don't think this is love." Her shoulders fell with the admission. "This is definitely more like lust." Her pulse raced whenever they were near, but that was just a surge of hormones triggered by sexual desire.

"Trust me." Amara's smile widened. "You will learn to love them."

"No, she cannot."

Nakomi was staring at them with a look so scorching, a lesser woman would've melted.

"What did you say?" she asked, hating how her voice shook. She didn't need to give Nakomi one more reason to try to intimidate her.

"I have held my tongue long enough." Nakomi lifted her chin like a regal African queen. "Humans and Amaroki are not meant to mate. It's an abomination."

Eilea was at a loss for words. An abomination? She had faced all kinds of prejudice in her life, but never had she been more offended, more pained, by Nakomi's insult.

"Excuse me?" Amara snapped. "My mom was human."

Nakomi skirted her mate's bed and wagged a finger in Amara's face. "And where is she now?"

"Dead, as far as I know."

"As far as you know?"

Amara looked out the infirmary windows. "We weren't close."

Nakomi let out a grating squeal of laughter. "Exactly. Humans are incapable of loving their shifter offspring." She snarled at Eilea, eyes shifting from mahogany to gold. "If she mates with your fathers, she will only bring heartache to them and any children they conceive."

"I beg your pardon." Indignation made her blood boil. "You don't know that. You don't know anything about me."

Nakomi gave Eilea a long look meant to intimidate, a look that said Eilea was no more significant than the mold growing under her shoes. "I know you are human, and that is enough for me."

"And what do you know of humans?" she retorted. How dare this wolf-girl pretend to know anything about her species.

Nakomi's full lips thinned into a wicked grin. "I know they are greedy and selfish and not like our kind."

That bitch! Of all the fucking nerve. Eilea had quit her career as an esteemed surgeon in Houston's top hospital and moved to nipple-biting, bear-shitting Alaska to help Nakomi's kind. Wasn't that proof enough she was anything but selfish? And what about Uncle Joe? He'd been so dedicated to the Amaroki, he'd ignored his own flesh and blood when she'd needed a father figure. Did their sacrifices mean nothing? "You're wrong."

"Am I?" Nakomi laughed. "You humans care more about celebrity gossip than helping your neighbors."

"Don't listen to her, Eilea," Amara said. "She's generalizing."

"No, I'm not." Though Nakomi spoke to Amara, she kept her wolfish gaze trained on Eilea. "I've had enough dealings with humans to know. You cannot mate with Amaroki." Her words were harsh. "You will not make a good mother."

Nakomi's accusation was like an arrow of venom shooting straight into her heart. "You might think you know humans, but you know nothing about me. After my loving mother was killed by a drunk driver, I was raised by a caring, sweet grandmother." She recalled her mother's gentle touch and grandmother's kind smile. Her gram was different than most grandmothers, a little quirky and sometimes embarrassing with her weird voodoo beliefs, but she had loved her. She'd died of a stroke ten years ago, leaving a hole in Eilea's heart the size of Texas. "If I ever have a child, I'll love that child as much as the women in my life loved me."

"You won't have a child if you mate with them." Nakomi crossed to Eilea, flashing the fingers of one hand. "You will have five, and you will have to raise them. Are you prepared to give up being a doctor?"

Amara slipped between them. "Step back, Nakomi." Amara's command was low yet powerful.

Silence stretched between them, mimicking the widening chasm in Eilea's heart.

Five kids? One or two, maybe, but five? No. Fucking. Way.

Nakomi laughed triumphantly. "I knew it."

AFTER MAKING THE ROUNDS, Eilea stole away for a moment to herself. Nakomi's words had shaken her so badly, she needed time to decompress. She snuck into her office, locking the door behind her, angry when she couldn't find her bag of dark chocolates to console her. She dug through the trash, not surprised to find the empty bag and wrappers. Jimmy had literally eaten everything in her stash.

Douche-nugget.

Surrendering to fatigue, she laid her head on her desk, berating herself when her eyes watered. She had no idea why she was crying. It wasn't like Nakomi had told her anything new. Eilea knew it would never work out with the Lupescu brothers, but deep in her soul, there had been a flicker of hope, a tiny ember in the chasm of despair and darkness. Now that ember had been snuffed for good. Even if she wanted to mate with the Lupescus, there would be other prejudiced shifters like Nakomi, determined to make her life miserable for thinking humans and shifters could mate.

Those few tears turned into a steady trickle. She sobbed into her arms, mourning the loss of the family she'd once had and the one she'd never have.

Why had her Christian god taken her parents? Why had the Amaroki gods taunted her with the hope of a new family?

At some point her tears turned into soft sobs, and then her sobs mellowed out into slow and steady breathing. Damn, she was tired. She closed her eyes. Maybe all she needed was some sleep. Maybe fatigue had burned out her adrenals, and her body was signaling she had to rest. Maybe she'd no longer be depressed after she recharged.

Chapter Nine

EILEA DREAMED SHE WAS floating across the clouds in an ethereal place illuminated by a glowing moon that hung low in the sky, like a giant bloated thumb. To the right was a stone well, swirling mists pouring out like a smoking volcano. In front of her was a buffet offering breads, cheeses, fruits, and meat. Beside that was an intricate iron table and two chairs. Just beyond the buffet was a shadowy forest, treetops lit by the moon's rays.

Mist flowed around her like the currents of a stream, tickling her bare feet. She was no longer wearing her hospital scrubs but a beautiful, silky dress with straps that looped around her neck and bared her shoulders. The straps dug into her skin, like they would in real life, and details were surprisingly clear.

A cloaked shadow emerged from the forest, floating to her as if being propelled on a current of air.

It pulled down a hood, revealing a beautiful woman with alabaster skin, dark hair, and silvery eyes. "Hello, Eilea." She gestured to the table of food. "Won't you join me for a repast?"

She warily eyed the woman. "Where am I?"

The woman piled a platter with food and set it on the smaller table. "You are in Valhol."

Eilea's stomach rumbled at the tantalizing smell of fragrant cheeses and meats. "What is that?" She vaguely remembered her uncle telling her something about Valhol being the shifter name for heaven, but no, she couldn't be there.

Her smile widened, revealing a dimple on either side of her mouth. "Think of it as heaven." She poured crimson liquid from a jug into two silver goblets.

"Heaven? Am I dead?"

"Certainly not." Her laughter was light and lilting. "You are a temporary visitor."

She looked over her shoulder at the mists that ran down behind her, falling over the edge of what appeared to be a cliff, then descending into darkness. A mournful howl coming from somewhere beyond the forest drew her attention. Was it a wolf or something more sinister? A terrifying thought struck her. If she was in the afterlife, were spirits here, too?

"Is Katarina here?" she blurted, her stomach twisting. The food no longer smelled good.

She shook her head. "If she was here, she wouldn't be haunting the Amaroki."

"Who are you?" Eilea asked sharply.

The woman splayed her hands and sat on the edge of the chair. "I am the Goddess Amara."

That was the Amaroki goddess who'd frequented Amara Thunderfoot's dreams. "You are one of the Ancients. My friend Amara is named after you."

The goddess nodded. "She is."

"Why have you brought me here?" she asked, fearing the answer.

"To talk." The goddess took a long sip from her goblet. She motioned to the chair beside her. "Please sit."

Eilea did so, prepared to bolt if things went sideways, though where she'd run to, she had no idea.

"Have some wine," the goddess said, pushing the goblet toward her.

She scowled at the swirling crimson liquid. "I'm on duty."

"Of course." The goddess laughed, "But you are dreaming now. A little wine in a dream won't hurt. It may even help." The goddess picked up her goblet and drank again.

She had a funny feeling in her stomach, like she was being tricked. "What's in it?"

"Wine spiked with the blood of my mates," the goddess said casually, as if drinking blood was an everyday occurrence.

"You're trying to feed me blood?"

Her red lips stood out against her porcelain skin. "You want to be like us, don't you?"

"I never said—"

The goddess held up a silencing hand. "No truer words are spoken than in the longing of one's soul."

"Wh-what?" she stammered, though she knew what the goddess was saying.

"You have always wanted a culture to belong to, have you not?"

She averted her eyes. "I never said that." But she'd thought it many times.

"You thought you'd find camaraderie among your fellow doctors, but they disrespected you because of your ancestry and sex." The goddess ran a fingertip over the rim of her goblet. "You searched for your heritage among the Africans, but they mistrusted your American birth. You sought acceptance from your uncle, but he always put the Amaroki people above you."

She swallowed the lump of granite that had formed in her throat. Had the goddess been reading her mind? If so, there was no use denying it. She'd always wanted to belong to something, anything. She'd lived a lonely life with just her eccentric grandmother, but there was no way she could change who she was. Could she? "What's your point?"

She tossed her curtain of black hair back. "How do you think I became a shifter?"

"I don't know."

"It is a very long story, one perhaps your mates can tell you, but I wasn't born a shifter. I became one through the blood of my mates."

"Hang on." Eilea abruptly stood, looking at the goblet as if it held poison. "You want to turn me into a shifter?"

"I'm offering you the blood of the Amaroki." The goddess gave her a pointed stare. "What you do with it is your choice."

If she was turned into a shifter, she could mate with the Lupescus. She would belong to them, and that was the crux of the problem. She didn't want to belong to any man. But how amazing her life would be as a shifter. She'd have an instant family she could rely on. "This isn't something I can decide in a second."

"I figured you'd be pragmatic about this," the goddess said and sighed. "Very well. I'll bring you back one more time. Think about it. Choose wisely. Once made, you will not be able to change your decision."

A KNOCK ON THE DOOR awakened Eilea. She sat up and checked the time. She'd slept two hours, probably not long enough to enter into deep sleep but enough to dream. What had she been dreaming about? She vaguely remembered a beautiful woman and clouds, but her mind was too fuzzy to piece together the rest.

When the knocking persisted, she stumbled to the door and unlocked it before falling into her chair.

Amara Thunderfoot hung over her like a mother hen. "Are you okay?"

"Yeah." Eilea yawned into her hand. "Why wouldn't I be?"

"You've been in here a long time." She took a closer look. "Have you been crying?"

"Crying?" Eilea wiped moisture from her face. "I fell asleep."

"Oh, good. I thought Nakomi upset you."

She grimaced, recalling the African shifter's harsh words. "She did."

Amara knelt beside Eilea and took her hands in hers. "Don't listen to her. I work almost every day as the tribal healer, and Rone watches the kids. You don't have to give up your career. I'm sure the Romanian tribe would appreciate a medical doctor who understands them."

She jerked free of Amara's grasp. "I'm not moving to Romania. After this is all over, I'm turning in my resignation and moving back to Houston."

"But why?" Amara cried in surprise.

"Nakomi was right. I don't want five kids. I don't want to be married to four controlling men."

Amara plastered on a forced smile. "I didn't either at first, but I love my life now."

"Amara, you're a shifter. I'm not. I'm not meant for this world." A vague memory flitted through her mind. She saw a goblet of red wine and a beautiful woman offering to turn her into a shifter. Where had that come from?

"If you'd just give them a chance," Amara pleaded. "They are only controlling when your safety is threatened."

"Which will be all the time." Amara would be upset for her fathers, but it couldn't be helped. She would not choose a life out of guilt.

"You don't know that," Amara said, sounding like a deflating balloon.

"No, Amara." Eilea turned up her chin, steeling her resolve. "It would never work, and I refuse to lead them on."

The beautiful woman's face appeared again, this time as a wisp of smoke in the window above Eilea's desk.

"You have until the next full moon." The woman's lips didn't move, but Eilea heard her voice as clear as day.

She pointed at the window. "Are you seeing this?"

Amara stood. "Seeing what?"

Eilea blinked hard, and the woman was gone. "My fucking insanity, that's what."

BORIS AND JOVAN WERE hulking white beasts outside, pacing the perimeters of the building with gleaming axes slung across their broad shoulders, looking into the forest with narrowed eyes like they expected the boogie man to come out and attack them. A white wolf Eilea assumed was Marius accompanied them. What the heck? Why were they in shifter form? Was it to ward off ghosts or something worse? She didn't see Amara's mate, Drasko, but she assumed he was somewhere out there, too.

Geri sat in the waiting room, chair propped up against the makeshift door, an axe lying across his legs. She thought about asking him what was going on, but decided she'd rather not know. She had enough to worry about. She could tell Geri was tired by the way his head kept bobbing toward his chest, his eyelids heavy. Hell, everyone was exhausted. Even Nakomi had finally agreed to take a power nap in one of the exam rooms, demanding that Eilea wake her in a few hours. She didn't want to anger the shifter, but she was sorely tempted to let her sleep the rest of the night. Maybe she'd wake in a better mood. And maybe shit-eating gremlins would fly out of Eilea's ass.

She made the rounds again, dismayed when not one patient had a reduction in fever. How could they sustain such high fevers for so long? Night had fallen. The days were rapidly getting shorter as winter approached. Eilea sure as hell hoped they figured out how to close the portal before winter swallowed them whole. Drasko had informed her they were relocating at dawn. She worried about the Spiritcaller alpha, whose oxygen level was critically low. How would he handle the move?

Raz was softly snoring beside one of her mates, curled up like a cat at the foot of his bed. How did the old woman have such flexibility? Amara looked after Nakomi's mates, keeping cool compresses on their heads. She was a great help, even if she couldn't access her healing powers.

Jimmy kept to himself, constantly telling everyone he had to check on supplies when he only went into the janitorial closet to let out gas. Sadly, he didn't wait long enough, and most of the smell followed him back out. Amara finally said something.

With an exaggerated pout, he stormed into the bathroom, slamming the door behind him.

Amara laughed under her breath. "Douche."

Jimmy emerged from the bathroom about an hour later, throwing an empty bottle of antacid medicine in the garbage.

He ambled around the infirmary, groaning and rubbing his belly while pretending to be helping, but mostly he just got in the way. Though Eilea tried to focus on her patients, she could feel his eyes boring holes in her skull. What the hell was the matter with him?

He circled the room, edging a little closer to her with each pass.

Jesus, the guy was creepy as fuck.

Finally, he was just one bed away, pretending to check a bed pad when she knew he had no intention of changing it. "Hey, sorry about earlier," he blurted.

She gritted her teeth. "About what?"

"You know." He shrugged, flashing a bashful grin.

She wasn't fooled "Let's see." She counted on her fingers. "You flirted with me, then stole my food, then nearly knocked me out with your flatulence."

"All of the above." His flush deepened, making him look like an overripe carrot with that fake tan. "I don't usually fart. Those fiber bars were really strong."

"Everyone farts, but whatever." She felt the elder Spiritcaller's pulse. It was weak but still there. His raised welts had scabbed over and turned a dark green, looking like dried up slugs. She was alarmed when she touched one, and it crumbled apart like dead leaves. If she didn't know better, she'd have sworn the man was petrifying.

"Do you have a thing for that shifter?" Jimmy said at her back.

She stiffened, speaking through tight lips. "The one who had you in a chokehold?"

"Yeah."

"Why is it any of your damn business?" This asshole was getting on her last nerve.

"I don't know. I just thought it was weird. I mean, I'm all for interracial dating, but people should stick to their own species."

She imagined she was channeling Nakomi's inner-wolf. "Can you stop talking now?"

"Is it because I'm white? Because color doesn't matter to me. Actually, I lied." He flashed a sideways smile. "It does matter. I prefer dark chocolate to white chocolate."

Her jaw dropped. "Excuse me?" She was so stunned, she didn't know what to say. Was this douche calling her a candy bar?

"You know what they say." He waggled his brows. "The darker the chocolate, the sweeter the flavor."

She blinked. "That doesn't make any sense. Milk chocolate is sweeter than dark chocolate." Surely nobody was that stupid. She wished he was a figment of her imagination. That would make sense, since she was currently living in a nightmare.

He had the nerve to lick his lips lasciviously. "Is it?"

"You need to work on your pickup lines." She pointed a thermometer at him, wishing it was a magical wand, and she could zap him into the next dimension, far, far away from her. "Actually, don't bother. I'm not interested in anything more than a professional relationship, and I never will be." She didn't even want that with this man. After she made her rounds, she was determined to call her uncle and get Jimmy the hell out of her clinic.

He turned so red, he looked like a volcano ready to blow. "Think you're too good for me because you're a fucking doctor?"

Oh, so he was one of *those* assholes. She knew his type. The short shits with the big attitudes. He probably had a micro penis, too. "You know what I think?" she said evenly so he wouldn't know how pissed off she was. "I think you should change the bed pads."

"Eh." He blew out spittle with an annoying face fart. "No thanks."

Amara clucked her tongue. Eilea worried Amara would tell her fathers about Jimmy's lack of respect toward her. The last thing she needed was four possessive, angry shifters getting involved. It would not end well for Jimmy—or for any of them if the government found out.

"Do you have problems taking orders from women or does that apply to everyone?" Eilea drawled.

"I don't have problems taking orders when they're fair." His pitch rose to a girly squeal, and the veins in his neck popped like raging rivers. Yeah, micro penis.

"It's not your place to determine what's fair." She impressed herself by keeping it together this long, and it was fun knowing her cool demeanor was making him angrier. "If I tell you to change the bed pads, you do it."

Shaking her head, Amara marched out. Eilea wondered if she was about to alert the Lupescus.

"Fine." He turned up his nose, looking like a disgruntled toddler who'd been sent to time-out. "Forget I asked you out. I'm no longer interested."

"Golly gee"—she snapped her fingers, heaving a dramatic sigh—"and I was so looking forward to an evening of cheesy pickup lines and noxious gas."

Jimmy was about to say something when Amara returned with her father, Geri, his eyes lit with determination. Before Eilea could stop him, Geri grabbed Jimmy by the neck and dragged him out the door. Amara returned to her patients, showing no alarm that her father had had a federal agent in a headlock.

She chased after them. "Geri, wait. What are you doing?" Jimmy was annoying, but she didn't want her mates charged with murder. No, wait, they weren't her mates, but murder was murder, and she couldn't condone it.

Geri emitted an ear-splitting howl that rattled her insides. She shielded her ears and then her mouth and nose when Jimmy let out an explosive fart, struggling in Geri's grip.

Geri tightened his hold on Jimmy's neck, releasing a string of Romanian expletives that she didn't recognize, with the exception of the word quallu.

The makeshift front door burst open, revealing two pale, hairy monsters with heaving chests and gleaming axes, and a snarling wolf beside them. Jimmy was so fucked.

Chapter Ten

JIMMY'S EAR-PIERCING scream alerted Drasko, who ran to the front of the clinic, the thunderous booms of his heavy feet rattling Eilea's brain. He stopped short of Boris and Jovan, every inch as large and intimidating as they were in his big ape-like form.

"What's going on?" he demanded, his deep bellow shaking the ground.

Bile projected into the back of her throat when Boris spun Jimmy around like a baton, dangling him by his ankles while Marius, still in wolf form, snapped at Jimmy's scalp.

Jimmy flailed like a fish out of water. "Help," he rasped, then yelped when Marius snapped at his neck.

Geri waved the axe precariously close to Jimmy's groin. "He was flirting with our mate, and when she rejected him, he insulted her."

"Y-your mate?" Jimmy wheezed. "I didn't know."

Eilea turned up her nose. "I'm not their mate."

Jovan looked at her with a grin so possessive, it made her flesh crawl. "You will be."

"You beasts listen to me." She craned her neck to glare up at the two big brutes. "I handled Jimmy already."

Boris let out a sinister chuckle. "But we haven't."

"I won't bug her again," Jimmy cried, snot dripping from his nose to his eye. "I swear."

Boris and Jovan laughed, revealing sharp fangs.

"He works for the government. I don't want you going to prison for me." She tried to appeal to their reasonable sides.

Jovan's smile widened. "Can't go to prison when there's no evidence."

Jimmy let out a wail, followed by a liquid fart.

Boris howled, fanning his face and trying to hand off his captive to Jovan.

Jovan backed up, waving Jimmy away. "What the hell is wrong with this quallu?"

"He might be a skunk shifter," Geri said.

"I'm sorry. I'm really sorry." Jimmy moaned, tears and snot dripping down his forehead. "I didn't know she was taken."

"It doesn't matter if she was taken," Geri snapped, swinging the axe at Jimmy's groin once more. "You don't talk to women that way."

"You're right." Jimmy turned pleading eyes to Eilea. "I'm an idiot. I'm so, so sorry, Eilea."

She stiffened. "Dr. Johnson."

"Right. Dr. Johnson." He sniffled, dragging a line of snot back inside his nose. "I'm sorry. I won't bother you again. Please don't let them kill me."

"Guys, let him go." She heaved a sigh, not sure if she felt pity or disgust for Jimmy. "I'm sure he'll be on his best behavior now."

Boris grunted and turned on his heel, stepping over the salt circle and heading toward the forest with long strides, Jimmy still in his grip. His brothers quickly followed.

Jimmy's wails grew louder.

"Guys!" She hollered.

Geri turned, pointing the tip of his blade at the salt circle, which was still intact. "Stay inside, Eilea."

She raced to the edge of the circle, careful not to cross it—not because she was obeying their orders, but because she was genuinely afraid of that ghost. "What are you going to do?"

"Don't worry," Jovan said over his shoulder. "We'll bring him back."

"Sure they will," she grumbled, turning pleading eyes to Drasko. "In how many pieces?"

"Meh." He shrugged broad shoulders and grinned. "Probably no more than six."

She clutched her churning stomach. Considering Jovan had ripped the head off a federal agent once before, she was afraid for Jimmy.

Amara appeared in the doorway.

"Stop them," she said.

"Why? He dishonored you."

She was frustrated and furious with these hard-headed shifters. "But your fathers can get in trouble."

"No they won't." Amara turned up her chin, revealing a too-confident grin. "Your uncle will make sure of it."

"If you say so." Eilea brushed past her and strode to the infirmary. Would Uncle Joe protect the Lupescus? Maybe because his world revolved around the shifter species but not because he cared about his niece's honor.

EILEA HAD A HARD TIME focusing on her patients while she worried about Jimmy being decapitated. Yeah, he was a first-rate douche, and she despised working with him, but she still didn't agree with murder. If ever there was any hope of Eilea forming a bond with the Lupescus, they'd ruined it. The thought saddened her more than it should have, and she berated herself for not doing more to stop them. She'd been so numb from shock that her critical thinking skills had gone right out the window.

She heard a commotion in the waiting room. Geri had returned with his gleaming axe, his green jacket stained with what appeared to be black paint. He sat in a chair beside the front door, whistling as if he hadn't a care in the world.

She marched over to him. "Where's Jimmy?"

He quirked an eyebrow, looking at her with a crooked, fanged grin. Of all his brothers, he seemed the most feral, an air of danger clinging to him like a shroud. She remembered he'd been the only brother to experience demon burn. She wondered what he was doing when he suffered the burn. She imagined he'd been hunting some foul creature. She'd no doubt by the way he held the axe, like an extension of his arm, that he'd seen his share of battles.

"Why do you care about him so much?" he said, with a subtle accusatory tone.

"I don't care about him." She averted her eyes, not because she was lying, but because the animalistic gleam in his eyes unnerved her. "I care about you getting into trouble."

His fanged smile broadened. "You have nothing to worry about."

"So you didn't kill him?"

"Not yet."

Her spine stiffened and she let out a curse. "I don't agree with murder."

"We know, lubirea mea," he said with a wink. "We would never do anything to hurt you. We just want to protect you."

Heat fanned her skin as he continued to look at her with intense silver-blue eyes. When he licked his top lip with an impressively long, thick tongue, she got lightheaded.

He leaned back in his chair, crossing wiry, muscular arms. "I don't need to read your mind to know what you're thinking. Your facial expressions give you away."

She froze when he set the axe on the floor and unfolded himself from the chair, rising like a phantom emerging from the grave. Leaning over her, he threaded his fingers through hers, whispering hot and heavy in her ear. "Let me take you into your office, mândră. I will show you what my tongue can do."

Heat pooled between her thighs. Her knees wobbled like two wet noodles and she had to drape her arms around his shoulders to steady herself.

When he leaned into her, nibbling her ear with sharp teeth, her head went back, giving him easy access to her neck.

"Stop," she pleaded, though she rubbed her taut nipples against his chest.

He trailed hot kisses down her neck, growling against her skin and making her soak her panties. Dear God, what was this man doing and why was she letting him do it? Amara and Raz had to be watching, and Nakomi would be furious when she found out, but she was so damned horny, she didn't care.

When he ground his hips into hers, and his denim-clad erection pressed into her belly, she just about orgasmed then and there. She lifted her leg, dragging it up his calf when he dug his fingers into her ass, branding her.

"Let's go to your office," he rumbled in her ear. "Let me give you pleasure."

"Yes, oh yes," she cried, going limp against him. She knew she wasn't thinking clearly, knew she'd regret surrendering to temptation, but she couldn't see past her much-needed orgasm.

He was leading her to the office when the makeshift door slammed open, revealing Drasko Thunderfoot in human form, grim determination in his eyes.

"Just got word the Moosenecks are sick; all three packs— elders, sons, and grandsons, plus their mates and babies. Hakon told them to go straight to the lodge. The feds are dropping supplies in the parking lot." He dangled a set of keys. "We need to get moving." He sniffed the air and gave Eilea and Geri the once-over. "Sorry if I interrupted something."

She was at a loss for words. Geri didn't help by staring at his feet, his pale cheeks turning crimson. She'd never been more ashamed in her life. Luckily, Drasko had deflated her libido with the news of sick children. She pulled away from Geri, ashamed at what she'd been about to do. What the hell had she been thinking? How could she give herself to him when she knew he was only using sex as a means to claim her as his mate? Correction, as a mate to four hot and horny brothers.

"The Spiritcaller pack is too sick to move," she said, worried they wouldn't survive the trip and desperately needing to say something to fill the awkward, deafening silence.

Drasko grimaced. "Jovan and I will move them." He brushed past them on his way to the infirmary. "I need to notify the others."

As if on cue, Jovan appeared. He, too, was back in human form and looking too sexy to be legal in faded jeans and an unbuttoned flannel shirt revealing a muscular, broad chest with a smattering of blond hair. Like his brother, he was smeared with black paint. He had globs on his cheek and chest. What had they gotten into?

He gave Geri an accusatory look, nostrils flaring.

Geri shot Jovan an apologetic look. "I wasn't going to take her virginity. Just mark her."

Um, take her virginity? She'd lost that long ago to her first boyfriend during freshman year of college. Jesus, she was almost thirty-five. Did they really expect her to be a virgin? Well, they were in for a disappointment. Not that they should judge. They had five children.

She gestured at the infirmary window, where her patients resembled corpses more than men. "I think this is a bad idea. We should bring more beds here, fill up the exam rooms."

"Every choice we make from here on out will be a bad idea," Jovan answered, "but some choices are less bad than others."

"Is dismembering a federal agent a less bad choice?"

"Who said we dismembered him?" Jovan chuckled.

She gave him a stern look she hoped would intimidate a man who could turn into a ten-foot hulking beast in the blink of an eye. "Where is he?"

"You sure you don't have a thing for him?" Geri asked.

"That farting little creep?" she said, aghast. "Do you hear yourself? How can I even think of other men when I compare them to...." She bit her tongue.

Jovan bridged the distance between them, grabbed her shoulders, and searched her eyes, his expression a mixture of desperation and desire. "To what?"

She turned away. "Never mind."

"Why do you deny this attraction between us?" He leaned into her. "Do you think I can't scent the desire between your legs? Imagine four men pleasuring you at your whim. You'd no longer have to use your showerhead."

He knew about that? How fucking embarrassing.

She struggled free, hating how turned on she became at the feel of his skin. "It won't work."

He jerked her against him. "You won't know unless you try," he cooed.

She wanted to give into temptation and let him try, but she would not surrender her independence to these shifters, despite the promise of mind-blowing sex at her command. "I'm not like you," she said.

"That doesn't matter to us," he said.

Would he feel the same way if he knew she wasn't a virgin? Would he be angry with her or her past lovers? How would his brothers react? When he tried to nuzzle her, she bit her lip so hard, she drew blood. The taste of it brought a vivid memory rushing back of a beautiful woman trying to coax Eilea into drinking blood-tainted wine. Holy shit! Was that a dream or had she been visited by a goddess offering to transform her into a shifter? Nausea overcame her and she went limp in Jovan's arms, barely aware of him calling her name and then carrying her to an exam room.

He laid her on the table, eyes shifting from blue to blinding white. "Are you okay?"

"I, um," She almost blurted that she'd just remembered almost drinking blood wine, but she thought better of it.

Geri held her hand to his heart. "She's been working too many hours. Humans don't have our stamina."

Truth be told, she was tired. Fucking tired. She got up on her elbows. "I'm fine," she lied.

Jovan's brows drew into a deep *V*. "No, you're not."

"I'll rest when we get to the lodge."

Geri scowled at his brother. "She's lying. She's going to tend sick patients first."

Jovan's features darkened. "Not if I can help it."

Their overbearing nature was enough to drive her insane. She grabbed Jovan's arm and pulled herself upright. "Yes, I'm tending to my patients first, but then I am resting. Promise." Had she just caved? Why didn't she tell them off for being controlling assholes?

She let Jovan help her back to the waiting room and lower her into a chair. "Stay here," he said, kissing her temple. "We'll load the patients and supplies."

She shouldn't have basked in the attention, but she did, maybe too much. Little things like Jovan kissing her forehead set her heart aflame. Damn her for falling for these shifters, and damn her for recalling her dream, for she was almost certain she remembered the goddess telling her she had one more chance to accept the opportunity to become a shifter.

LUC MOPPED HIS BROW after helping the last of the Moosenecks into his truck. Since his fathers had become sick, his pack had stepped up to fill the chieftain's role. He didn't relish the responsibility. He'd gone to almost every homestead close to the portal and sniffed out the sickest shifters. All of them had been able to drive except for the Moosenecks.

Not one of them had understood what was happening. They were all walking around in a daze while itching the scabs on their arms into bloody oblivion. Luckily their houses were close together. Luc had to make three trips to the lodge, starting with the youngest Moosenecks, including a seven-month-old baby flushed from crying. By the last trip, he was feeling disoriented, too. It took him longer than expected, as he kept having to stop to refocus.

After he'd helped the elder alpha Mooseneck into the front passenger seat of his truck, he sat at the steering wheel a long time, trying to remember where he was going.

He looked at the cardboard sign taped to the center of the dash: *Take the Moosenecks to the lodge.*

Oh, yeah, the lodge.

He started the engine and put the truck in drive, gently rolling down the hill toward the front gate. After he pulled out, he stared at the fork in the road. Which way was he going?

He looked at the cardboard sign again: *Take the Moosenecks to the lodge.*

Was it left or right?

The elder Mooseneck was slumped in the seat beside him. The man's paper-thin skin was ashen and covered in raised welts, his large nose and the sagging skin on his neck dripping with sweat. He looked like a plucked pelican, roasting on the spit.

"Do you remember how to get to the lodge?"

The elder raised a feeble finger and pointed right.

He drove slowly, hitting every pothole and narrowly missing trees. He kept stopping to mop his eyes and scratch his arms. Had he gotten into poison ivy? They itched like crazy. It consumed him so badly, he'd forgotten to drive and rolled to a stop at the edge of a ditch.

He scratched and scratched until he bled. Still, his skin burned.

He jumped at a sharp rap on his window.

He stared into the familiar face of a scowling girl with pretty blue eyes and long black hair. He knew her, didn't he? He rolled down the window, wondering if he was in a dream.

"What the fuck, Luc?" she snapped. "Why would you leave me behind?"

"Do I know you?"

"It's me, Annie. You don't know your own cousin?" Her eyes bulged when she looked at his arms. "Holy fuck, Luc." She jerked open the door. "Move over."

He tried to, but something was holding him back. Swearing, she unbuckled his seatbelt and pushed him over.

"Where are you taking me?" he asked.

"To Amara," she said.

"Oh. She's my mate," he said, proud of himself for remembering. He scratched again as he tried to recall his mate's face, but all he could visualize was her sobbing into her hands. Why would Amara cry? He had a sickening feeling in his gut that he'd somehow upset her. That sick feeling raced into his throat, and he vomited all over the dashboard, splattering the window with what looked like buckets of green slime.

The woman beside him shrieked, but Luc was too sick to care. He curled into himself and rested his head against a bony knee.

Chapter Eleven

THE CLINIC HAD BEEN emptied of everyone except Eilea. Now the time had come for her to go to the lodge. She looked around her empty clinic with a mixture of relief and sorrow. What she was sorry for, she had no idea. She was going to turn in her resignation anyway.

After expelling a quivering breath and shaking nervous energy out of her hands, she spied Jovan's borrowed truck barreling into the drive. She followed Boris outside, stopping when he thrust an arm behind him.

"Are you ready?" he asked over his shoulder.

She shrugged. "As I'll ever be."

Jovan barreled at her like a runaway train, swooping her in his arms before she could react.

The air expelled from her lungs when he dumped her in the passenger seat. He practically flew over the hood of the truck and jumped into the driver's seat, throwing the truck into drive and peeling out of the parking lot. She looked behind her to see Boris standing in the bed of the truck, holding onto the bars as Jovan practically drove on two wheels around each bend in the road.

"Don't you think you should slow down?" she asked, clutching the dashboard like a lifeline.

Jovan kept his gaze centered on the road. "*Nu*," he said tersely, then added. "Keep your eyes open for any signs."

"Signs of what?" she asked, then screamed when Jovan slammed on the brakes and a huge branch tumbled down in front of them.

Boris jumped out of the truck, shifting into beast form. He moved the branch with one arm and waved them forward. Jovan hit the gas again, not even waiting for Boris to get back in the truck. She was shocked to see Boris keeping pace.

Her jaw practically hit the floorboards when he soared through the air, first as a behemoth beast, then as a wolf, and finally landing in the truck bed as a naked human.

Jesus Christ, these shifters must spend a fortune on clothes.

He grabbed onto the bars again, bracing muscular legs while his flesh snake swung like a windsock in a hurricane. Her face burned when Jovan caught her looking at Boris's appendage.

He grinned wickedly. "All of the Lupescus are blessed by the Ancients, lubirea mea."

She turned away, shivering from a sudden icy chill. Oh, fuck.

Jovan stomped on the brakes again when a boulder rolled toward them.

Boris flew out of the back of the truck once more, stopping the boulder with a roar. Jovan kept on driving, and his brother caught up.

"Did this happen on your other trips?" she asked Jovan.

He grimaced. "Nu."

Holy fuck, they were being chased by a jealous ghost who was determined to murder Eilea.

"Well, don't I feel special?" she said wryly.

Jovan clutched the steering wheel with white knuckles. "You are a better woman than she ever was, and she hates you for it."

That was the wrong thing to say, because an ear-piercing wail filled the cabin. She cringed, covering her ears, then jumped at the sound of four large explosions. The truck made a jerky dip, then a metallic screech. The tires had burst. Jovan swerved, narrowly missing a tree before coming to a violent halt. She jerked against the seatbelt, and Boris flew over the hood, tumbling through the air as a white wolf and landing on the ground with a yelp.

Jovan jumped out, kicking the panel with a holler. "Get out. We walk from here."

She slid out the truck and into Boris's furry arms. A bloody gash in his forehead marred his white fur. "We need to take care of that."

He shook his heavy jowls. "No time." His deep baritone rattled her chest.

He ran so fast with her in his arms, the forest became a blur. A shrill demonic wail followed them. She was stunned when tall pines fell into each other. She had to close her eyes or risk losing the stale bagel she'd eaten for breakfast. When she heard a second set of heavy footsteps, she knew Jovan was beside them. She prayed to her god and their gods that they made it to the lodge before Katarina.

AFTER THEY STUMBLED into the lodge like a herd of wild elephants, Eilea heaved a sigh of relief. Chest heaving and furry brow dripping with sweat, Boris set her down, then shifted, thanking Nakomi, who handed him a robe. Jovan waved off Nakomi's offer of a clean robe and marched back outside to join his other brothers and Drasko on guard duty. Boris wanted to go with Jovan, but Eilea insisted they fix his wound first. Inside, the lodge was as chaotic as outside. The structure was more of a coliseum, with a circular auditorium that sloped like a theater. Instead of chairs, dozens of cots were arranged on the circular rows. The center was a control station with cameras and equipment. Guess Uncle Joe had come through with more supplies. There had to be close to fifty sick people, some of them children, and only Raz, Amara, and Nakomi to help them.

Eilea had no time to address Boris's injury, as she had to get to work administering IVs to the children, but she was grateful to Amara, who quickly healed his head wound.

She'd secured the first IV and ventilator on a seven-month-old infant when she heard a toilet flush nearby. Her jaw dropped when Jimmy came out. She had to slap a hand over her mouth to keep from laughing at his comical appearance. He looked like a skunk, covered head-to-toe in black paint or soot, with a long white stripe running down his backside and a bushy skunk tail pinned to his rear. He was carrying a bundle of bed pads, looking as haggard as a waiter at an all-night diner.

She was glad her mates hadn't killed him, and his skunk appearance fit his smell. Maybe next time he'd think twice before harassing women.

She berated herself for referring to the Lupescu brothers as her mates. Why did she keep doing that?

Jimmy passed by, keeping his head down and not so much as giving her the side eye. She'd thought the skunk tail was pinned to his bottom, but it appeared to have been shoved up his ass.

"That's a hell of a wedgie." Amara laughed and winked at Eilea.

He gave Amara a look that reminded Eilea of a starving dog begging for scraps. "I'm not allowed to remove it."

Ouch.

"Your new colors look good on you," Amara continued. "Spray-tan orange was so last decade."

He scowled but didn't answer. Eilea shot Amara a warning look. Jimmy had the look of a caged animal, with his shifty and wild eyes. The last thing she needed was for the agent to lash out at Amara.

"Stop provoking him," she hissed when Amara laughed.

"Why? It's so much fun. My cousin Annie killed a creep like him, ripped his neck wide open. He'd be a fool to fuck with shifters."

"That's the problem," Nakomi said as she went by carrying an armful of empty bottles. "He *is* a fool."

"Wise words," Eilea mumbled, not daring to voice her support aloud. Nakomi would probably take it as an insult.

"Amara!"

It was Annie, Amara's cousin. Beside her, Drasko carried Luc Thunderfoot, who hung limply in his brother's arms.

Her eyes filling with tears, Amara stood when Drasko descended the stairs two at a time and placed Luc on an empty cot.

Annie dropped on an empty cot with a groan.

"What happened?" Amara asked.

Annie said, "He fell ill when we were getting the Mooseneck elders."

Amara grasped Luc's flushed face, tears streaming. "Luc, darling, speak to me."

"Amaaaraa," Luc rasped. "The baby."

"He's fine." She wiped her eyes, turning to Drasko. "He didn't show me Luc getting sick."

Drasko frowned. "Maybe he was sleeping."

She set to work cleaning Luc with a wet rag. Drasko kissed her cheek. Then he leaned over his brother, nuzzling his shorn hair. "Be strong, brother. We love you." His voice cracked, and he quickly strode out the door.

Amara's face fell as she watched him leave. She quickly got back to work cleaning Luc, alternating between sniffling and then scrunching her face so tight, she looked ready to crack.

Eilea's heart hurt for Amara. She couldn't imagine the young mother's fear and suffering. She grabbed a wet cloth and knelt beside her, Annie following her lead. They wordlessly attended Luc. Eilea feared for him. He was burning up, and he'd been covered in green, sticky vomit. She checked his temperature, dismayed when the thermometer read 104°.

After forcing him to drink a few teaspoons of fever reducer, she wiped her eyes with her forearm, shocked to see she'd been crying.

Nakomi went by again, scowling down at Eilea. "Why do you cry for us?" she asked with a sneer. "We are not your people."

She was too depressed, too distraught to be offended. "I cry because I care," she said matter-of-factly. Nakomi could believe her or not. She no longer gave a shit what the African shifter thought of her.

Nakomi took dirty rags from Annie and gave her a fresh pan of soapy water. "We do not need your pity."

A wave of anger rolled over her. Knowing she was taking a risk, she stood, hands clenched into fists. "Amara and Luc are my friends. I'll cry for them if I want to."

Lifting her chin, Nakomi glared at Eilea through slitted lids. "Don't try to fool me with false compassion. You humans are all the same." She marched away.

"Don't listen to her." Annie wrung water out of a rag and cleaned Luc's leg. "She probably doesn't mean it."

"She's under a lot of stress," Amara said, laying a cool cloth on Luc's brow.

Eilea gritted her teeth. "Everyone's under stress, and she did mean it. She clearly hates me."

Annie rested a hand on Eilea's arm, looking at her with luminous blue eyes. "We don't all think like her."

"No, but I'm sure more Amaroki do. I need to check the others."

She held back a fresh wave of tears. Even if she wanted to mate with the Lupescus, tribal prejudice against humans might prevent that from happening. She remembered the goddess's offer. If she accepted, her genetic make-up, her biochemistry, her very life would change forever. Worse, she'd feel obligated to mate with the Lupescus. Was that what she wanted? She used to think her independence was more important to her than anything. Now she wasn't so sure.

EILEA WAS SO EXHAUSTED, she could barely see straight. After stumbling into a patient's bed and nearly stabbing herself with a needle, Raz and Amara insisted she go lie down. Her feet felt like they were encased in buckets of concrete as she trudged toward the private room they'd set up for her.

She felt guilty leaving when more and more Amaroki were piling into the lodge. They needed her, but more importantly, she was terrified she'd have another dream. What if the goddess visited her again? She wasn't ready to decide if she wanted to become a shifter. Was Amara right that Marius would watch their babies so she could continue being a doctor? And wouldn't it be amazing to shift into a wolf? To defend herself against creeps like Jimmy? To have a family to come home to each day? Four strong men who wanted to protect and love her? Men who made her libido go wild?

In the end, fatigue won out. She'd be no good to the sick if she didn't rest. Besides, those who hadn't succumbed to the sickness yet acted as nurses, and Eilea had more help than she could've hoped for.

Her room had a bed and a bathroom with a shower. After she washed the smell of sickness off, she ate a few jerky sticks and a granola bar, then crawled into bed. It wasn't much bigger than the cots the patients were using, but it felt like heaven, with soft flannel sheets and a fluffy down comforter. She'd just snuggled into her pillow when the door cracked open. Geri stalked toward her like a wolf cornering a rabbit.

She shot up, pulling the comforter close and wishing she was wearing more than a hospital gown.

"What do you want?" she barked, then felt bad for being so harsh. Geri wouldn't hurt her. She was terrified he'd finish what he'd started earlier. Goddess save her, she wouldn't have the willpower to stop him.

He pulled a woolen cap off his head, looking sexier than should be legal, with disheveled hair and that crooked, fanged grin. "I've come to say goodbye."

Her heart seized, then quickened. Were they finally taking her advice and returning to Romania? The thought tied her guts in a knot. Though she wanted them far away from this virus, she never thought she'd be so torn up over their leaving. "You're going home?" she asked, unable to keep the sorrow from her voice. What if they were contagious? What if they made the Romanian tribe sick? Even worse, she wouldn't be there to help them.

"No." His smile widened. "But I'm glad to see you don't want us to go."

She flushed. Damn. Next, they'd be expecting her to be their barefoot, pregnant, breeding bitch.

"Now that Luc is sick," he continued, "I'm volunteering to check on the rest of the tribe and see if I can root out the witch."

She worried her lip, thinking of him out there alone. What if Katarina attacked him? What if a demon did? She'd seen them with axes and knew they were expecting something far worse than the jealous ghost of their dead wife.

"And you can't get infected because you've had demon burn?"

"It's what Amara tells me." He sat on the bed. "Is it true you're leaving the clinic?"

She scooted away from him, pressing her back against the wall. Why did he think he could sit there? "Where did you hear that?"

"From Amara, who heard it from Tatiana."

Damn that Tatiana. Well, no use hiding her intentions. Maybe she could make them realize how important her medical career was to her, that she wouldn't be tied down to a boring job or a mundane marriage. "I'm not needed here."

"We don't have a good healer in Romania. Perhaps you'd like to open a clinic there."

"You can't be serious."

He nodded eagerly. "We've already said we'd allow you to open a clinic in Romania."

What the ever-loving fuck? "Oh, you'll allow me?" She shook a fist at him, rage making her blood pressure rise. "How generous of you."

"We are not used to human women, but I think you are being sarcastic." He scratched the back of his head. The confused expression on his face would've been comical if hadn't he just made himself out to be a total ass. "Have we done something to offend you?"

Un-fucking-believable. "The mere notion of being your breeding machine offends me."

His face fell. "Then you do not desire us?"

"I didn't say that." She cursed her traitorous hormones as an uncomfortable ache throbbed deep in her groin.

"Good, because you'd be lying." He leaned closer. "I can still smell your desire."

When he placed a hand on her knee, she thought she'd expire from lust. His fingers practically burned holes through the fabric, setting her skin on fire.

"I can't help it."

"Neither can I," he said and slid over, brushing his lips tenderly across hers. "Should we continue where we left off?"

"We shouldn't." But desire rebelled against reason, and her legs fell open, allowing his hand to slide down her thigh.

He nibbled her ear, making a sound that was a cross between a purr and a growl. "It will help you sleep."

"Your brothers will be angry." She thrust her hips toward him, gasping when his hand slid lower.

"I will not take your virginity," he cooed. "I'll just give you pleasure with my touch."

Her virginity? Aw, fuck. She'd forgotten about that. She should tell him the truth, but then his hand moved to her mound, cupping her through the fabric, his finger gyrating against her sweet spot.

She threw back her head with a moan. How long had it been since a man had touched her there? She'd missed it badly. "This is a bad idea." When he stroked faster, she sank into the bed with a shudder.

"Are you sure?" He chuckled, sliding a hand under the blankets. His eyes widened, his fanged smile making him look like the devil himself when he discovered she wasn't wearing underwear. He slid his index finger down her slick ribbon. "You're so wet."

It was true. She was wetter than a Texas thunderstorm. She'd started gushing the moment he walked into the room.

He kissed her softly. Greedily, she opened her mouth to him, threading her fingers through his corn-silk hair. When he slipped his tongue in her mouth, she spread her legs wider, letting him brand her with his touch, and consequences be damned. He tasted like spice and some earthy, unfamiliar scent. Not bad, just different. Arousing. Like his spit had pheromones that made her libido come alive. Crying into his mouth, she clenched his hair by the roots when he stroked her slippery ribbon faster.

The intense pressure deep inside her built. Her clitoris felt like a balloon, inflating bigger and bigger with each stroke.

When he trailed hot kisses down her neck, she surrendered to the pleasure. "Oh, god."

"Your god isn't here, Eilea," he rumbled in his wolf voice, making her even wetter.

Straddling her, he nudged open her robe with his nose, scraping his teeth across one pert breast, then the other. She panicked when he took her hard nipple in his mouth, then moaned in delight when he suckled her like a baby drawing milk, sucking, licking, nipping her sensitive flesh, until she thought she'd die from the pleasure. Just as she was about to expire, he released her and kissed his way to the other breast, teasing, stretching her nipple with gentle tugs of his teeth before releasing and licking away the pain.

When he slipped a digit inside her swollen pussy, she stilled, unable to breathe. He tunneled inside her while trailing kisses down her belly. If he sucked her clit, she would come undone. Her pussy swelled around his finger, then tensed when he slipped in another digit.

His fingers were thick, too thick.

"Easy." She reached for his wrist. "It hurts."

He scraped her thigh with canine teeth. "Relax. You'll get used to it."

She swallowed hard and forced herself to relax, to submit to the pleasure. Her tight sheath gave way, opening to him like a flower. He dove into her, his tongue darting across her sensitive flesh, his thick fingers probing her.

She thrust her hips, calling his name, giving in to euphoria as he fucked her with his fingers.

Her world shook, rocking so hard, she gasped for breath as a powerful climax gripped her. His fingers were deep inside her, thumping against her slick channel like a pulsating cock. Her sheath contracted, suddenly becoming too tight. She scurried up against the headboard, trying to free herself, but he followed her, jamming his fingers into her with deep, choppy thrusts.

"I'm not done with you," he growled, his eyes canine slits and his nose lengthening as he circled her nub with his thumb.

Holy fuck! Was he shifting in front of her? He looked part demon. He finger-fucked her harder, faster, eyes glowing, canines extended. She should've been terrified, but she'd never been so damned turned on in her life.

He continued ramming into her, rattling the bed and making the springs squeal in protest. Clutching the headboard for support, she threw back her head with a plea on her lips as another powerful climax built. Without warning it spiraled through her, setting off a chain of orgasms so powerful, she couldn't breathe as they shot through her, electrifying every nerve from head to toe. Sated and spent, she fell back in a puddle of satisfaction.

Geri removed his fingers and sucked her juices off them, making her pussy weep all over again. They settled on the pillow, and he kissed her neck while whispering Romanian words in her ear. She slumped against him, his thick erection jutting into her like a two-by-four. She thought about returning the favor, but she was so warm in his embrace, and so tired.

"Eilea," he said. "What happened to your barrier?"

She stiffened, her eyes flying open. Aw, fuck. "Geri." She cleared her throat, relieved she didn't see judgment in his eyes. "I lost my virginity ages ago."

Thunderstorms brewed in his eyes, his nose lengthening. "We will kill the man who raped you."

She got up on her elbows. Feeling self-conscious, she pulled the blanket over her breasts. "I wasn't raped." Her heart sank when the light in his eyes dimmed.

"You chose to offer yourself to another?" Funny how his question sounded more like an accusation.

She cursed under her breath, shame washing over her. She'd known he wouldn't be pleased about this. "It's what human girls do."

"I'm not sure how we will complete the bond without your virginal blood." He frowned. "Did you love him?"

"I thought I did." Her shoulders fell with the admission. Her first boyfriend was one of three failed relationships, all because they'd become too controlling.

"Was he your mate?"

Eilea wasn't sure if his idea of mate was the same as hers. "For a time."

"For how long?" His look of disappointment made her more than uncomfortable.

"A few years." She cringed at his heavy sigh and wondered if his heart was breaking as much as hers.

"And you didn't have offspring?"

"No." She blew out a deep breath, her heartbreak slowly replaced by annoyance. How could he have expected her to remain a virgin for thirty-five years? Besides, he wasn't a virgin. Talk about a double-standard. "We were students."

His brow hitched, and for the first time, he looked mistrustful. "Where is this mate of yours now?"

"Last I heard?" She tried to recall Devin's features. It had been a lifetime ago. "Married with three kids."

His cheeks reddened, thick veins standing out on his neck. "So he claimed your virginity and then left you for another?"

She vigorously shook her head, her frustration growing. "It was a mutual separation."

"I'm trying to understand this." He leaned into her, confused. "It's not common among the Amaroki. Was he the only human you mated with?"

She clenched the blanket, trying to find the right words. Then she realized she didn't have to sugarcoat her life for him. If he didn't approve, too damn bad. "There were two others."

His jaw dropped, and he looked at her as if she'd just set fire to a bus full of nuns. "His brothers?"

"No." Her left temple throbbed, and she sensed the beginnings of a migraine. She worked hard to unclench her teeth. "Different guys. They didn't know each other."

"And these men weren't angry with you for giving yourself to others?"

The incredulity of his tone would've been comical if Eilea didn't feel so fucking judged. "Do you know nothing of humans?"

He shook his head, his sharp features looking less sexy by the second. "Only what I've heard."

"And what have you heard?"

"That they are whores, and I guess they were right."

Her breath hitched as she waited for him to tell her he was joking, but he'd said it with a straight face. Holy fuck! He was serious?

She pointed at the door, tears threatening at the backs of her eyes. She would not let him see her cry. "Okay, you can leave now."

"Have I said something wrong?"

No guy could be that fucking stupid. "Just go."

He stood, shoving his hands in his pockets and looking like a wayward child who'd been sent to time-out. "I do not keep secrets from my brothers, but I will not tell them you've already given your blood to another until after we've closed the portal. They have enough on their minds."

"How thoughtful of you," she said tightly. "Please leave."

"You are offended by my choice of words?" His question sounded more like a statement.

Maybe the dumbass was finally getting it. "Ya think?" She faced the wall when a tear slipped from the corner of her eye.

"I'm sorry for offending you. It was not my intention."

She refused to look at him. "Could've fooled me."

The sound of his retreating footsteps was followed by the soft click of the door. Only then did she give in to the torrent of tears she'd been holding back. She could never mate with the Lupescus, and not because of prejudice from shifters like Nakomi or the domineering nature of Amaroki males conflicting with her need for independence. She couldn't mate with the Lupescus because they thought she was a whore.

Chapter Twelve

DRASKO PACED OUTSIDE the lodge in protector form, refusing to take any chances in case Katarina had summoned more demons. Clutching his silver-tipped axe like a lifeline, he stared up at the full moon through the trees. The air was stagnant, stifling. The forest's silence was almost deafening. Drasko's wolf-touched senses were attuned to every nuance of the forest, yet not even an owl hooted. It was as if the evil that permeated the air had driven away the woodland creatures. Or maybe they, too, were sick. Drasko prayed they weren't. An icy chill swept across his nape, and he heard his name on the wind. *Drassssko.*

"Fuck you, bitch!" he roared, shaking his axe at the trees.

He dodged a falling branch, then laughed. "Your days on this plane are numbered. Prepare to meet your fate."

The breeze died down in an instant. He hoped the Ancients had a special punishment prepared for Katarina after the death and destruction she'd brought to his tribe.

He heard the familiar hum of his brother's truck approaching. Other than Amara's fathers, Hakon had said only the sick or immune Amaroki were allowed near the lodge.

Drasko raced over when they rolled to a stop in the parking lot. His heart thudded a warning when he saw his mother and sister slumped inside. Hakon was hunched over the steering wheel, and Rone was bent over a bucket while the babies cried in back.

Hakon was the first to stumble out of the truck, looking disoriented.

Drasko grabbed his arm when he fell against the side of the truck. "Hang on, brother. Let me help you."

Hakon looked up at Drasko with bloodshot eyes. "The fate of the Amaroki is in your hands now." He wiped a bead of sweat from his brow.

"Luc and Annie have called on almost every pack. There is no sign of this witch."

Drasko whistled to the Lupescus, relieved when they rushed toward the truck. The Romanians helped the women, Rone, and the babies into the lodge.

Drasko lifted his brother in his arms, an easy task when he was in protector form. So why did it feel like he carried the weight of the world?

His throat constricted as he looked into his brother's wan face.

"Wait." Hakon placed a trembling hand on his shoulder. "The Cloudwalkers. Luc couldn't get to them."

Drasko frowned. Of all the packs in the Amaroki, the odd Cloudwalkers were the most likely to have a witch among them. Both elder and young packs lived in the same cave. The goddess had said the witch was a female; maybe she was one of the Cloudwalker mates. "I will send a party after them."

Hakon shook his head, sweat trickling down his face. "They are too close to the portal. It may be too late."

Drasko ducked inside the lodge's massive wooden front doors, which were etched with carvings of the Ancients. "I will handle it, brother." His mind raced, searching for a plan. Who could he send on what might be a suicide mission? The number of healthy shifters was few. Who would guard the lodge if Katarina caused more trouble or demons emerged from the portal?

Drasko marched down the stairs toward his waiting mate, who stared at him with such hopelessness in her eyes, it broke his heart.

She fell to her knees when her father laid Rone down on a cot. Clasping his hands, she fell onto his chest. Drasko set Hakon in the cot next to Rone, his heart twisting when Amara turned and wrapped her arms around Hakon.

"My mates!" she sobbed. "Oh, Ancients, please save them!"

Drasko placed a hand on her shoulder. *Amara, do not let the others see you upset. They follow your lead.*

She blinked at him with wet eyes. *Are the babies okay?*

They're fine. They must have enough of your human blood to stay well.

She nodded, dabbing her eyes before laying her hand on Hakon's forehead. "You're burning up."

His eyes opened. "Don't worry about me," he rasped. "Take care of the others."

She hiccupped. "You need me."

"Please, Amara." He punctured each word with a low whine.

She stood, shoulders sagging in defeat. "Okay." She turned to Drasko. "There's something I need to show you."

She led him to the bottom of the lodge steps. He had to duck his head when she took him down a narrow hall.

"What is this about?"

She gave him a grim look. "It's the Strongpaws."

He shot her a questioning look when she brought him to the locker room. "Change into your jeans. If you go in there as a protector, she will think you're there to kill them."

"What the fuck, Amara?" Why would he want to kill the Strongpaws?

"Just change." She pushed him inside.

He pulled on his pants and checked his cellphone, feeling a mixture of relief and apprehension when he noticed Johnson hadn't called or texted in several hours.

Amara took him to a private room. Nakomi Strongpaw was quietly tending to her three mates.

He looked at the sick shifters, who were as still as statues, their pallor deathly gray. "What am I looking at?"

Nakomi's eyes flashed red. She rose, her fingers extending into long claws as she let out a deep growl. "I will crush him if he tries to hurt them."

Amara held out a staying hand. "I just want him to see." She nudged him toward a bed. "Touch Albert."

Ignoring Nakomi's low growls, Drasko touched the shifter's skin, then pulled back, dark, depressing memories suddenly surfacing. "He feels like petrified wood."

Amara licked her cracked lips. "That time you almost turned into a were-wolf, your skin felt like this."

Nakomi pushed his hand away, shielding Albert from Drasko's scrutiny. He didn't blame her for her protectiveness, but if Albert turned into a were-wolf, Drasko would have no choice but to kill him.

The reality of the situation settled in his stomach like a lead brick. "Fuck me."

"Drasko, what if they all turn? There are over 300 sick shifters out there, and more will come."

Drasko's head was ready to explode. What if this epidemic turned every Amaroki into a werewolf? How would Drasko kill them all? And what about his brothers? His mother, sister, and fathers? Did he have it in him to kill them, too? They had to find the witch, even if she lived near the portal.

Determination stiffened his spine. "We don't have time to wait for the witch to reveal herself. I'll send a party to go after her."

"Who?" Amara asked.

"I don't know yet." He wracked his brain for a solution. He was the most capable shifter at the moment, immune to the sickness and with the power to turn into a protector should a demon emerge from the portal. But they needed him at the lodge, too. What if Albert turned? Who would keep his family safe?

He was startled by a sound outside. He held out a silencing hand before jerking open the door.

The little weasel named Jimmy emerged from the shadows, pocketing his phone and scurrying up the stairs.

Drasko let out a string of curses. "I think we have a spy."

"Do you think he heard about the werewolves?"

"I don't know." But he suspected Jimmy had.

"You need to stop him," Nakomi hissed.

"And do what?" Drasko snapped. "What will the government do if anything happens to him?"

She unsheathed long talons. "What will they do if he tells them they're turning into werewolves?"

Drasko blinked at her hands, which were now tipped with claws. He must've imagined talons. The stress from this virus was taking a toll on his mental health.

"Sheath your claws," he commanded in his protector voice. "We will not kill any humans today." He pulled Amara out the door. "Come on."

"Slow down," she cried, digging her heels in.

He dragged her into a utility closet. Time was not on their side, and he had to know she would be safe. He slammed the door and switched on the solitary lightbulb overhead. "If we can't find this witch—"

She jerked away. "I'm not leaving my mates."

His vision tunneled. If he lost her and the babies, his life was over. "If we stay, we will all die." He enunciated each word, hoping to get through to her. "Our babies will die."

"I'm not discussing this." She turned from him, shoulders stiffening. "Find that damn witch."

She threw open the door and ran up the stairs. Slumping against the wall, he felt powerless. Fool that he was, he didn't stop her. What kind of protector would he be if he couldn't save the woman he loved? What kind of chieftain if his people perished under his watch?

His phone buzzed in his pocket, making him yelp. He swore when he saw Agent Johnson's name on the screen. Jimmy *had* heard them talking about the werewolf virus. His people were fucked.

BORIS ROLLED HIS SLEEVE down to conceal the rash, ignoring the burning pain that raced across his skin like wildfire. If his brothers saw it, they'd insist he lie down. It was one reason why he stayed in human form. The red welts would certainly stand out under his white fur. He refused to give in to the demon illness without a fight. As long as he had the use of his legs and his mind, he would do whatever it took to protect his family. Luckily, his younger brothers were inside the lodge. Jovan, who was in protector form, didn't comment on Boris's decision not to shift. Boris hoped it was because he was too concerned with threats from the eerie forest to pay attention to him. Or else Jovan knew about Boris's impeding illness and chose not to comment.

Jovan paced the gravel walkway leading to the lodge's massive double doors. "I don't like that smell."

Boris stopped, frowning at the familiar stench that left an unpleasant coppery taste on his tongue. "Neither do I."

Jovan gave him a pointed stare. "Do you remember it?"

He swallowed. "I do."

"Who do you think it is?" Jovan asked.

"The elder Eaglespeakers."

Jovan nodded. "Tor should've removed their bodies when he found them by the portal."

"They were too disoriented." Boris shook his head. "I'm surprised they made it out of there."

"So you think they met the same fate as the Devoras?" Jovan slapped his palm with the flat side of his gleaming axe.

Expelling a shaky breath, Boris rubbed one arm across another in a discreet attempt to scratch the unbearable itch, hoping his brother didn't notice. "Ancients, I fucking hope not." Damn, his arms burned so badly, he wanted to scrape off his skin with the sharp end of his blade.

"We need to close that portal." Jovan glanced at Boris's arm, then quickly looked away.

He knew Boris was getting sick. Damn. Boris didn't want his brother worrying about him. "The goddess told Amara only the witch can close it." His chest felt tight. Was the sickness settling in his lungs?

"Then where the hell is she?"

"The goddess said she'd reveal herself when she's ready." Boris hoped she'd do it soon.

The massive doors flew open, and Drasko emerged as a human, clutching his cellphone in one hand and an axe in the other. "Fuck that! She needs to reveal herself now."

Annie followed close behind him. "I agree."

Drasko pocketed his phone. "Get inside, Annie. It's not safe out here."

She stood her ground. "Someone needs to go after the witch."

"I know that!" he boomed. "Get inside."

She didn't even flinch. "I'm going after the witch."

"I'm not sending a woman."

"Who the hell do you think saved Luc and the Moosenecks?" She narrowed her eyes at him. "Drasko, I saw the Strongpaws. I heard your thoughts."

"What is happening with the Strongpaws?" Boris asked.

Hopelessness swirled in Drasko's golden eyes. "They are petrifying."

An icy chill tickled the nape of Boris's neck. He wasn't sure, but he thought he heard the ring of Katarina's grating laughter in the wind. "Petrifying?"

"The same thing happened to me when I was bitten by the Devora werewolf."

The burning of Boris's skin became a dull throb. They were turning into werewolves. *He* was turning into a werewolf, which meant none of the tribe was safe. Eilea, Amara, his grandchildren... he was a threat to those he loved most. He absently rubbed his arm, numb from shock and grief. Finally, he summoned enough brainpower to manage one coherent thought. "We need to find this witch."

"It has to be Geri." Drasko grimaced. "I'm the only protector immune to the virus. I'm not leaving my people."

"We can't send our brother there by himself," Jovan protested.

When Jovan looked to Boris for confirmation, Boris had to look away. What other option did they have?

"We have no choice," Drasko said. "We need to find the witch."

Annie stepped between Drasko and Boris, tossing her long, black curtain of hair over a shoulder. "I'll go with him."

Drasko's eyes lit with fire. "Like hell you will."

"You do realize that if we don't find this witch, we're all dead? Either I die helping Geri, or I die later. Which is it?"

Damn, the girl had a good point. Boris didn't envy Drasko's decision. It went against the Amaroki code to willingly put their women in danger.

He handed his axe to Annie. "Go, but run at the first sign of trouble."

She took the weapon, slinging it over her shoulder like it weighed nothing. "I'm not leaving Geri."

"Yes, you will." Geri emerged from the shadows.

Boris studied his brother. Something in him had changed, and he smelled like Eilea? When Jovan gasped, Boris knew he'd picked up on the scent of Eilea's fluids, too.

Geri gave his brothers an apologetic look. *We did not mate, brothers. Peace. We have bigger problems.* He turned to Annie. "You're running, Annie," he continued. "You're not coming with me otherwise."

"Fine," Annie huffed. "Where do we start?"

"Start with the Cloudwalkers," Drasko said.

Annie's features scrunched. "They're fucking weird."

"Exactly," Drasko said. "The goddess said the witch was a woman. If anyone in our tribe is a witch, it's their mate."

"Fine." Annie waved at Geri. "Let's get going."

"Do you remember where they live?" Drasko asked.

"I know my reservation. We're wasting time." She waggled her fingers impatiently. "Keys."

When he pulled them out of his pocket, Geri stepped in front of Annie. "I'll drive."

She reached around him, snatching the keys from Drasko and running for the truck.

Geri gave Boris a hopeless look. Grasping Boris's hand, he noticed the faint bumps circling his wrist. *Brother, you are unwell.*

Boris choked back the lump of sorrow that had suddenly formed in his throat. *As long as I have breath in me, I will fight.*

Geri's eyes glossed over, but he didn't shed a tear. *And I will fight for you, for all of us.* He hugged Boris and then Jovan before jumping in the truck with Annie.

Boris's breath hitched when they pulled out of the drive, tires spinning and gravel flying like she was being chased by the hounds of hell. Then again, maybe she was. Maybe they all were.

He pulled his sleeve down and said evenly, "What if they can't find her? What if our people start turning into werewolves?"

"They will have to be killed," Drasko said flatly, his eyes as cold as stones.

Boris didn't want to die, but he'd rather do that than be a threat to those he loved. "You think you can kill them all? Your brothers? Your mother and fathers?"

Drasko shook his head, his eyes softening. "The government knows. They have a backup plan."

"Was that who you were talking to on the phone?"

"Yes." Drasko's mouth draped in a heavy scowl, his glowing eyes narrowed to slits. "It appears they've been alerted by someone on the inside."

Jovan's eyes and nose shifted. "We should've killed that skunk when we had the chance."

"Leave him alone." Drasko leveled Jovan with a stern look. "If anything happens to him, they won't hesitate to press the button."

Boris's heartrate came to a slow, grinding halt. "Press the button?"

"The humans will not put their own at risk." The lack of inflection in Drasko's voice was unsettling. Had he already intuited that their survival was hopeless?

Boris's jaw hardened, the tension winding around his shoulders and neck so tight, the pain was the only thing rooting him to the ground. "They're going to nuke us, aren't they? What about Eilea and the immune shifters?"

"I will make sure they escape," Drasko answered.

"Did they say when?" Jovan asked, his voice as rough as sandpaper.

Boris felt Drasko's fear in the marrow of his bones.

"We have eight hours to close the portal," Drasko answered, "or we're all radioactive."

"YOU'RE STAYING IN THE truck when we get there," Geri told Annie as she put the truck in four-wheel drive. He looked at the full moon that peeked from behind the trees, a premonition making his hairs stand on end. They were running out of time, but they should travel at night.

He cringed, clutching the grab bar when she swerved sharply, narrowly missing a pothole. In all his years, he'd never been driven by a woman. Never mind how inappropriate it was for him to be alone with a female destined for another pack. The Alaskan tribe was on the brink of extermination. They were past right and wrong.

"I'm not staying in the truck," she said. "The Cloudwalkers live off-grid. Even if you find them, they won't recognize you."

Damn her, she was right. He didn't want to have to rely on her. If anything happened to her out there, he'd never forgive himself. There'd been a few packs like the Cloudwalkers in Romania once upon a time, mistrustful of outsiders. Too feral to acclimate to the growing population of humans, they'd been killed by poachers. His thoughts shifted to Katarina, the dead mate who'd been killed by a gun. Had her violent death caused her to turn into a tornaq or had she always been evil? Probably the latter. She'd always been a selfish bitch, nothing like Eilea, who worked tirelessly helping others.

He remembered hurting her. His definition of a whore had always been a human who slept with many different humans without bonding with them. The Amaroki looked down on that kind of behavior, but he thought humans enjoyed being whores. Why would they refuse to acknowledge the name assigned to their actions?

When Annie continued talking, he wondered if it was just a diversion to mask her fright. As she rambled, he sensed the undertone of fear in her voice. She went on about her plans to spend the summer with her brother, who'd been transferred to Texas, and how Amara was teaching her photography. Geri let her talk, only half-listening, constantly thinking about Eilea crying in bed. He'd seriously fucked up.

"Drasko said the Cloudwalkers live near the portal," she said pulling Geri from his thoughts. She clutched the steering wheel, her face scrunching as she focused on the road.

Near the fucking portal? Why hadn't anyone mentioned that to him before they left? The portal was a dangerous place. Had he known, he'd have said goodbye to Eilea or at least tried to make amends with her. "What do you know about the Cloudwalkers?"

"I know they're fucking strange. Both generations live in a cave and rarely come out as humans."

In that case, he needed Annie. The Cloudwalker males wouldn't respond well to another man coming near their mates.

She stopped the truck and clutched her hair.

After scenting the air, he reached for the axe at his feet. The smell of dark magic was strong. Had she smelled something else? "What is it?"

She turned to him. "What are you thinking?"

He squeezed the wood of his gleaming axe. "What do you mean?"

"I haven't heard your thoughts since we got in the truck."

He tried to make sense of her words, then remembered Amara telling him that Annie was a mind reader. "You've been listening to my thoughts?"

"No. That's the point. I can't hear a damn thing. First Amara stopped having visions, and now I can't hear your thoughts. Are you thinking anything?"

"I have a lot on my mind, but it's none of your business."

Ignoring her hurt gasp, he wondered what her waning powers meant and if Amara would soon lose her power to heal common sickness. Or worse, what if the Amaroki lost their ability to shift? Damn Katarina for bringing this curse to their people. What would happen if they couldn't find a witch to close the portal?

"Are you going to drive, or do you need me to?"

She put the truck back in gear. "You don't know where you're going." She peeled out, her face a mask of stone as she kept her gaze centered on the road.

Great. He'd pissed her off, too. What was one more woman angry with him?

Chapter Thirteen

EILEA STOOD ON THE precipice of fate, staring at what she knew would seal her destiny and her doom. She glided across the mist toward the table with the solitary goblet on it as if she, too, was made of vapor. Why did she move toward her undoing? Why didn't she turn and run? She had no idea if she was being propelled forward by her own free will, by a higher power, or by her desire. Not just sexual desire, but the longing to have four caring men put together the shattered pieces of her life. To fill the void in her heart left by her dead family. To never abandon her when she needed protection and comfort.

She gazed into the swirling red liquid. The blood of the Ancients. Her ticket to a strange new world. Her body would forever be changed, her life forever altered.

She traced the rim of the goblet, her heart pounding wildly in her ears.

Could she throw her life of independence away for four brothers whose prejudice might not let them reconcile with her human past? Four shifters who'd risked their own lives to protect her? Dear Goddess, what should she do?

The goddess's words came racing back. *I'll bring you back one more time.*

This was it, her one chance to become a shifter. If she didn't drink it, she'd remain human and very different from the men claiming to be her mates. Men she was inexplicably drawn to.

She reached for the goblet, pulled back, then reached again, but it was no longer within her grasp. What was happening?

She was being pulled backward across the mist. She fought it, kicking and pleading to be let go as the goblet disappeared from view. Then she fell through clouds that descended into darkness.

She woke with a silent scream on her lips, staring into the scowling face of Nakomi Strongpaw.

"Wake up, human." The shifter violently shook Eilea's shoulder. "You have rested long enough."

Her dream came back: the heavenly mist, the goblet, the goddess's warning that she'd have one more chance. Had the prejudiced she-wolf destroyed her one opportunity to become a shifter? To finally belong?

"Omigod!" She shot up, shaking Nakomi off her. "The blood wine. I didn't get to drink it."

"You're making no sense." Nakomi flexed her fingers, her nails lengthening and lips pulling back in a feral snarl. "I smell your mating fluids. Did you have sex with a Lupescu?"

Was the bitch trying to threaten her? Eilea refused to be intimidated. She turned up her chin, eyes narrowing. "It's none of your business."

Before she could react, Nakomi had her by the throat, pressing her into the wall and digging her nails into Eilea. She struggled against her captor, but the more she fought, the deeper Nakomi's nails went.

Fearing the crazed bitch would puncture her jugular, she stopped fighting, and that's when she got a good look at the shifter's face. She looked more like an eagle than a wolf. What the hell? She didn't know the Amaroki could shift into other creatures.

Nakomi loosened her hold. "Did you have sex?" she hissed. "Because if you did, I'll peck your tits off."

What? "N-no."

Eilea thought she saw a flash of sorrow in the shifter's hooded eyes, right before her beaked nose retracted. The goddamn bitch was a bird shifter? What kind of magic was this?

"Did you not hear what I said?" Nakomi snapped. "Human and Amaroki unions are an abomination."

"I heard you," she choked out, worried she'd run out of air when Nakomi tightened her hold, her nose once more turning into a beak before retracting again.

Nakomi released her. "If you let them take your virginity, I will kill you."

Clutching her neck, she inhaled a shaky breath, trying not to lose her composure when blood ran over her fingers. "You don't have to worry about that, because I'm not a virgin."

"You have already given yourself to another?" Sheathing curved talons, Nakomi's eyes lit with amusement.

After wiping blood on the blankets, she reached for the bottle of water by her bedside. "Long time ago."

"Why am I not surprised?" Nakomi chuckled. "Humans are whores."

She was unable to control the trembling in her hands as she uncapped the water, sloshing it down her neck. "I've already heard that. Thanks."

"Good." Nakomi gazed at her blood-tipped fingernails. "You cannot bond with Amaroki without virginal blood."

Eilea nodded for no other reason than to get the crazed bitch away from her. "Do you mind getting the hell out of my room now?"

She wiped more blood off her neck and tried to recall everything she'd learned about the Amaroki. Never had she heard of bird shifters, but she knew without a doubt she'd seen a beak and felt Nakomi's talons. How was Nakomi able to transform into other creatures? Could she be the witch? It made no sense. If Nakomi was the witch, surely she would've closed the portal rather than watch her mates suffer. At least Eilea sure as hell hoped so.

GERI WAS GETTING USED to Annie's driving. Truthfully, it wasn't all that bad. He realized his nervousness earlier was unfounded. Perhaps he'd judged her harshly because she was a woman. Perhaps he'd misjudged Eilea, too. He couldn't get the look of Eilea's heartbreak out of his mind. He shouldn't have called her a whore, but he'd thought humans didn't mind such labels.

He remembered Annie had lived among humans most of her life. He wondered if she could help him understand what had happened. "Can I ask you about human women?"

She gave him a smug once-over before turning back to the road. "Sure."

"Is it offensive to call them whores?"

She made an odd snorting sound. "Um, yeah."

"Oh." He wondered how he could repair the damage he'd done. "How offensive?" He prayed he hadn't ruined his pack's chance to claim Eilea as their mate, even if they couldn't complete the bond.

"Very offensive." She shot him a look of derision. "Why would you think it wouldn't be?"

"What about a human woman who slept with different human men and had no intention of bonding with them?"

Annie gaped at him as if he'd grown a second head. "Please don't tell me you called Eilea a whore."

Maybe he shouldn't have told Annie about this. "She's been with three men." His voice rose along with his ire when he thought of them touching his woman. He regretted the words as soon as they left his lips. He shouldn't have told Annie about her men. Eilea hadn't told him he could share. He silently berated himself. How else would he screw up this night?

"Do you understand what a whore is?" she asked.

"A person who does not commit to a pack."

Annie let out a bunch of expletives he wasn't used to hearing from a woman, especially not one so young. "It's a derogatory term. Very derogatory. Eilea is a medical doctor. In her world, she is treated with respect, reverence. Being called a whore is the worst insult imaginable."

"I didn't know that." He looked out the side window, shame flushing his cheeks. "She was very angry."

"Of course she was angry." She laughed. "Jesus, you wolves are thickheaded. How could you not know this? Don't they have televisions or computers in Romania?"

"We had one television in our house. Our mate watched it."

"And you didn't?"

"I don't care for technology. I have farm work to do. Besides, our mate didn't like company when she watched her shows." Actually, Katarina hadn't liked their company at all, not after she'd discovered soap operas. Geri hadn't liked competing for Katarina's affection with a television. They'd fought about it more than once, making him resent the technology even more.

"Well, your ignorance shows," Annie said. "You're going to be in the doghouse for a while."

He contemplated her words. Perhaps she didn't realize the complications from Eilea's lost virginity. Their pack might not be able to seal the bond with her. The bond enabled them to telepathically speak with her. He'd heard rumors of other packs sealing the bond after taking their mate's virginity before the ceremony, but he wasn't sure if it could be done. Not that they were sure if they could anyway, being that she was human. Geri had been upset when he'd called Eilea a whore, but he didn't realize what that might mean to her. Or maybe deep down he did. Maybe he meant to insult her, repay her for her infidelity. But had she been unfaithful? She hadn't known Geri and his brothers then. Geri had been unfair and unkind, punishing her for her past, maybe even for Katarina's past. Great Ancients, what had he done?

She pulled over and turned off the truck.

"What are you doing?"

"This is as far as we can go by vehicle." She gazed at a worn path cutting through the forest. "We'll have to go the rest of the way as wolves." She slipped off her seatbelt and got out.

Geri grabbed his axe and joined her. The smell of dark magic was strong here. No way was he going into that forest without a silver blade, the only thing that could kill the demons that manifested in haunted forests. The hairs on the back of his neck stood when he caught a familiar scent. His stomach roiled. He'd only smelled that odd coppery smell once before, the night the Devoras had emerged from the Hoia Baciu as werewolves.

"I can't shift," he said.

"Why?" She took off her jacket.

"Because I need to carry my axe." He slung it over his shoulder, the silver blade gleaming in the light of the full moon. "So do you."

She shook her head. "We'll never reach them."

She was pulling off her shoes when the stench of blood and rot hit him.

He held out a staying hand. "Hang on."

She made a spluttering noise behind him. "What's that stink?"

"Great Ancients." He breathed in deeply, recognizing at least three decomposing bodies mixed with the dark, coppery stench of evil. "I recognize it. Get back in the truck."

An unearthly howl shattered the stagnant air.

Clutching his axe like a lifeline, Geri said, "Get in the truck!"

"Not without you." She tugged his arm.

He shook her off. A slanted pair of blood-red eyes blinked at him from within the trees. He had barely enough time to push Annie to the ground and swing his axe when a demonic creature with patches of gray, matted fur, a wide, bony ribcage, and an emaciated waist sprang from the shadows, blood and poison dripping down the distended fangs, sizzling when it splattered the ground.

Geri barely registered Annie screaming when his axe went into the demon's chest. The beast lurched, then let out an eerie wail, grasping the handle before Geri swung around him, driving the axe farther in and jerking it out the creature's spiny back.

The monster looked at the gory wound in its chest with a slackened jaw. It tipped over, its body breaking in two pieces. Annie scrambled back when the creature shattered on the ground in a cloud of dust and smoke.

She looked at Geri in horror. "What the fuck was that?"

"A werewolf," Geri answered grimly. "And there will be more." He thought about retreating, but he refused to bring werewolves to the lodge, endangering his family. Besides, they had to get that witch. He prayed she hadn't been eaten.

Annie jerked her axe out of the truck. "I'm ready."

He admired the girl's bravery and sent a prayer to the Ancients her courage wouldn't get her killed.

When three more werewolves emerged from the forest, he braced for battle. "You ready, kid?"

"Not really." The tremors in her voice revealed her fear. "But I won't go down without a fight."

"Get in the truck bed," he said. "Aim for their necks."

He didn't have time to see if she followed his orders because a werewolf sprang at him. With a roar, he drove his blade into the beast's neck, slicing off his head with a sickening crunch. The monster turned to dust before the head hit the ground.

He whirled when Annie screamed, driving his axe into the ankle of a beast that had climbed up on the hood of the truck. The monster howled, scrambling over the top of the vehicle, right into her axe. She drove the blade through its skull, making disgusted noises when green goo splattered her. The monster rolled off and hit the ground in a cloud of smoke.

"Look out!" she yelled, pointing.

He spun around in time to duck when a drooling beast swiped at him with elongated claws as sharp as razors. A sickening screech rent the air when the monster sliced open the side of the truck, peeling back the steel panel in long curls.

She jumped away from the creature when it snapped at her. Geri drove his blade into its back, dragging his weapon down the ridged spine, like he was slowly opening a zipper. It arched back with a squeal, its spine curling around Geri's hands before falling out of the open cavity, clattering on the rocks like wooden bowls.

The werewolf looked over its shoulder, whimpering, then curled into a petrified ball.

Geri scented the air for any more threats. When he didn't find any, he leaned his axe against the truck tire. Wiping sweat and goo off his brow, he looked at Annie. "Are you okay?"

She was hunched over, clutching her knees. "I think I pissed my pants."

"You were amazing," Geri said, impressed with her stamina and bravery.

She flung goo off her clothes and face. "Thanks."

Funny how he'd once thought of Amaroki women as vulnerable and in need of protection. Maybe because Katarina had always acted helpless, relying on her mates to do everything for her. He realized it had been unfair to judge other women based on Katarina. His dead mate had been a special kind of selfish.

"You sure we can't reach the Cloudwalkers on foot?" he asked.

She slanted a smile. "We're going to have to, because no way in hell am I giving up my axe."

Chapter Fourteen

AFTER CLEANING HER wounds and donning fresh hospital scrubs, Eilea returned to the main hall, relieved when she didn't see Nakomi. In fact, her mates' beds were empty. What had happened to them?

She searched for Amara among the sick, dismayed when they vomited in buckets, on the floor, and even on themselves. Family members were doing their best to take care of loved ones. How horrible they must feel to know they would soon succumb to a sickness with no cure. And their numbers had doubled since she'd gone to sleep. She felt helpless.

You have it in you, Eilea, a voice whispered in her ear. No one was near her. Had she imagined the voice?

She spotted Amara Thunderfoot, but it took a long while for her to work her way through the crowd, as she checked on babies and administered fever reducer and fluids, hoping to make a small difference to those who needed her most.

When she finally made it to Amara, her heart slammed against her ribcage when she saw that Hakon and Rone Thunderfoot had become ill. Her blotchy face marred with tracks of dried tears, Amara stoically took care of her mates and in-laws, changing their cold compresses and checking their fluids. Her two babies cried in a crib nearby, begging to be held.

"Amara," she said, her heart so heavy it felt near to bursting as she took the smallest child, Alexi, in her arms. "I'm so sorry."

"Not your fault." Amara smoothed a hand across Rone's brow. Her mate didn't respond. Other than his ragged breathing, he lay motionless on his cot.

She checked the baby's temperature, relieved to see it was normal. She hated how he cried when she set him down, but she had to check his brother, Hrod. Both children had normal temps, but they appeared dehydrated.

"Amara," she asked. "Have you had time to nurse?"

"I haven't had time to eat, much less feed them." She nodded to Tor, his legs so long they hung over the short cot. "My father-in-law's temperature is too high."

Hating herself for ignoring cries for help, Eilea pushed her way through the throng and found a bag of MREs, as well as formula and bottles, diapers, and wipes. After shoving the stuff in a bag, she took the stairs two at a time and handed Amara two MREs and gave each baby a bottle. "Eat," she said to Amara, holding Alexi. "You will be no good to anyone if you pass out."

Nodding, Amara slumped on Rone's cot and hastily ate her meal.

Eilea sat nearby with Alexi in her lap. The baby sucked down his bottle too fast and greedily took another. Balancing the baby in one arm, she opened an MRE and spoon-fed Hrod macaroni and cheese. "Where are the Strongpaws?" she asked and held her breath, afraid to hear the answer. Had they succumbed to their illness?

Amara's face blanched. "We moved them to a private room while you were sleeping."

"Why?"

"Albert is petrifying," she whispered, eyes wide with fear.

Eilea helped Alexi burp. "What?"

Alexi let out a cry that yanked at her heartstrings and held out his arms to his mama. Amara took him, stricken when he crawled over her lap to snuggle against Rone. The unconscious shifter struggled for each ragged breath, unaware of the baby who wrapped his pudgy arms around his neck.

Amara stifled a sob. "I don't know how much longer I can do this."

Eilea picked up Alexi, bouncing him on her hip and trying to distract him when he reached out to Rone, calling "Dada." She held him tighter, whispering soothing words in his ear. She was suddenly transported to the moment she'd awakened alone in that hospital room, calling for her father, but he never came. She rocked Alexi and sang a lullaby her grandmother had taught her. She'd probably screwed up most of the words, but it didn't matter. The baby didn't need lyrics.

Despite the sounds of sickness and beeping of equipment around them, Alexi finally fell asleep. Amara took him from her, kissing the top of his head before laying him in the playpen beside his brother, who'd also fallen asleep.

"Rone was such a good daddy." Amara sniffled, wiping her eyes. "I don't know what I'm going to do without him."

She laid a hand on Amara's shoulder. "He's not dead yet." She cringed at her words. She knew there was little hope for the sick.

"We believe Albert Strongpaw is turning into a werewolf." Amara blinked back tears, biting on her knuckles as she stared longingly at her mates. "They all are."

"Jesus," Eilea said, sinking down on a cot, a knot twisting in her stomach.

Boris, Jovan, and Marius weren't immune to this sickness either. It was only a matter of time before they succumbed to the disease, then what? For over a year, she'd fought the notion of getting together with the shifter brothers, worried they'd be too controlling. Now it appeared they'd never have a chance to mate. The thought made her heart ache so badly, she had to clutch her chest, breathing in through a hiss to manage the pain. She hadn't spent much time with Jovan and Marius, but from the little time she'd shared with Boris, she knew he was a good man, putting her needs before his, caring too much about her wellbeing. He would've made a good mate and a wonderful father, but she'd never get to experience any of that with any of them except maybe Geri, the one brother who'd pleasured her and then called her a whore.

"If you want to leave, I won't blame you," Amara said.

"I'm not leaving." No way in hell would she abandon the Amaroki when they needed her most.

Amara narrowed her eyes to slits. "What happened to your neck?"

Her hand flew to the scratch on her neck. The pain was nothing compared to the suffering of the Amaroki.

Amara's lips twisted. "Did Nakomi attack you?"

Eilea heaved a groan and rose to her feet. "I need to make my rounds. I don't want to get into it."

Amara's arm shot out, blocking her from going. "At least let me heal you."

She felt selfish for even considering taking the shifter's offer when there were others far worse off than her. "I'm fine."

"You don't want my fathers seeing your injury." Amara said coolly. "There's no telling what they will do to Nakomi."

Awareness was like a cold bucket of water. "Christ. Fine."

Amara offered Eilea the faintest of smiles before placing a dry hand on her neck.

Closing her eyes and lifting her chin, she waited for the magic to soak into her skin. She held her breath, waiting, and felt nothing. The look of panic in Amara's eyes told her all she needed to know.

Amara looked down at her hands as if seeing them for the first time. "I-I don't understand what's happening. It's like my magic has dried up."

"I'll tell you what's happening," a crackly voice said behind them.

Raz peered at them, deep lines crinkling her foggy eyes. The matronly woman pointed at Amara with a crooked finger. "The portal is poisoning you, stripping you of your powers. Soon it will affect all of us, and we won't be able to shift."

"Great Ancients." Amara's hand flew to her throat. "I thought I was immune."

Raz clucked her tongue. "Immune to the virus maybe, but not to the powers of the veil. This entire region will be like the Hoia Baciu unless we close that portal."

Lowering herself on Rone's cot, Amara hung her head. "Let us pray to the Ancients that Annie and my father are successful."

Eilea was so petrified, she went numb. "Geri told me he was going to root out the witch, not close a portal."

"That's right." Amara blinked up at her. "He went to find the witch."

Eilea slowly lowered herself onto a stool. "Why do I feel something horrible will happen to him?"

"Because you are a loving and concerned mate," Raz answered.

Eilea blushed. She did care for Geri, even though he'd been a first-rate jerk. She hoped his insult was a cultural misunderstanding and not an attempt to hurt her. Dread grew like a virus when Amara looked away.

"There's something you're not telling me." Eilea leveled Amara with a hard stare.

"They went in search of the Cloudwalkers," Amara said. "We suspect one of their women may be a witch." She paused, then spoke on a rush of air. "They live close to the portal."

Eilea's veins solidified, her heart slowing to a dull thud like her veins were filled with sludge. "And Geri and Annie went after them alone?"

Amara threw up her hands. "Who else could go with them?"

"How dangerous is it?"

When Raz and Amara shared dark looks, warning bells went off in Eilea's head.

"There are usually demons near a portal," Amara said quietly.

Eilea's world came to a grinding halt. "Oh god."

Raz shook her head. "Your god can't save them now."

AFTER OVER AN HOUR of hacking through brush and climbing dangerous, steep terrain, Geri and Annie finally arrived at what was left of the Cloudwalker dwelling.

They were going to find the shifters had perished. He'd smelled their blood for miles. What he wasn't expecting was the extent of the carnage. Limbs and heads of what appeared to have been two packs of wolves were strewn everywhere. Even the protectors had been in wolf form, which meant they'd been caught unawares. Hadn't they scented the werewolves approaching? Wouldn't their instinct have warned them of the danger? Only one of the wolves had an intact head, though he'd been gutted, his innards strewn across the ground as if his killer had used them to play jump rope. That wolf would need to be burned to ensure he didn't turn into a werewolf. Actually, they all should be burned, just in case.

The wind shifted, bringing with it a thin, pungent mist. A strange fog filled his brain. What was he doing again? He looked down at the mauled bodies of wolves. Why were they dead, and why had he come here? He looked at the axe in his hand, which was encrusted with dried green splatter. When he spotted a pile of green splat similar to the stuff on his axe, he wondered if he had killed the wolves. No. He wasn't a monster. Was he?

"Excuse me?"

He looked up at the sound of a raspy girl's voice. She clutched an axe to her chest. She was covered with the same green gunk. The girl looked familiar, with her long black hair, alabaster skin, and blue eyes. He suddenly remembered her face from the scrolls.

"You are the goddess!" He knelt, bowing before her. Had he died and gone to Valhol?

"No, I'm not." She scratched her head, looking lost in thought. "I'm Annie, or maybe Takaani. One of those two names. I don't remember which."

He straightened as a strange mist blew past her, blurring her face for a moment. He swatted the mist, which tickled his nose. "What are we doing here?"

"I don't remember." She frowned. "But something bad happened."

Geri stepped back, nearly tripping over a severed wolf head. "Something very bad."

"I think we should leave."

When she held out her hand to him, he shrank back. What if she was the demon who'd slaughtered these wolves? But no. Something in the recesses of his mind told him this girl was his friend, that whoever the butcher was, he'd already been killed.

He stepped over a bloody leg and a long rope of entrails. "We need to search the bodies. I think we were looking for someone."

"We can't." She reached for him again. "It's dangerous here."

A child's cry cut through the thick fog in his head.

Her eyes bulged. "Did you hear that?"

He nodded. "What is it?"

"It sounds like a baby." She surged ahead of him, jumping over puddles of blood, heading toward a dark, narrow cavern.

He lunged and jerked her back. "We shouldn't go in there."

A foreboding feeling told him a demon lurked inside, eager to slaughter them, as it had done to the wolves.

The child's wails grew louder.

She pulled free and ran into the cave.

He followed her and stumbled over slick rocks, nearly falling face first onto the gleaming axe he held. What was happening? Why were they running? He tripped again, dropping the axe and slamming into the girl.

She howled. "Watch what the hell you're doing."

He fell to his knees, scrambling for his weapon. That's when he saw three pairs of wide eyes staring at him from under a ledge. Before he could get to his axe, a child grabbed it and dragged it back into the shelter, crouching down in front of two younger boys, one barely a toddler.

"Hello, sweetheart. Are you okay?" The girl knelt beside him, flashing a kind smile and holding out her hand to the kids.

Who was this girl? He felt he should know her.

The oldest boy tried to lift the axe but ended up dropping it on his foot. He cried out as the weapon clanked to the ground. Geri took that opportunity to snatch it up.

The boy gasped, pushing his brothers against the wall.

"Are you going to eat us?" he cried.

The girl shook her head. "We don't eat children."

The boys wore ragged clothes, and had mops of black hair, and grimy hands and faces. "What are you doing under there?" What was he doing here, for that matter?

"They ate our family," the oldest boy blurted, tears spilling down his dirty cheeks.

"Who?"

The boy blinked at him. "Why are you acting so stupid?"

Geri growled, thinking he needed a reprimand, but the child was right. He was acting stupid. There was a weightless feeling in his head, and his thoughts were jumbled.

"We need to leave this place," the girl beside him said. "Will you come with us?"

The boy dragged the back of a hand across his nose, smearing snot and dirt all over his face. "Where will we go?"

The girl looked at Geri, who had no response. He didn't know where to go. He didn't even know where he was.

She shrugged.

"Will you take us to our chieftain?" the child asked.

"Da." Geri eagerly nodded. "That sounds like a good idea." Though he didn't remember who their chieftain was, instinct told him they'd be safe if they found him.

The child looked from Geri to the girl. "Do you know your way out?"

He shook his head.

"We do." The child stepped forward, pulling the smaller children with him. "Follow us."

Geri felt as dumb and useless as a cow, mindlessly being herded toward the slaughterhouse.

When they emerged from the cavern, the children let out pitiful wails.

Geri blinked at the carnage. Had these wolves been the children's parents?

The girl scooped up the smallest child in her arms, kissing his filthy cheek. "We should burn the bodies," she said with a sob, rocking the crying toddler.

"No." Geri grimaced. "This place is evil." Though his reason had fled, dark memories of snarling werewolves with venom dripping from their fangs slipped in and out of his mind, like glimpses of sunlight shining through patchy clouds.

For some reason, the oldest child appeared to have all of his senses.

"Show us the way out," Geri said.

The child sniffled once, then screwed his face up tight and directed them to a worn path that wound down the steep side of a hill. Geri led the way, gripping his axe tightly and sending up a prayer to his ancient gods that they would find a way to escape the cursed prison that had trapped his body and mind.

"WHAT IS IT, JOVAN?"

Boris's brother's pale brow was furrowed as he gazed into the forest, looking like he'd lost something inside the stagnant foliage. No leaves rustled in the wind. No animals moved. They could've been looking at a painting, the night was so eerily still.

"I don't hear Geri anymore." Jovan's wide nostrils flared, his long fangs digging into his lower lip as his frown deepened. "I've been reaching out to him and nothing."

"I haven't heard him in a long while. The foul stench is getting thicker. It's blocking everything." He prayed to the Ancients Geri was safe, hating himself for his infirmity. He wouldn't be able to help Geri if he needed him.

He wiped sweat off his brow, trying not to become alarmed as his internal temperature rose. Now he knew how a chicken felt, slowly roasting over a fire. Was this Katarina's evil plan? Kill everyone with demon sickness so she wouldn't be alone?

"Is it true only a witch can close the portal?" Jovan asked.

Boris ignored the hammer banging at the back of his skull. "That's what the goddess told our daughter." An iridescent fog hung above them like a blanket tossed over the trees.

"Unless we can convince Katarina to go through the portal."

Bitter laughter rose in Boris's throat. "She never listened to us in life. Do you think she'll listen in death?"

"Why is she doing this?" Jovan's luminous eyes shone with pain.

Though he'd always tried to hide his emotions behind a stony veneer, he knew his brother's heart ached for the mate they'd lost. He'd been the one to discover her body, murdered by a corrupt federal agent, and he'd always blamed himself for not saving her in time. Now the Amaroki tribe was paying for it.

"Because she's a vindictive bitch." Katarina had been killed because she deliberately put herself in danger for attention. That had always been her way. Sadly, her selfishness and cruelty were magnified in death.

"She could be listening," Jovan hissed.

Marius trotted up to them on all fours, a whimpering white wolf with tail tucked between his legs. *Brother, do not bring any more of her ire on our heads.*

Turning his gaze to the sky, Boris pounded his chest. "I don't care!" he hollered. "Do you hear me, Katarina, you unfaithful, evil *catea*? You can kill us all. It won't change what you are. The only thing you're accomplishing is making us hate you more."

His baritone bounced off the trees like a boomerang. It was as if no sound could penetrate the thick fog in front of them. If Katarina's ghost was near, she didn't answer. The deafening silence was almost as tormenting as her temper.

He was sweating like a pig. He wiped his face with a trembling hand, innards churning. He suspected his sickness, and not his ire, had brought on the sudden wave of dizziness.

The heat that raced across his back was more than he could bear. Stripping off his shirt, he threw it to the ground, his eyes filling with frustrated tears.

Boris, your arms, Marius thought.

"I know." He leaned against a tree, startled by the cool veneer of the rough bark. "I'm not down yet." He blinked when sweat dripped into his eyes.

"You should go inside," Jovan said.

"Did you hear me? I said I'm not down yet." He glared at them, then his legs abruptly gave way, and he crumpled to the ground like a puppet with cut strings.

His brothers ran to him, calling his name, but he was so disoriented, their faces blurred, then spun. He was so dizzy, he felt sick.

The pounding of feet shook the ground, and Drasko appeared, hovering over him in guardian form.

Boris clutched Drasko's furry arm. "Promise you will guard our women."

His massive brow drew down. "With my life."

Sighing, Boris finally gave in to the sickness that consumed him.

THE FARTHER DOWN THE hill they went, the clearer Geri's mind became. By the time they reached the truck, and he saw the piles of ash and green goo, he remembered why he was here. He'd come in search of the Cloudwalkers and found them slaughtered by werewolves, leaving behind three orphaned children. His heart had never been heavier. So much death and destruction, all because his selfish dead mate refused to pass into the afterworld.

With a feeling of detached dread, he watched Annie loaded the children into the truck. He wondered why they hadn't been affected by the confusing mists, then recalled a tribal elder once telling him the veil shrouding Romania's haunted forest had a disorienting effect on older shifters, and the younger the shifter, the less likely they were to be affected. Their innocence protected them from evil. That would also explain why the elder Eaglecallers had died while hunting near the portal, but the younger Strongpaw pack had emerged alive.

A cool wind tickled his nape. *Geriiii,* a familiar sibilant hiss whispered in his ear.

A line of mist rose from the forest floor like smoke from a forgotten fire, tendrils lazily swirling until the outline of a woman took shape. In the familiar sinful curves was the image of his dead wife, a blonde beauty with pale eyes and a sultry smile. The curvă who'd bewitched him and his brothers over twenty years ago, stealing their hearts and then their sanity when she betrayed them.

"Geriii." She held a hand out to him. "Come to me, my love."

"I am not your love anymore, Katarina."

She produced a familiar pout, the one she'd used so many times to get her way.

"Go into the afterworld, Katarina. Close the portal before you destroy any more lives."

Tendrils of smoke wafted from her crooked finger as she beckoned him to her. "I will if you come with me."

"No, Geri! Don't go."

He paid no heed to the plea in Annie's voice. The witch was dead, and there was no other way to close the portal. If Katarina refused to go through, the Alaskan tribe would perish.

He stiffened when the smoke from Katarina's fingers reached him, tickling his nose with the familiar scent of her perfume.

"Take the children to the lodge," he said over his shoulder, attention fixed on the wicked spirit.

"No," Annie cried, latching onto his elbow. "Come with us."

"Tell my brothers and my children I love them." He swallowed the rock of emotion lodged in his throat. "And tell Eilea I'm sorry." He was sorry for so many things, but especially about how he'd wrongly judged her and made her cry. He was specifically sorry he'd never get the chance to love her.

Shaking her off, he ignored her cries and threw his axe into the dirt. He put his hand in Katarina's and followed her into the forest.

"Geri!" Annie screamed. She trailed after him, slicing through the mist with her blade.

Katarina hissed, fangs extending as she transformed into a smoky serpent. He watched in horror as she sucked in a breath, her sides expanding.

"Run, Annie!" he hollered right before Katarina unleashed a stream of blue fire.

Annie howled, shifting into a wolf and yelping as she ran away, blue flame licking her hind legs.

"Stop," he cried. "Enough wolves have died on your account."

"Wasss she your lover?" she hissed, her serpent tongue darting back and forth.

He vehemently shook his head. "She is destined for another pack."

The serpent reformed as his dead mate, traces of the snake still visible in her cold eyes. "Come with me." She crooked her finger again, black smoky tendrils flowing from her hand.

He wanted to flee. If he went with her, he'd never break free of her. But he could not let his family perish. The smoke wrapped around his wrist like a noose, swirling around him in a cocoon that smelled of her. An unnatural chill wracked him, so paralyzing he fell to his knees. Frigid pain shot through his veins. He prayed to the Ancients his death would be fast, and he wouldn't be bound to Katarina for an eternity, but it was a price he was willing to pay to save those he loved.

Chapter Fifteen

"EILEA," JOVAN BOOMED from the doorway, "you have another patient."

She looked up and her heart seized. Jovan thudded down the stairs as a giant, white beast, Boris in his arms, and a howling white wolf following them.

No, no, no!

Her legs felt encrusted with concrete, her body numb from shock and pain as she trudged toward them. The cries and moans of the sick, the beeping of machines—it all faded into white noise as her attention centered on Boris, who looked like a child pressed against Jovan's broad chest. Jovan laid him down on a cot, wrapping him in a blanket with the tenderness of a father swaddling a newborn babe.

Amara reached her fathers first, holding a bucket for Boris, rubbing his back while he leaned over and vomited. Marius curled up beside Boris's bead, whining softly and resting his chin on his paws.

Eilea watched helplessly as Amara took care of him. Without thinking, she scratched Marius's ears. He nuzzled her hand, his nose surprisingly dry. She looked into his glossy eyes. "Marius, are you getting sick, too?"

He answered with a whimper. "Shift," she pleaded, "so I can examine you."

He shifted, still curled in a ball. She felt his forehead, alarmed at the heat radiating off him. He closed his eyes, moaning when she brushed a lock of bushy hair out of his eyes.

Not fazed by Jovan's intimidating size or the teeth that hung over his lower lip like two, sharp tusks, she asked, "Can you please put Marius in a bed?" She pointed at the empty cot next to Boris.

She covered his nude body with a sheet, then took his temperature: 104°.

Marius looked up at her through heavy-lidded eyes. "I'm sorry to be a burden to you, lubirea mea. I'm supposed to be taking care of *you*."

She bit her lip, repressing a retort. Funny how his chauvinism didn't bother her anymore. She could've said she was a big girl and would take care of herself, but she sort of liked the idea of this big shifter looking after her. It beat the alternative, which was losing Marius to this virus. She didn't know how she could go on if her handsome shifters died. Blinking back tears, she forced a smile. "You are no burden."

He traced the curve of her face, the longing in his eyes making her heart beat with a dark, deep depression, one she hadn't felt since her parents died.

"You have beautiful eyes and a kind soul." His smile was pained. "You would've made us happy. Not having the chance to love you will be my biggest regret."

"Marius, please don't speak like that." She held his hand, kissing his damp palm. "I can't bear it." She clamped her lips shut, unable to say more.

When his eyes rolled back, and his hand went limp in hers, it took all her willpower not to fall on top of him with a sob, as Amara had done with her mates. Dear lord, she cared about him too much. She cared about all the Lupescus. If given the chance, she could love them, too, but that chance might never come.

He barely moved when she gave him fever reducer and hooked him up to an IV. She did the same with Boris, brushing his hair out of his eyes while longingly looking at his wan face. She struggled to breathe when she realized they might be dead soon, because she had no idea how to cure them.

"She blinked at Jovan. "I-I don't know how to stop it."

He cupped her chin. "There is nothing we can do, lubirea mea, but pray to the Ancients."

She could've gotten lost in the love and kindness in his pale eyes. This giant beast was no monster. For the first time, she fully appreciated why they were called protectors.

He dropped to one knee, his brow furrowing as he traced a line down her jaw with a thick finger. "What happened to your neck?"

She slapped a hand over her bandage. "Never mind me. I have patients who need me." His frown deepened. "Did a shifter do that?"

She looked away, unable to meet his eyes. "Nakomi." She regretted naming her attacker the moment the name left her lips. What good would it do?

He jumped to his feet with a roar, then went down the steps two at a time.

Oh, fuck! Why had she told him?

"Jovan, wait!" She chased him, unable to keep up with his long strides.

When he reached the bottom step, his eyes rolled back and he toppled to the floor with a violent tremor, narrowly missing a shifter, who skirted him with a shrill scream.

Eilea fell beside him. "Jovan." She cupped his cheek, turning his big, furry face toward her.

His eyes opened. "I can't defend you. I'm sorry."

"I don't need anyone defending me, and you don't need to apologize. Can you shift? I don't think we can carry you."

He shifted with a groan, his human body red with welts. He looked up at her with baleful puppy dog eyes. "I'm sorry, lubirea mea. This wasn't how I imagined our courtship."

Raz knelt beside them and draped a blanket over him from the waist down.

Two men nearby carried Jovan back up the steps to a cot beside his brothers, though they could barely lift him. Sweat dripped down their faces. She made them go lie down after depositing Jovan. Then she hooked him up to fluids while Amara coated his arms with the homemade concoction Raz had made.

"Eilea, Amara, you need to leave." Jovan got up on his elbows, his head bobbling like he was drunk. "There's dark magic in the air. All these sick shifters are turning into werewolves."

After releasing a shaky breath, she regained her composure and wagged a finger at him. "Now you listen to me, Jovan. As long as you and your brothers need me, I'm not leaving."

"You have to." He fell back. "Go with Geri when he returns. They're going to nuke this place."

"Who?" she demanded. "When?" But he was unconscious.

She raced outside in a panic. Spotting the big, brown behemoth, she waved him down. "Drasko!"

He marched up to her with long strides, giving her a grunt of acknowledgement.

"Boris told us they are nuking this place." She hoped to read shock in his expression.

When he nodded, her heart sank.

"How long do we have?" she asked.

"Your uncle gave us eight hours to close the portal and halt this virus," he said, "and that was about four hours ago."

Well, fuck.

"UNCLE JOE," EILEA BARKED into the phone.

"Why in hell haven't you answered your calls?"

She flinched at his sharpness. "Are you going to nuke the Amaroki?" she demanded. She wasn't reassured when her question was met with silence. "Uncle!"

He let out a bunch of expletives. "We've had reports that the sick are petrifying. That they are turning into werewolves."

"I haven't seen anyone turn into a werewolf," she answered honestly.

"Have you seen petrified bodies?"

"No." Another honest answer. Sort of. Though she'd heard about Albert Strongpaw, she hadn't seen him.

"Don't lie to me, Eilea."

"I'm not lying." Technically, she wasn't, but if she told him she'd heard about Albert's condition, they'd speed up the bomb.

"I'll be there in an hour. Pack your things. You're leaving."

Pack what, and how did he expect her to leave when a demonic ghost would probably kill her at the first opportunity?

"But Un—"

He cut her off by ending the call.

How could he do this to her? How could he involve her with this strange species, let her surrender her heart to a pack of shifters, then take it all away? Didn't she mean anything to him? Didn't the Amaroki? He'd given up his family and dedicated most of his life to serving them. Was he just going to discard them without proof they were a threat?

SWALLOWED BY THE WHITE mist, Geri lost his sense of smell and direction. Fog made it impossible for him to see beyond his nose. He only knew where to go by listening to Katarina's lilting voice, imploring him to follow her and promising eternal happiness in her arms.

His feet felt like they were dredged in quicksand as he followed what he knew to be his eternal doom. But he had to do it. There was no other way to save the Alaskan Amaroki and his family.

He stopped, startled, when the image of a behemoth black protector materialized beside him. He recognized the ancient god, Amarok, from the scrolls.

What are you doing? Amarok demanded.

Though his mouth didn't move, Geri heard the protector in his thoughts.

Geri wondered if Katarina could see and hear the god as well. "Saving the Amaroki."

She called, "Geriii, why do you stop, my love? Come to me."

He had his answer. She couldn't see the god.

Amarok's heavy jowls punctuated a frown. *This is not the way.*

"Geriii...."

Ignoring his late wife, he gazed at the apparition. "But the witch is dead."

The witch is not dead. Amarok's thick brow drew low over his eyes. *She has yet to be revealed.*

Geri gaped at the Ancient, barely hearing anything beyond the wild beating of his heart. "I don't understand. We've looked everywhere."

Do not sacrifice your soul for Katarina. She will lead you into the abyss, and you'll never see your family again.

"What do I do?"

Amarok's brilliant white eyes shifted to gold and then a blinding orange. *Run!*

He ran and saw a pinprick of swirling light ahead. He reached for it, calling on Amarok's help to escape his unearthly prison.

"Geri, come back to me!"

He pushed himself harder, straining for the exit. He had to make it out.

"Geriii, do not betray me."

He stopped, his heart pounding so hard he feared it would burst when Katarina's snarling spirit materialized in front of him.

"You cannot leave me, Geri."

"No, Katarina." He turned up his chin, determined not to let her see the dread and fear in his soul. "You must go without me."

"I can't go in there alone."

"You have to, Katarina. You're dead. I'm not."

"Don't you want to be with me?" She floated close, teasing him with tendrils of smoke that smelled like her cloying perfume. "Don't you miss me?"

Geri swallowed back a lump of regret. Instinct told him to lie, but he couldn't. "You were unfaithful. You lied to us."

Her large luminous eyes became narrow, dark slits. "I smell her on you! Is that why you won't follow me? You'd rather fuck that human bitch?"

Again, Geri should've lied. But there had been so much he'd wanted to say to her before her death. He gritted his teeth, looking into the endless black chasms in her hollow eyes. "You drove me to her."

She let out an ear-splitting howl.

Run! Amarok thought to him from a distance.

Ignoring the chill that swept down his spine and twisted his innards, he jumped through Katarina's spirit and kept going.

A serpent's hiss filled his ears, and he yelped as flame licked at his heels. Bursting through the swirling vortex, he sprinted for the road, feeling a mixture of dread and relief when he saw Annie and the truck were no longer there. He'd have to escape on foot.

He leaped back when a tree limb twice his height fell, nearly crushing him. Another limb fell, and another. He looked over his shoulder and saw a smoky serpent with Katarina's face slithering though the branches. Her sibilant laughter echoed through the forest.

The crack from above was so loud, it filled his skull. In a panic, he tried to duck out of the way but moved too slowly. A heavy weight fell across his back, driving him to the ground. Something ground into his back with the blinding pain of a thousand stinging serpents.

"Now you will have to join me." Her maniacal laughter made him cringe. "And when your brothers come for you, I will take them, too."

Chapter Sixteen

EILEA WAS CHECKING Boris's temperature when Annie stumbled into the lodge with three children in tow. She looked like she'd been dragged through the flames of hell. Her clothes were torn, and green gunk stuck to her hair and face.

Eilea stood on shaky legs and looked over Annie's shoulder. "Where's Geri?"

Amara said at almost the same moment, "What happened?"

When the baby in her arms vomited down her shirt, Annie didn't even flinch. She handed the child to another shifter and stripped down to a tank top and her dirty jeans. She left the children with two women shifters who'd yet to succumb to the virus. Annie had bad news about Geri. Eilea could tell by the way Annie's lower lip quivered.

Eilea sank onto Boris's cot when Annie walked over to them. The first thing she noticed was a powerful smell of sulfur and sickness.

Amara fanned her face. "Dang, Annie."

She shrugged. "I'm used to it. Werewolves ate the Cloudwalkers. These children are the only survivors."

"Werewolves?" Amara clutched her throat. "Then our worst fears have come true."

Annie solemnly nodded. "Geri and I killed them."

Eilea scanned the entrance once more, hoping Geri would make his appearance any moment.

"Where is he?" Amara asked.

Annie burst into tears. "He didn't make it."

Eilea could've sworn the world stopped turning at that moment.

"What do you mean?" Amara pleaded. "What happened to him?"

Annie wiped her eyes. "Katarina took him. She said she'd close the portal if he went with her."

Eilea shot to her feet. "No!"

"If the portal was closed, wouldn't I have my healing powers back?" Amara frowned at her hands. "I feel nothing."

Annie scowled. "She lied to him. I told him not to go."

"Then what did she do with him?" Amara asked.

Eilea's world spun, then rocked as images of Katarina torturing or killing Geri flashed in her mind. Eilea felt sick. Not Geri. Not any of her mates! Wrapping her arms around herself, she hung her head between her legs, trying and failing to steady her breaths. Geri had left her on bad terms. They hadn't had a chance to make up, and now he was gone.

"Eilea, he asked me to tell you he was sorry."

"What for?"

Annie shrugged, flashing an apologetic smile. "He just said he was sorry."

When Amara sat beside her, they fell into each other's arms, crying on each other's shoulders. Amara would've been Eilea's daughter by marriage if Eilea had been able to complete the bond with her mates. Now they were lost to her, and she feared nothing would save them.

A succession of thunderous booms made her head snap up.

Drasko Thunderfoot, whose last name suited him perfectly, was stomping down the stairs as a towering protector. "Dr. Johnson, your uncle is on his way to get you."

She straightened. "I know, and I'm not leaving." No way was she leaving the sick Amaroki by themselves. No way was she leaving her mates.

"Yes you are," he boomed. "Amara and Annie, you and the babies are going with him."

"No!" Amara jumped to her feet. "I'm not leaving my mates."

He let out a low, menacing growl. "You are getting in his truck if I have to force you."

Eilea jumped up, pointing an accusatory finger at Drasko. "You can't force me to go."

His eyes lit with fury, and he lunged for her.

She dodged, missing the swoop of his big maw. Then she scrambled to her feet and ran. Where she was going, she had no idea, but she couldn't let them take her.

She tore off down the hallway that led to her room. Chest heaving, she slammed the door behind her, relief sweeping through her when she didn't hear Drasko's heavy footsteps in the hall.

A familiar silver goblet was on the table beside the bed. Could it be? No. She'd lost her chance.

She approached the drink, fearing it was just an illusion. When she looked at the swirling red liquid, her heart skipped a beat.

"The witch isn't dead. You can save them," a familiar voice said as if speaking in a dream.

Without hesitation she snatched the goblet and swallowed the wine in huge gulps, barely registering the coppery taste of blood mixed with a sweet, heavy syrup.

After she'd finished the last drop, she set the goblet down and belched, blinking at the old patchwork curtains hanging over the window.

A feeling of weightlessness came over her. She stumbled to the bed when the room spun. The room became a vortex, and she was the axis on which it spun. She draped an arm over her eyes, crying out as a wave of sickness overcame her chest so tight, she thought she was going into cardiac arrest. *I'm going to die, and I haven't even lived yet!*

"Please make it stop."

Your god is no more, Eilea, a voice whispered in her head. *You are Amaroki now.*

EILEA WOKE TO THE UNMISTAKABLE sound of pants being unzipped.

The fuzzy figure before her slowly came into view. Where was she and what had happened? She licked her lips, tasting a mix of blood and wine.

The blurry figure leaned over and squeezed her breasts.

"Ouch!" she yelped. "What the hell?"

She knocked the hands away and blinked until Agent Parelli's snarling face came into view. "Jimmy? What the fuck are you doing?"

He dropped his pants, something no larger than a thumb poking through the slit in his boxers. "Settling a score."

What the fuck? Was she about to be raped by the world's smallest penis?

She scrambled to her knees with surprising alacrity and strength. "Get away from me."

"Or what?" He chuckled. "Your mates are dying or dead. They can't help you."

He leaped on top of her so fast, she hardly had time to react. When he smothered her scream with a sweaty hand, her bones turned to liquid, then reformed. She bit his hand, snarling and shaking until she felt a snap, followed by the crunch of bone.

His agonized scream filled the room, the sound so grating, she released him. He fell back, clutching a bloody hand to his chest. When he scrambled off the bed and reached for the holster on the table, she sprang into action, biting his other hand until bones crunched. He tried to grab her in a headlock. She scratched his face and chest until he cried for mercy. The smell and taste of his blood filled her senses. In fact she could smell everything, even the foul odor of his crusty underwear. Gross! The stench of hundreds of sick shifters hit her. What was she doing here when they needed her?

"What the hell is going on?" Annie was in the doorway, gazing at them in surprise.

Eilea sat back on her haunches. *What does it look like?* she wanted to say. *I'm kicking rapist ass.* But when she opened her mouth to speak, all that came out was a howl. She looked down at black furry legs. Holy shit! She was a goddamn wolf.

Jimmy stumbled to his feet, and she jumped between him and his gun.

"Okay, okay," he cried. "You win." One limp and bleeding hand pressed to his chest, the other trying to hold up his pants, he stumbled to the door.

Annie growled at him when he tried to pass. He ducked, jammed his shoulder into the doorframe, and slipped past her.

Eilea looked in a cracked mirror hanging above the iron headboard. She was a large wolf with a long snout, fur the color of midnight and eyes a blinding silver.

You have Amarok's coloring. A great honor, a familiar voice said in her head.

Thank you, goddess, she answered.

"Dr. Johnson, is that you?" Annie walked over and stroked her ears.

Eilea whimpered, unsure how to shift back.

As if reading her mind, Annie said, "Envision yourself as a human."

In seconds she was a naked human, blinking at Annie.

"It *was* you!" Annie shrieked.

"Yeah," Eilea grumbled. "And that son of a bitch just tried to rape me."

"Want me to finish him off?"

Eilea shook her head. "I doubt he'll be a threat with two broken wrists."

"No offense, Dr. Johnson, but how in the fuck?"

Eilea laughed joyously. "Let me get dressed, and I'll tell you all about it."

She remembered the goddess telling her the witch wasn't dead, and she could save them. She wasn't sure how, but with her suddenly heightened senses, she was determined to root out the witch.

AFTER EILEA TOLD ANNIE what happened, they found Amara in Hakon's cot, crying against her sleeping mate's shoulder. She clung to his neck when Annie tried to pull her away.

Annie shook her cousin's shoulder. "Get up."

Amara clung more tightly to her alpha. "I'm not leaving him."

Eilea's heart plummeted at the sight, which only made her more determined to find the witch. She couldn't let these people die. Her people now.

"Dr. Johnson just spoke to the goddess. The witch isn't dead. We can still close this portal."

Amara looked at Eilea with red-rimmed eyes and scrunched her nose. "You smell different."

"I know. The goddess turned me into a shifter." She waved impatiently when Amara gaped at her. "No time to explain. Is it common for Amaroki to turn into eagles?"

"What?" Amara released her mate and sat up. "I've never seen any shifters turn into birds. Why?"

She squared her shoulders. "I saw Nakomi turn into an eagle." She wasn't sure how that indicated she was a witch, but it was her only lead.

Annie and Amara shared looks, then Annie grimaced. "That's impossible."

"Unless she's the witch," Eilea said.

"She can't be," Annie said, taking the fussing Hrod from his pen. "Her mates are petrifying. She would have already revealed herself."

"Why hasn't she gotten sick?" Eilea asked, frustrated.

Amara sat up, taking the squirming toddler from Annie. "I think she said she's already had demon burn."

Annie scratched the back of her head. "Did she say it?"

"Maybe I assumed it, since she's not sick, but now that you mention it, they don't have haunted forests in Africa." Amara stood, balancing the child on her hip.

"Are you sure?" Annie asked, pulling Alexi from his pen.

"Yes, I'm sure. My grandmother told me. There are a few in Europe and North America, but nowhere else."

"So why is she immune to the virus?" she asked.

"A protection spell," Amara said in amazement. "My mates' great aunt was the last of the Amaroki witches. She could cast spells to protect our tribe from viruses."

"Why would she protect herself and not the rest of us?" Annie looked affronted, voice rising as her cheeks reddened. "Or her mates?"

"It doesn't make sense," she admitted. Nakomi was a raging bitch, but she appeared to care for her mates. Why wouldn't she save them if she could?

Balancing the baby on her hip, Annie marched down the stairs with purpose in her stride.

Eilea and Amara followed, rushing to keep up with her.

Annie burst into the private room where Nakomi was taking care of her mates.

Eilea whimpered at a horrid stench so thick it fogged her eyes. Great Ancients, it smelled worse than a rotting cadaver.

Nakomi mumbled beside Albert's bed, but at their entrance, she jumped to her feet, shielding her sick mate with extended claws. "What do you want?"

"What were you chanting?" Annie demanded.

Nakomi's eyes flashed gold. "A prayer."

"Or a spell?" Annie accused.

"Our people are dying." Amara stood beside Annie. "Your mates are petrifying. Why haven't you told us you're the witch?"

"Will you let us all die because of your foolish pride?" Annie bit out. Alexi cried a little in her embrace, struggling in her arms.

"Back away, bitch, before I rip out your throat." Nakomi jutted a claw toward Annie. "I am no witch."

"Then how is it you are not sick?" Amara demanded. "And don't tell me you've had demon burn. There are no haunted forests in Africa."

Nakomi backed up defensively. "My secrets are mine alone." She snapped at Annie and Amara, her fangs distending.

Annie and Amara shielded the babies. Eilea lurched in front of them, anger turning to shock, then horror when she saw that Albert's gray skin was covered with patches of matted fur. His legs and arms extended past the small cot, his ribcage was as wide as a barrel, and his face contorted in a mixture of human and beast.

He was turning into a werewolf.

"Tell us!" she demanded, instinctively unsheathing her claws, her voice dropping several octaves.

"Well, look who has claws," Nakomi snarled. "You suddenly sprout fangs and call me the witch?"

"The goddess changed me."

"How kind of her," Nakomi said with a bitter laugh.

"Are you going to tell us or what? I've seen your eyes turn red. If you're not a witch, then you're possessed." She refused to let the bitch get to her. They had more pressing matters.

"I am neither witch nor demon."

"Then what the hell are you?"

They engaged in a tense stare-down, Eilea's veins pumping wildly as she waited for Nakomi to strike. She wouldn't get away with it this time. If she so much as raised a claw, Eilea would attack. Much to her surprise, Nakomi backed down.

"I've never been demon-burned before." Her voice dropped to a whisper. "My birth mother was human."

"I didn't know that," Amara said.

Nakomi's eyes sharpened. "You didn't know because it's none of your business. She was an American doctor, and she looked too much like you." She pointed at Eilea. "The Ancients bewitched her and my father in order to create an abomination."

Nakomi's hatred for Eilea suddenly made sense.

They all stared at each other for several stressful heartbeats until Amara's babies broke the silence by crying.

"You are not an abomination, Nakomi." Amara said with pity.

Nakomi looked from Amara to Eilea. "Then why did my mother leave me?"

"I-I don't know," Eilea answered, feeling an odd sense of guilt for a crime she didn't commit. "I imagine she was scared."

"She left me to a life of misery." The hurt in her eyes revealed the lonely, abandoned child she must have once been. "My stepmother called me a cursed child. She resented me for having to hide the secret of my birth."

"I'm sorry," Amara said. "I know what it's like to have a stepmother hate you. Mine was the same way."

"But did she raise you?" Tears spilled from her eyes. "Did she beat you for the slightest offense?"

Amara shook her head. "My birth mother abused me. Now look at what my stepmother has done to all of us."

"My grandparents didn't want me. Nobody did." Nakomi sank onto Loki's cot, casting a woeful glance at her sick mates. "I never knew love until I found my mates."

"It's safe to say we've all had shitty lives," Annie crossed her arms. "Maybe yours was harder than others, but that's no excuse not to close the portal."

"If you don't, we'll all die." Amara said. "Is that really what you want?"

Nakomi threw up her hands. "How many times must I tell you I am not a witch?"

"Then what is your power?" Amara demanded. "Annie can read minds. I can heal. The Ancients said those of us with a lot of human blood have special abilities."

Whatever it was, Eilea knew red eyes had something to do with it.

Nakomi pulled back her shoulders, reminding Eilea once again of that regal African queen. "I can shift into more than just a wolf."

"What do you mean?" Annie asked.

"An elk, a cougar, a protector." Nakomi shrugged. "I can become any animal. Some of my birds have red eyes." She gave Eilea a look, challenging her to refute her story.

"Wow." Amara breathed. "I'd like to see that."

Nakomi's eyes narrowed to slits. "But I am *not* a witch. I do not know spells, only ancient prayers."

Annie patted Alexi's back when he snuggled against her. "So who is the witch?"

Eilea was at a loss. She wracked her brain, trying to recall what the goddess had told her.

The witch isn't dead. You can save them.

She heard a familiar voice in her head. It wasn't the goddess. It was old, scratchy, but sweet. Her grandmother. Memories washed over her. The line of sick people at her grandmother's door every morning. The chants her grandmother sang to cleanse their home before each full moon. Everyone in their small Louisiana town had called her a *kurioso,* a witch. She'd healed them with potions and spells, an ancient magic she'd taught Eilea. A magic she suddenly remembered. All of it. Every recipe and chant flooded back.

Grasping Amara's forearm, she slowly lowered herself onto a chair. "Holy shit! I think I'm the witch."

She recalled the chant her grandmother had used to drive away spirits and knew without a doubt, she had the power to close the portal.

Amara knelt beside her. "Eilea, what are you saying?"

She smiled when Baby Hrod wrapped his fingers around hers, giving her a look that was wise beyond his years. "My grandmother was a *kurioso.*"

"A what?" Annie asked.

"People used to come to her for potions and spells when they couldn't afford a doctor. She considered herself a spiritual healer. She practiced *brua,* a Caribbean witchcraft. She taught me her spells when I was young, but I rebelled against them because they weren't science-based. I was ashamed of her." She regretted the way she'd rejected her grandmother. "I thought I'd forgotten them, but they suddenly came back to me."

Amara said excitedly, "Do you know a spell to close the portal?"

She nodded enthusiastically.

Albert thrashed, letting out a howl.

Nakomi screamed. "No, my love!"

Eilea hurried to his side, placed a hand on his brow, and muttered a sleeping spell. He fell quiet, eyes closing. She released a shaky breath. "Take me to the portal."

"At once." Annie handed Hrod to Nakomi.

"You two are going alone?" Amara asked.

Annie nodded. "Who else are we going to take? Drasko needs to stay here in case...." She glanced at Albert, whose snores filled the room, his chest rising and falling with disturbing violence. His snout had elongated to a crooked point. Eilea didn't know how long the sleeping spell would last, but Annie was right. Drasko would need to deal with him and the others should they turn.

Amara grabbed Nakomi's wrist. "I'm sorry, but I need to get my children out of here."

Nakomi solemnly handed Hrod to Amara and looked at Eilea pleadingly. "Please hurry before it's too late."

"I'll do my best." She grabbed Annie's arm. "Drasko will try to stop us."

"I know." Annie grimaced, then patted her pocket. "But I still have the keys to his truck. We'll go out the back way."

As Eilea followed her, the reality of her situation sank to her gut like a brick. They were going out into the wilderness to close a portal to the afterworld. Assailed with the memory of the time Katarina's spirit had brutally choked her, Eilea shuddered. Never mind the potential werewolves that threatened to kill them. She was more worried about the vengeance of a jealous, vindictive ghost. She sent a silent prayer to the goddess, asking her to infuse her with the strength she needed to battle this spirit. Otherwise the Amaroki were doomed.

Chapter Seventeen

JIMMY'S HANDS ACHED so badly, he couldn't think to reason.

Damn that bitch. I'll kill her and all those fucking dogs.

Cradling damaged hands, he stumbled down the road, forcing his legs to propel him forward, though he was beyond exhausted and had to keep stopping to pull up his pants. It took all his willpower not to collapse face-first in the dirt. As soon as he made it to safety, he would get his revenge. There was an outpost at the edge of the reservation. He'd phone Headquarters and report a massive werewolf outbreak. His government would nuke every last mongrel.

Maniacal laughter bubbled in his throat. That stuck-up bitch would regret ever fucking with him.

He paused at a rustle in the overgrown bushes beside him. Odd. He hadn't heard a peep in this forest for hours. He moved faster. Only a few more hours, and he'd be safe.

A low whimper made the hairs on the back of his neck stand up. "Whatever the fuck is out there better back off!" he hollered. "I'm a goddamn federal agent!"

The bushes rattled again.

"I'm warning you! My government will skin your hide if you lay a fucking finger on me."

Grunting, he stumbled over a rock and tumbled into the dirt. Swearing, he clutched his throbbing arms and rolled on his side. A silent scream died on his lips when he found himself looking into the blood-red eyes of the most frightening creature he'd ever seen. It had a distended, pointy snout and razor-sharp teeth dripping with green goo that sizzled when it hit the ground. The creature loomed over him, one long, crooked arm raised as if to strike.

"You wouldn't da—" Jimmy rumbled right before the creature sliced through his eyes with claws like blades.

Blinded by blood and pain, Jimmy screeched and kicked the creature between the legs with all his strength. The beast grunted and fell on top of him. Jimmy frantically pushed him off, gagging on the monster's putrid breath. Mewling in agony, he stumbled to his feet and fled.

A roar behind him prodded him to move faster, fumbling through branches and undergrowth. A howl chased him deeper into the woods moments before his back was ripped open. He lunged forward and rolled like a ball until landing with a bone-sickening crunch.

Curled in a fetal position, Jimmy moaned as his lifeblood drained into the forest floor.

THE DRIVE DOWN THE dark winding road was filled with a deafening silence. Annie, who was driving, stayed alert, watching for signs of the ghost. Eilea alternated between marveling at the claws that extended and retracted from her fingers at will, and thinking about Geri. Had he gone with Katarina because he missed his dead mate or had he sacrificed himself in hopes that she would close the portal? If so, was it too late to get him out? Because Eilea refused to close the portal without trying to save him.

"I wish I knew what you were thinking."

Sheathing her wondrous claws, she recalled Uncle Joe telling her Annie was a telepath. "I thought you could read minds."

"I can, but my powers have failed me."

What if she lost her spell-casting powers? She summoned the words to the banishing spell, quietly reciting them to herself. She remembered her grandmother's memory spell and recited the words, hoping the chant was enough to preserve her spells.

"Well, Dr. Johnson?" Annie prodded. "What are you thinking?"

She decided it was best not to mention her concern about losing the spells. "I'm worried about trapping Geri in the portal."

"I knew it." Annie smacked the wheel. "You're going in after him, aren't you?"

"I have to try."

"What if you both get stuck there?"

That thought had crossed her mind, but she did her best to subdue her fear. "I won't let that happen."

Annie side-eyed Eilea. "Do you know what happens to your mind in the portal?"

"No."

"You completely lose it—your memories, everything."

Aw, shit. She murmured the memory spell again.

"What are you doing?" Annie asked.

"Reciting a memory spell," Eilea told her.

"You'd better pray it works."

She continued her incantations. The spell had to work. She refused to fail the Amaroki.

PLACING LUC'S HAND over her abdomen, Amara whispered, "You must recover for your child, my love." She choked back a sob and gently brushed her lips across his feverish forehead. "And for me."

He responded with an eyelid twitch, nothing more. She didn't even know if he could hear her. She moved over to Rone, checking his fluids and bed pad. Taking care of her sick family and keeping her babies fed and happy was the hardest thing she'd ever done. She had no time for sleep when so many needed her, but she considered herself fortunate. Other families had no nurses, so they languished with no one to help them. She wanted to offer assistance to those families, but she was spread too thin with her family. Raz turned out to be a miracle nurse, moving from pack to pack with amazing alacrity for an octogenarian. If it hadn't been for her, the weakest shifters would've succumbed to dehydration.

Amara resented the government's reaction to their plight. The humans had dropped supplies but not sent help. Jimmy was nowhere to be found. If they survived this ordeal, she was going to file a formal complaint with Agent Johnson.

She moved to her in-laws and wiped vomit off Mihaela, looking up with a start when the massive lodge doors slammed open for Drasko as a big, intimidating protector, eyes blazing gold. Agent Johnson was behind him. Hrod and Alexi howled, startled by the noise.

"Shh, babies." She hurried to their playpen, which was positioned between Luc and Rone's beds, and leaned over them. Annoyed, she handed Alexi his bottle and Hrod his sippy; she'd just put them to sleep.

Chest heaving, Drasko pointed an axe at her. "Time to go."

Ignoring him, she swaddled her boys, attempting to soothe them back to sleep. "I already said I'm not leaving."

Drasko stomped down the steps three at a time. "I'm not arguing with you."

Amara's heart sank. She couldn't fight a massive wall of muscle and fur. "Give Eilea a chance to close the portal."

"My niece went to close the portal?" Alarmed, Johnson rushed down the stairs. "Is she insane?"

Amara held her ground. "She's the witch."

Drasko's heavy jowls fell. "You're not making sense."

"The goddess turned her into a shifter, and she has magical powers."

"Turned her into a shifter?" The wrinkles around Johnson's eyes deepened. "How?"

"Eilea drank the blood of the Ancients."

Johnson had a look akin to horror in his eyes. "My niece drank shifter blood?"

"Yeah," Amara huffed. "Now she's got our cooties."

Johnson rubbed a hand over his buzzed, gray hair, looking as if he was waking from a dream. "I-I didn't mean offense. This just caught me off guard. I don't understand how this means she can close the portal."

"She remembered her grandmother's spells," Amara answered plainly, as if drinking Ancient wolf blood and suddenly recalling witchcraft was an everyday occurrence.

"Those spells weren't real."

Amara snickered. "The spells work for Eilea. I watched her put Albert to sleep with one."

Drasko's eyes bulged. "Albert woke up?"

Amara froze. Fuck, what had she done? "It's fine. He's asleep now."

Drasko latched onto her shoulder with a bruising grip. "Did he turn into a werewolf?"

She struggled to shake him off. "He's sleeping. He can't hurt anyone. As soon as the portal is closed, I can heal him."

Glowering, Drasko pushed her aside and stomped down the stairs.

"Drasko, wait!"

But he'd already reached the bottom step and was heading for the hall that led to the Strongpaw's private room. Johnson followed him, a hand on his holster.

She tried to catch them, but fatigue slowed her movements.

She faltered when an ear-piercing scream rent the air. Heart beating double time, she finally reached their room, breathless and dizzy.

Drasko leaned over Albert Strongpaw's bed, axe raised.

Nakomi was sprawled across her sleeping mate, glaring at Drasko with distended fangs. "You lay a paw on him, and I will rip your throat out!"

"I don't want to, Nakomi, but he's a threat to all of us."

"He's a threat to none of us," Nakomi hissed.

Amara peered around Agent Johnson. Great Ancients, Albert looked even worse. He had fully transformed, snout jutting like a beak, fingers curved into massive claws. And the stench! She covered her nose, stomach turning over. He smelled worse than week-old roadkill. His brothers also appeared to be changing, their skin a deathly gray, noses twisting and eyes sunk in their sockets.

She understood Drasko's reaction, but she didn't want him to kill them yet. They were so close. Eilea had it in her to save them.

Pushing ahead of Johnson, Amara said, "Let Eilea close the portal, then I can heal him. All I'm asking is for you to give him the same chance I gave you," she pleaded.

He turned, a low rumble rising from his chest. "I told you to kill me then, Amara."

"You did, and we wouldn't have Alexi if I'd listened." She held out her hands. "Lower your axe, sweetheart. Give Eilea a chance."

"Please," Nakomi cried.

Agent Johnson stood in the hall, gun in one hand, phone in the other. "I have to call this in."

"You do, and we all die." Amara said. "Your niece included."

Johnson pocketed his phone with reluctance. "If he wakes, you have to kill him," he said to Drasko.

"I will." Drasko lowered his weapon. "You have my word."

"You will have to kill me first," Nakomi shrieked.

"If that's what it takes." Drasko grimaced. "I'm not putting my family or my people at risk."

Ignoring Nakomi's angry gasp, he ushered Amara out of the room. "One hour. If the portal isn't closed by then, you're leaving and I'm taking care of Albert and the rest of them. Do you understand me, Amara?"

She nodded. Great Ancients, please guide Eilea.

"KEEP YOUR EYES OPEN for werewolves," Annie said as she slammed the door.

Eilea clutched a hatchet, digging into the wood until her knuckles ached. "And ghosts," she said breathlessly, scanning the canopy.

How odd the air was here—even more stifling than at the lodge. It was as if a vortex had sucked out all life, and they were moving through a painting.

Annie led her along a worn path. The only sounds were their labored breathing as they trudged through air as thick as soup. The farther they journeyed, the louder her heartbeat. Her knees were so weak from fear, she was surprised she could walk at all. She blinked at a strange pinprick of white light, a beacon in the shadows. "Is that what I think it is?"

Annie didn't answer, arms hanging limply at her sides, looking like she was trying to catch flies with her mouth.

Eilea waved the axe in front of her face. "Earth to Annie."

The girl gaped at her. "What are we doing here?"

"Saving the shifter race. What's wrong with you?"

Annie turned in a slow circle. "I feel weird."

Annie had lost her mind. Eilea didn't know if she should feel relief or apprehension that she still had her senses. She hoped that meant the memory spell had worked. Damn, she should've performed the spell on Annie.

A low groan up ahead drew her attention. With her sharpened senses, she honed in on the source and breathed in a familiar scent. Geri!

She left the path and ran deep into the forest, heedless of her own safety.

"Wait, Dr. Johnson!" Annie called. "Where are you going?"

But Eilea wasn't listening. She had to get to Geri. Her limbs iced over with fear when she saw his denim-clad legs poking out under a massive tree branch.

Throwing down her axe, she grabbed the end of the branch and tried to heave it off him. "Help me move it," she cried to Annie.

Annie joined her, and together they pulled the heavy limb off him.

He was covered in cuts and bruises. "Geri, my love." She cupped his face. "Can you hear me?"

When he didn't answer, she closed her eyes and summoned a healing spell. She wasn't even sure if it was one her grandmother taught her, but it felt right. "Elements of healing and health, keepers of scriptures and tomes, restore this ailing body and mend these broken bones."

Warmth infused her fingers and flowed into Geri. His cuts faded. She recited a memory spell for good measure. She wanted to do the same for Annie, but the young shifter had left her to gaze, transfixed, at a strange buzzing tunnel of mist.

"Don't get too close to it," she said. She didn't want to have to take care of both Geri and Annie.

Geri groaned and blinked at her. "Eilea, what are you doing here? It's not safe."

She smiled. "And yet you're here?"

She braced herself for some sexist comment and was pleased when he chuckled. When he held out a hand, she helped him sit up. "Are you okay?"

He checked, running his hands over his limbs. "I think so. Just sore." He breathed her in, smiling as if she was some rare perfume. "You smell different."

"That's because I am. Can you stand?"

"Give me a minute." He dragged a hand down his face. "Where are my brothers?"

"Sick." She turned to the swirling tunnel of white mist. "I need to close this portal before they get worse."

"How are you going to do that?"

"Long story, but I'm a shifter now, and I'm also a witch."

He edged closer, sniffing her as if she was his own personal crack. "That explains the new smell."

She arched away. "Is it bad?"

"It's even better than before."

After she helped him to his feet, they stood there for a long moment, unspoken words in the air between them.

"Eilea, I'm sorry." Geri finally said, thrusting his hands in his pockets like a contrite child. "My words were unkind."

She impatiently tapped her foot. "They were."

His luminous eyes shone silver in the moonlight. "I know I don't deserve your forgiveness, but I promise to try harder not to offend you."

Eilea fisted her hands until nails broke skin—anything to stop the urge to kiss him senseless. She'd been royally pissed, but at the moment she was more relieved than anything. She thought she'd lost him forever. Still, this was her chance to assert herself. If she was going to mate with this man and his brothers, she had to establish boundaries. "Just don't say stupid things."

He flashed a rueful smile. "My brain turns to porridge when I'm around you."

She reached for his hand. "Annie told me you went into the portal."

Pulling her hand to his lips, he kissed her knuckles, making her already wobbly legs go weaker. "I thought it was the only way to save the Amaroki, but Amarok told me the witch wasn't dead and helped me escape."

"Thank the Ancients," she said, leaning into him, drawn to his scent like a moth to flame. What was it about this shifter that made her want him so? Had she truly been bewitched by the Ancients, or was she falling in love?

When he traced her bottom lip with his thumb, she clutched his collar. Though he smelled of sweat and blood and something foul, under that was the scent of her mate, the man who'd risked his soul to save them.

She leaned up to kiss him, then gasped when he pushed her to the ground. She hit the dirt so hard, the air was knocked out of her.

"Eilea," he hollered. "Look out!" He rolled her out of the way of a massive limb that fell on top of him.

"Geri!" She scrambled to her feet as another limb crashed down. She ran to Annie, jerking her out of the way of the assault.

"What's happening?" Annie cried.

Sprinting through the trees, she glanced over her shoulder. The forest was being destroyed in an effort to kill them, and she didn't know if Geri was okay.

They reached the edge of the swirling tunnel, suspended about a foot above the ground. A low hum reverberated from its translucent walls.

"Dragon!" Annie screamed.

A massive white dragon descended upon her, red eyes glowing.

"Cătea!" the demon screeched. "I will kill you!" The serpent reared back, black smoke pouring from its snout.

Pushing Annie out of the way, Eilea stumbled back and fell into the tunnel. She jumped to her feet and ran through a fog so thick, she couldn't tell where she was, but the flames licking at her heels indicated she was going in the right direction. The feeling of weightlessness in her legs was disconcerting, and unlike anything she'd ever known.

"Come back here. Let me show you what happens to whores who steal my mates," the demon hissed.

Fear flowed through her, igniting a panic attack. "I didn't ask to bond with them, Katarina. It was the work of the Ancients."

"Do you think I care?" Katarina's laugh reverberated, though the demon wasn't visible. "Either way you must die."

"And then what?" The fog was so thick, she could barely see her hand in front of her face. "Be reunited with Geri in the afterworld? Do you think he'll come with you if you kill me? Or his brothers for that matter?"

"I will make them come," she answered.

"How?" Eilea asked. "What leverage will you have over them if we're all dead?"

Katarina hissed, red eyes shining through the mist. The serpent slowly came into view, a creature made of smoke, circling Eilea as if preparing to strike.

Eilea backed up, praying she was moving in the direction she'd come.

"Think about it, Katarina," she continued, hoping to appeal to the spirit's reasonable side, though she doubted Katarina had one. "If you kill us, we'll go to Valhol, and you'll be alone again."

"My mates will come with me, I'm sure of it."

No, she wasn't. Eilea heard the doubt in each word. "You don't think they'll be angry with you for murdering the entire Alaskan tribe?" She retreated several more steps, the feeling in her legs slowly returning. Was she nearing the exit? "Their daughter? Their grandchildren?"

The serpent loomed over Eilea, black smoke billowing from her nostrils. "Their daughter is the spawn of a whore!"

"That may be true," Eilea conceded, not wanting to argue with the crazed bitch on every point. "But they still love her. I'm not sure they'll forgive you if you cut her life short." Her gut twisted as the demon advanced.

"Then what would you have me do?" Katarina spat.

Eilea stepped back again, doing her best to quell the shaking in her limbs. "I suggest you do what my grandmother taught me."

Katarina's thick neck fanned out like that of a cobra. "I will *not* give them up."

"I'm not asking you to." She fought to maintain control of her temper. The bitch wasn't getting any of Eilea's mates. She'd go to hell and drag them out of Katarina's clutches if she had to. "My grandmother taught me a poem." Backing up another step, she forced a smile as the feeling returned to her limbs. "I think you'll understand."

The demon looked down at Eilea, black smoke pouring from the slits above her mouth. "A poem will not bring me back from the depths of despair."

Eilea raised her hands and chanted the banishment spell, praying to the Ancients Katarina didn't realize what she was doing.

"Wandering sprits who've denied your plight, hear my command and go to the light."

"What are you saying?" Katarina demanded, her eyes starting to fade.

"Release the hold of your mortal state, embrace your death and face your fate."

Katarina arched back with an ominous cry, her neck expanding, more smoke and steam pouring from her nostrils.

Eilea raised her hands and channeled the buzzing energy flowing through her to the tips of her fingers.

"Ghouls, demons, and monsters of fright, you are banished to hell and eternal night."

Katarina released her dragon fire, and Eilea let fly, knocking the flame back and hitting Katarina's chest. The demon fell back with an ominous squeal, a cocoon of flame enveloping her.

Mist swirled at Eilea's feet, rushing past her like the current of a river, sweeping Katarina with it. The demon's mournful cry echoed through the forest as the portal retreated, sucked up into a vortex of light, like water circling a drain. The funnel turned into a small ember of light, then blinked out like a candle flame doused by water.

Eilea fell to her knees as realization slowly dawned. "Well, that's something you don't learn in medical school."

Holy shit! She'd faced a vengeful demon and survived.

Wait a minute. Geri!

Jumping to her feet, she raced through the forest, relying on her sense of smell to locate him. Panic gripped her when she reached a carpet of fallen branches. How would she find him in this mess?

Hearing the call of a wolf, she spotted a bushy tail stuck up through the debris.

"Annie!"

The wolf popped up, barking.

Throwing off her scrubs, Eilea shifted into wolf form and dove into the branches. Ignoring the pain from thorns and twigs, she crawled around until she reached them.

Annie lowered her head to a massive branch. She barely made out Geri's pale skin and fair hair. She and Annie grabbed wood with their teeth, dragging it away piece by piece for what felt like an eternity.

When they finally reached him, they saw his gut had been punctured by a sharp branch. After shifting into human form, she felt his pulse. It was there, but barely.

His eyes open briefly, then shut. "Eilea, you're alive."

"Don't speak," she said, struggling to remain calm. Losing her cool would not help the situation.

Rolling him onto his side, she swore when she saw the point sticking out his back. Annie whimpered and shrank back, tail between her legs.

There was no way she and Annie could take him all the way to the truck without injuring him further. Even if they did manage to carry him out, the movement would cause more damage.

If she was in the operating room, she could save him, but out here she had no surgical tools.

You have your spells, a voice whispered in her head.

Her confidence in her newfound magical powers faltered. What if she failed to save him? Blood steadily flowed from both puncture wounds. He'd bleed out by the time she got him into surgery.

She grabbed hold of the stick. "Geri," she said, "this is going to hurt."

He screamed when she pulled it out, and then he collapsed with a shuddering breath, a crimson bull's-eye fanning out on the dirt under him.

She placed her hands over his injury, dismayed when blood soaked her fingers. Conjuring up the healing spell, she closed her eyes, focusing on the slow pounding of his heart as he bled out. She chanted the spell over and over, fingertips tingling. That tingling turned into a throb as she continued, forcing herself to tune out the sound of chirping birds returning to the forest, crickets calling to one another, and Annie's low whine.

Channeling all of her energy into the spell, she barely remembered to breathe, intent only on saving Geri. *Please don't die,* she begged, too afraid to open her eyes and see if her magic was working.

"Did you close the portal?"

Her eyes flew open, and she looked into Geri's bright eyes. She ripped open Geri's shirt and frantically searched his stomach, amazed when she only felt the faint trace of a scar. She smiled when he took her hand in his, blinking at her as if he'd just woken from an afternoon nap.

"Well?" he asked.

She looked down at her bare breasts, remembering she'd discarded her clothes when she'd shifted. "I did."

Heat crept into her cheeks when he flashed a wicked grin.

He got up on his elbows, showing no signs of pain as he casually draped a hand across her bare thigh. "How?"

Eilea heard Annie's heavy sigh before she trotted off.

She knew his touch was no accident. If Annie hadn't been nearby, she'd have ripped off his pants and taken him right there.

"You going to answer me, lubirea mea?"

She felt his back, relief sweeping through her when she found a scar similar to the one on his gut. Placing her hands on his shoulders, she searched his gaze, unable to control her laughter when his wicked smile widened.

She brushed her lips across his. "Shut up and kiss me."

Chapter Eighteen

AMARA BRUSHED RONE'S mop of hair out of his eyes, stroking his forehead and committing his full lips and boyish face to memory. She gently pressed her lips to his, her tears falling on his lashes.

"I'm sorry we never conceived children," she whispered, exhausted beyond words but unable to sleep. "I would have loved to bloom with you." She kissed him once more, then moved to Hakon.

According to the clock on her phone, Eilea had two minutes to close the portal before Drasko would Force Amara to go, and just a few hours before the Alaskan Amaroki would be nuked. Two more minutes, and Amara would lose her mates forever. Unable to voice a goodbye, she simply held his hand. "I'm sorry you won't live to see your son grow. I will make sure he knows how much you loved him."

She winced when the doors to the lodge creaked open. When Drasko said her name, she refused to look up. If he wanted her, he'd have to come and drag her away.

At the sound of him stomping down the stairs, her heart cleaved in two. She threw herself on Hakon with a sob. She couldn't leave him. She wouldn't! She was stunned when she felt a familiar tingle in her fingers. Her skin pulsed with energy.

"Amara," Drasko said urgently. His eyes were brimming with tears as he held a furry hand down to her. "It's time."

She vehemently shook her head, backing away from him. "My magic. I feel it!"

Climbing on top of Hakon, she straddled his waist and took his face in her hands. "Hakon, baby, please wake." She channeled her healing magic into him. It trickled slowly at first, making Amara worry she'd been mistaken, but the tempo picked up, and there was no mistaking her magic was awakening.

When he groaned, she threw back her head, the magic bursting through her like a geyser. The jolt nearly knocked her off her mate. She slid off him into Drasko's arms.

Drasko grabbed her hands, holding them up in front of her. Her fingers were blistered and bleeding, but she shrugged off the pain. All that mattered was saving her family.

Hakon groaned again. "Amara."

She smiled at Drasko, her heart bursting with joy. "It worked! The portal is closed." Freeing herself from his arms, she returned to Hakon, taking his hand in hers.

"What happened?" Hakon drawled.

The noose of fear and worry she had carried so long unraveled when she felt his cool forehead. "You were sick," she choked out. "But Eilea closed the portal, because my healing magic is working again."

Drasko shifted into a human and sat beside her. He clasped his brother's shoulder. "How do you feel, Hakon?" His voice sounded as watery as a busted pipe, his eyes red-rimmed from crying.

Hakon flung an arm over his forehead. "Give me a minute to wake up."

Hanging his head, Drasko silently nodded.

Amara didn't realize how much Drasko had been suffering, too. She suddenly understood his terrible position, having to order the execution of his family and entire tribe in order to save his mate and children. She leaned into him, wrapping an arm around his waist.

He shuddered. "You're not angry with me?"

"No," she said, wiping tears from his cheeks. "You did what had to be done. You should go tell Johnson. I need to heal Albert."

"Don't go to him without me."

"I won't," she promised, then froze when a powerful and eerie howl rent the air.

Drasko shifted and hurried down the stairs toward the sound.

Holy shitfire! Albert is awake!

Hakon jerked upright, throwing his blanket off. "What was that?"

She struggled to stand, exhaustion nearly overpowering her. "Albert has turned into a werewolf."

She grabbed onto a chair, forcing back a wave of dizziness and trying to ignore the throbbing in her fingers. Before she could take a step, Hakon had shifted into a giant protector. "Stay here," he boomed and left.

She tiptoed after him. No way was she staying put when she had the power to save Albert.

By the time she made it to the Strongpaw's room, she wasn't shocked to find the door had been ripped off its hinges and the opening widened as if her mates had busted out the frame. She *was* surprised when she saw a hulking gray rhino pressing a crazed werewolf against the wall with its massive horned head. Drasko was behind her, axe raised, demanding she let go of the creature.

The rhino Amara assumed was Nakomi answered with a grunt, steam pouring from her snout. Hakon stood behind them, disoriented and rubbing sleep from his eyes.

"Amara, stay away," Drasko said, holding out a staying hand.

Hakon blocked her, trying to herd her back to the hall.

"Please," she begged. "You have to let me try."

"What if he bites you?"

She smiled. "He won't, because you won't let him."

The beast howled and tried to break free. Hakon latched onto Amara's hand and pulled her forward. "Let her try, Drasko."

Drasko used the axe handle to pin the creature's arm against the wall. "You have a few seconds, Amara, and then I start chopping."

She cringed when she touched Albert's skin, which reminded her of tree bark. He bucked and howled with such ferocity, she was terrified to close her eyes, but she knew she wouldn't be able to concentrate otherwise.

Hakon at her back brought a sense of comfort. "You can do this, Amara."

She closed her eyes and felt the magic stir. Her fingers ached as warmth spilled out, though not as badly as before. Clasping Albert's arm, she felt tree bark give way to rubber and finally to soft skin. She looked into Albert Strongpaw's frightened eyes.

"What happened?" He looked at the rhino pinning him down. "Nakomi?"

She backed away with a grunt, releasing him, then nuzzling his neck. He wrapped his arms around her thick neck, staring deep into her eyes. They were speaking telepathically.

Drasko lowered his axe and nodded at the other two Strongpaws. She healed them quickly.

Dizzy with fatigue and emotionally drained, she let Hakon carry her out while Nakomi and her mates reunited. She'd never been so relieved in her life. Now all she needed to do was heal the rest of her family.

"I'm so proud of you," Hakon whispered in her ear.

She sank against his broad chest when he brought her to the main hall, which was packed with hundreds of sick shifters. How in Ancients' name was she going to heal them all?

EILEA DIDN'T LIKE THE look in Geri's eyes when they got out of the truck. If he'd been a cat, she'd have imagined his hackles being raised. Though the portal's thick fog had lifted, and birds were chirping once again, she was alarmed at the deafening silence inside the lodge. Uncle Joe's truck was parked in the lot, and she hoped things hadn't gone from bad to worse.

"What is it?" she asked Geri.

He raised his nose. "Something doesn't smell right."

She scented the air. For the first time in days it finally smelled fresh and piney. "I don't smell anything odd."

"I'm a tracker, Eilea." He grabbed an axe from the truck, his expression grim. "My sense of smell is better than yours."

"What do you smell?" she asked.

"Blood and dark magic."

Eilea's stomach churned.

"I smell it, too," Annie said, giving Geri a knowing look. "Werewolf."

Well, fuck.

"Do you think Albert Strongpaw woke up?" she asked Annie.

Annie shrugged and fetched an axe. "I don't know, but I'm not taking any chances."

As they approached the entrance, Eilea felt magic balling up in her fingers. She didn't know a spell for chasing away werewolves. Her magic did feel stronger, though, pulsing through her, a fire in her veins. Unarmed, she let Annie and Geri to go through the doors first.

They burst through at the same time, weapons ready, twin howls heralding their arrival.

They were met by Hakon Thunderfoot, transformed into a mighty protector and gazing at them with a fanged grin.

"Hakon!" Geri threw down his axe and held out his hand. "Glad to see you're alive."

Hakon engulfed him in a hug. "I could say the same for you." He laughed, patting Geri's head.

Swatting him away, Geri stepped back, pulling Eilea to his side. "I owe my survival to my mate."

"Dr. Johnson." Hakon bowed to her as if he was addressing a queen. "I suppose I have you to thank for closing the portal."

She flushed. "I had help."

Annie waved her away. "It was all you."

"She was magnificent." Geri puffed up his chest, a goofy grin on his face. "You should've seen her."

The hard planes around Geri's mouth and eyes had softened. For the first time she didn't think of him as a feral or intimidating wolf, but as a man, a very attractive man.

Crossing one leg over the other, she repressed her desire. Her libido picked seriously shitty times to spring to life.

When he cast her a sideways look, she knew she'd been busted. Damn her scent.

"My daughter and brothers?" Geri asked Hakon.

"Your brothers still sleep. Amara is too tired to heal anyone else. She's not happy that I've forced her to rest."

"I will heal them." Eilea surged forward with determination, even though she had no idea how to heal so many at once.

Hakon raised a bushy brow. "You're a healer, too?"

She pulled back her shoulders, feeling like an imposter again as she struggled with the best way to heal them all. "I am."

"Eilea!"

When Uncle Joe came barreling toward her, she didn't know if she should stay or run, given the manic look in his eyes. She was completely taken by surprise when he took her in a fierce hug.

She stiffened under the weight of his touch. All these years she'd longed for a hug from him, and she didn't know how to react. "You can call off your nukes, Uncle," she whispered, unable to mask the hurt in her voice.

Pulling back, he searched her eyes. "I already did, and they weren't my nukes. I never wanted to bring harm to the Amaroki." He squeezed her again. "Thank god you're all right."

She wanted to melt into his embrace, pretend it was her daddy hugging her instead.

"Your god had nothing to do with it, Uncle," she grumbled. "The Ancients helped me."

He cupped her cheek, moisture in his tired eyes. "It's true then. You're one of them now?"

Embarrassment flushed her face, though she wasn't sure why. "I am."

He stared at her a long moment, then broke into a wide grin. "Eilea, I've never been more proud of you than this moment."

She wondered if he was proud that she'd saved the Alaskan Amaroki or that she was one of his special shifters.

She turned away from him. "It's nice to see you finally care." Though she didn't want to have this conversation now, she knew there would never be a right time, and he needed to know how badly he'd hurt her.

She looked at Geri, who stood stoically beside her. She was relieved he was there. His presence said everything.

"Eilea," Uncle Joe said, "forgive me. I know I haven't always been the best uncle."

Twenty-four years of hurt and rejection she'd bottled up inside her suddenly bubbled to the surface, like an awakened volcano. "You were my godfather, and you left me."

The lines around his eyes and mouth deepened. "Now that you've met the Amaroki, maybe you can understand why I couldn't turn my back on them. The government was frightened of them, and I didn't want that fear to lead to genocide."

She shot him an accusatory glare. "Like nuking the Amaroki?"

"This time it was different." His face fell. "This time they were turning into werewolves. Once upon a time, the government didn't understand the difference between shifters and werewolves."

Eilea hadn't realized they had distrusted and feared the Amaroki. Her uncle had always been at ease with them. For the first time she realized that his involvement with the Amaroki might have been the reason they trusted the shifters. She shared another look with Geri. He held her hand and smiled.

The weight of her childhood rejection lifted. The Amaroki needed Uncle Joe more than she did. If it hadn't been for him, there might not even be an Alaskan species. The thought both humbled and terrified her, and she finally appreciated her uncle's dedication. "I'll admit I used to be angry with you for leaving me, but after getting to know the Amaroki, I finally understand why you put them first."

He sniffled. "It was not an easy decision. If you hadn't had your grandmother, I would've given this up for you."

Her throat tightened with emotion. "I'm glad you didn't." She hugged him, sinking into his embrace when he hugged her back. "I would've never met my mates."

Rocking her in his arms, he held her for a long moment. "You are my only family. I love you, niece."

She sighed, the pain from all those years of rejection disappearing.

Though she was loath to break the hug, she had work to do. "Speaking of my mates, if you'll excuse me, I need to heal them."

She took Geri's hand and marched into the lodge, surveying the mass of beds and sick shifters. Raz was holding a child's hair back while the girl vomited into a bucket. The portal had closed, but they were still sick.

Raz gestured to a bundle of sage at the foot of the bed. "That's what you need."

Eilea agreed. She somehow knew just what to do. She lit the sage and walked around the room, chanting the healing and banishment spells, smiling when the patients began to wake.

Chapter Nineteen

EILEA LET MARIUS HELP her into the truck after leaving the Badger-hunter pack. They were the thirteenth pack she'd visited that day, and she was exhausted. She'd been mistaken to think every pack had gone to the lodge for medical attention. Many had chosen to stay home, either out of stubbornness or fear, or they'd been too sick to drive. Luckily she was able to heal every one of them. She didn't know how she'd handle finding a dead family. There'd already been enough death among the Amaroki, thanks to Katarina.

When Marius checked her seatbelt to make sure it was fastened properly, she swatted his hand. "Coddling, babe," she reminded him. "I'm not two."

"Sorry." He grinned. "I just want to make sure you're safe."

She cupped his cheek, planting a delicate kiss on his nose. "I'm safe. We all are."

Blushing, he scooted in beside her.

Marius's constant attention would've been annoying if she hadn't realized she needed him as much as he needed her. He was so doting and considerate, he'd make a fine father to their children. Odd how she was starting to think about children now, a whole pack of little shifters. She'd truly lost her mind.

Geri sat on her other side, wrinkling his nose.

"What is it?" she asked.

"There's still a strange smell."

"It probably won't go away until every last pack is healed," Boris said, climbing into the front seat.

Geri glared out the window. "I hope you're right."

"Luc and Hakon buried the Cloudwalkers. Every last one was accounted for," Jovan said. "Including the werewolf."

Her heart was heavy when she recalled the story her mates had told her that morning. Sadly, Hakon had been forced to kill the werewolf when it tried to attack Luc. Boris reassured her it had been for the best. The wolf wouldn't have wanted to live without his mate and brothers. Their children were orphaned, but luckily, their mother's parents were flying to Alaska to get them.

She leaned forward, grasping Boris's headrest. "How many more packs do we have to visit?"

"That's all for today." He put the truck in drive. "Tomorrow we finish the rest. Amara will be rested and able to help us."

She heaved a sigh of relief. "Thank you for coming with me."

Marius kissed her palm with a wink. "Where else would we be but by your side?"

Heat flamed her face and a zing shot straight to her lady parts when he kissed her palm again, a mischievous gleam in his eyes.

She would've pulled back a few days ago. Now she wanted to rip off his clothes and straddle him right there in the backseat, taking turns with each brother. She wondered, though, why they were so attracted to her. Was it because they'd been bewitched by the goddess, or did they truly feel a connection to her?

"Why?" she asked.

Boris looked at her in the rearview mirror, arching a brow. "Why what?"

"Why do you want to be with me?"

"Because you're our mate," Boris answered.

She fought the urge to smack the back of his head. "So you want to be with me because my scent tells you to?"

"That's not the only reason, lubirea mea," Marius said, resting a hand on her knee.

She turned to him. "Then why?"

"Because you're beautiful and brave," he said matter-of-factly.

"And selfless," Geri added. "You sacrificed everything for the Amaroki, even though you weren't one of us."

"Don't forget intelligent," Boris said. "Smart enough to be a doctor. Plus, your magic is amazing. You're everything we want in a woman."

"Oh," she said, heat creeping into her cheeks.

Jovan leaned over the seat. "And you have a nice round ass."

She swatted his arm, laughing so hard she snorted.

Marius traced a circle on her knee, batting his lashes and looking ten shades of sexy. "What do you think of us, Eilea?"

"What do I think?" Tapping her chin, she pretended to be lost in thought. "I'm wondering if Romania could use a witch doctor." She could hardly believe she'd said that. Leaving her luxuries in America behind and moving to a foreign country? Had she gone insane? Yes, yes, she had, because she couldn't imagine a life without her shifters, and she knew it was asking too much to uproot them from their sons and farm.

Jovan's eyes widened with shock. "I know we could."

The others voiced their agreement, reminding her of salivating dogs begging for a bone before breaking out into a cacophony of howls.

"Okay." She released Marius's hand. "But I have to set some ground rules before I agree to mate with you."

"We knew you would," Jovan said, not sounding bitter in the slightest.

They looked at her expectantly, and she cleared her throat, doing her best to quell her nervous energy. She'd been practicing this speech all day. She shouldn't have been worried, but a nagging voice in the back of her mind feared they'd reject her proposals. Then what? Could she live with them if they didn't give her the freedom she needed? Could she live without them?

She counted on her fingers. "I don't need your permission to drive or work. If I can get a medical degree, defeat a demonic ghost, and close a portal to the afterworld, I can do without the Amaroki's nineteenth century sexist shackles." Relief swept through her when not one of them flinched.

"Of course you can," Boris answered. "We wouldn't have it any other way."

Wow. She hadn't been expecting them to be so agreeable. "And I get an equal say in all family decisions."

"Da," Jovan nodded, "we will allow that."

Gritting her teeth, she leveled him with a glare. "You will *allow* it?"

"Forgive us, Eilea." Jovan smacked his forehead. "We are still learning."

"But you are open to learning?"

"Da," they answered.

She couldn't help but laugh. "Then I think we can make this work."

AMARA WOKE AFTER WHAT felt like an eternity asleep and stretched, then looked over at Drasko, who gave her a sleepy grin.

He kissed her nose. "Good morning, sweetheart."

"Good morning." She looked out the window. It was still dark. She checked the time on the blinking alarm clock. Half past eleven? Was it still nighttime?

They sat up, and she leaned into him.

"How long do you think we slept?" she asked.

He traced a lazy circle around her shoulder. "I have no clue, but I've never been so tired in my whole fucking life. I don't even remember going to bed."

"Me neither." Her rumbling stomach reminded her it had been a long time since she'd eaten.

Someone knocked, and Rone came in, carrying a steaming tray of food. "You up?"

Amara waved him forward. "Yes, sweetheart."

He set the tray on the nightstand beside their bed. "You hungry?"

Amara's stomach rumbled again. "Famished."

"How about dinner in bed?" Rone handed them each a platter piled high with smoked salmon, potato salad, green beans, and cornbread.

"Looks heavenly." She licked her lips. "How long did we sleep?"

"About twenty-four hours."

She shared a wide-eyed look with Drasko. "Damn. Our people need me."

Rone held out a staying hand. "Relax, Dr. Johnson is taking care of it."

"Thank the Ancients," Amara said, then dug into her food.

She and Drasko ate in silence and probably much too quickly, but she couldn't help herself. She washed down her food with juice, belching into her fist.

"How are the babies?" she asked Rone.

He wiped her cheek with a napkin. "Both happy to be home. I put them to bed hours ago."

Emotion suddenly overwhelmed her. "I don't know what I'd do without you." She draped her arms around his neck and nuzzled his cheek. She was relieved to have him alive, but she couldn't shake her panic. She'd almost lost him.

He sat back, wiping her cheeks. "No tears, my love."

"I can't help it." She hiccupped.

When Luc and Hakon came in, she kicked off the covers and patted the bed beside her. They went to her, taking turns holding her. When Hakon kissed her forehead, his lips lingering for an overly-long time, she clung tightly to him, the harsh reality that she'd almost lost all her mates hitting her hard.

"It's okay." He smoothed a hand down her back. "Everything is okay."

She knew it now, but she couldn't shake the memories of her despair, the horror that Katarina had brought down on them. She prayed Eilea had closed the portal for good.

Drasko said, "What's been happening?"

"Dr. Johnson has been making the rounds, healing those who were too sick to come to the lodge," Hakon answered. "Luc and I buried the Cloud-walkers."

That could've been her family. How thankful she was they'd survived.

"You found them all?" Drasko asked.

Hakon and Luc shared dark looks. "Yes," Hakon answered. "One of them turned. He was about to attack Luc. I had no choice but to kill him."

Drasko's features were screwed up so tight, Amara didn't know if he was about to cry or rage. "It was probably for the best," he answered solemnly. "I wouldn't want to live without my brothers and my mate." His voice cracking like shattered glass, he turned away.

Hakon went over to Drasko's side of the bed, sitting beside him. "I want to thank you for what you did for us."

"I was going to let our government nuke you."

Hakon clutched his shoulder. "You put the safety of Amara and the babies first."

"We wouldn't expect any less," Luc said.

Drasko solemnly nodded. "It wasn't an easy choice."

"I know," Hakon answered, patting his brother's back. "One day you and I will be the chieftains of our tribe. I couldn't ask for anyone stronger by my side."

After a group hug, Amara was fed up with sadness. They should be celebrating their survival. "You know what? We all need a drink."

Rone frowned. "I can make you an herbal tea, my love."

She patted her belly, remembering the child growing inside. "Perfect. You guys need something stronger."

Hakon smiled. "Are you trying to get us drunk?"

She gave him a teasing grin. "Yep. So I can take advantage of you."

"You don't need to get me drunk for that," Rone said, pointing at the growing bulge under his zipper. "I'm ready to make love to you right now."

Hakon rubbed her back. "Amara, you need rest."

"What I need is you." She flung off her top, letting her mates get their fill of her bare breasts. Squirming on Drasko's lap, she smiled when she felt him growing beneath her. She planted a tender kiss on his lips. "Would you like to be first, my sweet protector?"

He shook his head, thunderstorms in his eyes. "I want to watch you get fucked."

If ever there were magic words to cause massive flooding in Amara's pussy, those were it.

When Hakon tugged on her pajama pants, she climbed out of Drasko's lap and draped her arms around his shoulders. Drasko toyed with her nipples until milk pooled around his fingers. Hakon kissed down her spine.

Falling into Drasko, she arched back with a groan and Hakon probed her pussy with a thick finger.

Drasko stroked her cheek. "Keep looking at me." She surrendered to Hakon's thick cockhead with a hiss, eyes locked with Drasko's.

When Hakon slammed into her, she groaned and closed her eyes.

"Look at me, Amara," Drasko growled.

Her eyes flew open, and she watched him watching her get fucked. Luc toyed with her breast, bending over to suckle her milk. Crying out, she wrapped an arm around his shoulders, falling into rhythm with Hakon, the pressure inside her building. Rone suckled her other breast while Drasko held her captive with his golden eyes.

Hakon wasn't gentle, and she didn't want him to be. When he dug thick fingers into her ass, she slammed into him.

Hakon's release was her undoing. He stilled with a roar, spilling his seed, triggering her pussy walls to clench him like a vice, milking her desire. Drasko whispered words of love against her lips while she came.

Her mates drank from her breasts, triggering another powerful orgasm. Hakon pushed deeper, groaning as her sheath tightened even more, squeezing every last drop of cum from his thick cock.

She heaved a shuddering breath when he slid out and Luc slid in. Luc was more gentle, probing her pussy and spreading moisture across her anus until it was slippery and pliable. Keeping her eyes locked on Drasko, she slid onto Luc slowly, inch by agonizing inch, until he was buried to the hilt. He fucked her anus with short, choppy thrusts, building her orgasm quickly while Rone continued to play with her breasts.

The climax that gripped her came without warning, pounding Luc's cock like a drum, squeezing him so tight, he hissed in pain.

She broke eye contact with Drasko when Luc slid out. "Sorry, sweetheart," she said to Luc.

He nibbled her neck. "I'm not."

She giggled when he pinched her breast.

Drasko turned her to face him, giving her a warning look.

They locked gazes when Rone toyed with her slit. Rone had become a master of foreplay, learning how to work her into a climax with his fingers or tongue. He traced delicate circles around her nub until it swelled and ached. Luc and Hakon nursed from her breasts, relieving the pressure that made them ache like too-full water balloons. She relaxed into Rone, letting his fingers work their magic. It didn't take her long to achieve a sweet and easy release that rolled through her like a gentle wave.

Rone groaned behind her, his thick shaft pumping her like a piston until he spilled his seed deep inside her pussy.

Amara stared into Drasko's eyes while Rone mopped her up with a towel. Then she climbed into Drasko's lap and slid onto his erection.

"Don't close your eyes," he said.

"I won't," she promised, taking his thumb in her mouth and sucking all the way down, then up, matching the tempo of their fucking.

"Come for me, my love," she begged, their wet junctures slapping together with each thrust.

He wrapped her hair around his fist. "We're coming together," he commanded.

She gladly obeyed, surrendering to the euphoria that wrapped her like a shroud, causing every nerve ending to come alive.

He flipped her on her back, plundering into her with such ferocity, she bit her lip and clung to him, steeling herself against the pain. Pain turned into such intense pleasure, she threw back her head with a gasp.

"Look at me when I'm fucking you!" he said in his protector voice, slamming into her harder.

Her eyes flew open, and her heart skipped a beat when she saw his eyes had transformed into golden animal slits. The peak that had been building started to crest.

"Oh, Drasko," she cried. "I'm coming! I'm coming!"

She cried out when the orgasm swept through her, holding her captive for several pounding heartbeats.

He panted into her mouth as he came. He rolled off her and kissed her affectionately while stroking her hair.

"Thank you, Amara."

"No, thank you," she said. "I love you beyond words."

She cuddled and kissed her mates, working each of them into a frenzy until they made love to her once more. She had never felt so cherished and grateful to be in their arms.

Chapter Twenty

EILEA WOKE TO THE DELICIOUS smells of frying meat and freshly brewed coffee. With her newly heightened senses, everything smelled better. Everything felt better, too. Her eyes bulged when she saw the vibrator on her nightstand. She'd forgotten to put it away last night after giving herself seven orgasms. Seven. When she'd been human, she was lucky if she could rub out one. After last night she finally understood how she-wolves could mate with so many males. They needed that many just to keep up with their libidos. She couldn't wait until their bonding ceremony tomorrow night. She was more than ready for sex with a real penis. Correction, penises. Four gloriously large ones. Even though she had seen them, she hadn't yet had the pleasure of feeling them, because Boris insisted on behaving like a gentleman, leaving her languishing until she'd finally taken matters into her own hands last night.

Marius was in her small kitchen, cooking a breakfast big enough to feed an army. It had been this way every morning, and after a long day of healing, she came home to a delicious home-cooked meal. Marius even took care of the dishes and laundry. She could get used to this.

Marius had found the extra leaf for the table and piled it high with eggs, ham, toast, and something that looked like coffee cake sprinkled with almonds. Rubbing the sleep from her eyes, she sat in a chair, then gasped when Jovan pulled her onto his lap. She would've swatted him, but she enjoyed feeling rough denim rubbing against her bare thighs.

"What is this you're wearing?" He hiked up her oversized T-shirt and ran a finger under the string on her hips.

"Booty shorts with a G-string underneath," she said with a wink. "You like?" He pinched her ass so hard, she slapped his hand. "Ouch!"

"Yes, I like," he growled.

"You could've taken them off last night if you'd come to bed with me," she purred.

He nuzzled her neck. "Believe me, I wanted to. Tomorrow night," he whispered. "I'm going to take you hard."

Oh, damn. Moisture flooded her underwear. She thanked Marius when he handed her a cup of coffee, relieved to have something else to focus on instead of sex. If Jovan kept teasing her, she'd soak through her clothes and his. Palming her cup, she sipped, pleased when she tasted just the right amount of creamer and sugar. Yeah, she could definitely get used to this.

"Good morning." Boris walked in and kissed her cheek before going for the coffee. "How was your night?"

"Good," she answered, thanking Marius again when he placed a steaming platter of food in front of her.

"I imagine so, after listening to the hum of your artificial penis," Boris said with a wink.

She choked on her coffee, spewing a great deal down her shirt. "Omigod, you were listening?"

"We're wolves, Eilea," Geri said as he sat across from her, stabbing a piece of ham with a fork. "We have a keen sense of hearing."

When Marius handed her a damp towel, she wiped up the stain. "I wouldn't have needed it if you'd have come to bed with me last night," she pointed out.

"We're not taking you until after the bonding ceremony." Boris wagged a finger. "We have too much respect for you to do otherwise."

Damn. She'd been hoping they'd take her before, if for no other reason than they wouldn't be shocked at the ceremony when they learned she wasn't a virgin.

She looked at Geri, who gave her a blank look. Had he told his brothers yet about her lost virginity? "There's something I need to tell you."

Boris waved away her concern. "Geri already told us you're not a virgin."

She slouched, relief washing through her. "And you're okay with it?" Not that she cared what they thought. They weren't virgins either.

Jovan said, "It fills us with jealousy to know other men touched you, but we don't blame you."

Why would they blame her? Were they that thickheaded? "How kind of you." She didn't bother masking her bitterness.

Jovan said, "We sense you're being sarcastic."

She shook her head. "Good deduction, Einstein."

They shared looks, and she realized they were telepathically speaking. She couldn't deny feeling a stab of jealousy. Amara had told her that all packs communicated telepathically, and she'd hear her mates' thoughts after they'd taken her virginity. If the bonding ceremony didn't work, she'd never hear their thoughts. Not that she wanted them in her head, but she sort of did. If she was going to be one of them, she wanted the full experience.

Boris gave her that alpha dominance look he'd tried on her numerous times to get his way. "Once you bond with us, you will not have eyes for other men, just as we have eyes for none other but you."

"Guys." She rolled her eyes. "I haven't looked at other men since I first laid eyes on you."

They broke into massive shit-eating grins. She smiled into her mug, not wanting them to see how pleased she was with their declaration. She had four blond gods with gloriously large dicks wanting her and only her. How could she not be happy?

She heard her uncle coming up the porch steps and then she scented him. She quickly pulled down her booty shorts, wishing she'd worn sweats. She swatted Jovan when he latched onto her hips and forced her back into his lap.

"Uncle Joe is here," she hissed.

"I know." He tickled her ear with his breath. "I don't want him to see this." He shifted, stabbing her ass with something she realized was too big to be his cellphone.

"Control yourself."

"It's so hard."

She slapped a hand over her mouth, laughing at the double meaning. These wolves were going to drive her insane.

Marius must have scented and heard her uncle, too, because he quickly crossed to the door, opening it just as he had his hand poised to knock.

"Good morning, Agent Johnson," Marius said, taking his coat. "Would you care for some breakfast?"

Her mates stood, each offering him their seat.

Uncle Joe went over to their small table, awkwardly rocking on his heels. "No thanks." He waved for them to sit down. "I already ate with the Thunderfoots."

She loved how respectfully her mates treated her uncle, just like he was her father.

Not wanting to be the sixth wheel, he'd been staying with the chieftain's family since the Lupescus had insisted on staying with Eilea. This was his first appearance at the house since he'd left.

"Hope I'm not interrupting," he said.

"No, not at all." She slid off Jovan's lap and into a nearby chair, feeling like a naughty teen who'd been caught making out with her crush.

She gave Jovan a sideways grin when he scooted closer to the table to conceal a massive boner.

Uncle Joe shoved his hands in his pockets. "Tomorrow's the big ceremony?"

Eilea beamed. "Tor told me you can be there."

Boris wiped his mouth with the back of his hand. "No human has ever witnessed a bonding ceremony."

"I realize this is a high honor," her uncle said, "one I will not take lightly."

Marius handed him a cup of coffee, then pulled out a stool and forced him to take a seat. "We are happy you can be there."

He sat, hiking up his pants. "As am I."

Something about him seemed awkward. She couldn't help but feel he'd come with bad news. "What's on your mind, Uncle?"

He heaved a dramatic sigh. "We still haven't found Agent Parelli." The subtle look he shot her mates would've probably been overlooked by the human eye, but she suddenly understood the purpose of his visit.

Boris drummed his fingers on the table. "And you think we had something to do with his disappearance?"

"I didn't say that." He didn't have to say it. His body language gave him away.

Leaning back in his chair, Jovan gave him a cool look. "I can sense it in your tone."

Uncle Joe flinched and looked away.

"We already told you the werewolf probably ate him," Boris said through clenched teeth. "Believe me, we've looked everywhere for that quallu."

"He was a werewolf snack," Geri added. "I would've scented him by now."

"He tried to rape our mate." The chill in Jovan's even tone gave Eilea goosebumps. "If he is alive, and we find him before your agents do, we will avenge her honor."

"That's what I was afraid of," her uncle answered. "If we find him, he will stand trial."

Jovan stood, leaning his knuckles on the table and giving Uncle Joe a look that could melt lead. "You should know by now that the Amaroki believe in swift justice, not foolish trials." He nodded to Eilea. "We sense deception, and we know our mate is telling the truth."

She wanted to hug Jovan so hard. Her mates were a special kind of awesome, and she had absolutely no regrets telling them what Jimmy had tried with her.

Her uncle jerked back as if slapped. "As do I."

"Then it's settled." Boris rose, voice dropping to a deep protector baritone. "If he's not already dead, he'd better pray you find him before we do."

EILEA WAS WITH AMARA in a changing room, frowning at her reflection in the mirror. She'd always envisioned something different for her wedding day. Instead of a beautiful white gown, she wore a shimmery blue cocktail dress, the one good dress she owned. She was more of a jeans and boots girl when she wasn't in her scrubs.

"You look beautiful," Amara said, pinning flowers in her hair.

Eilea's frown deepened. "I look like I'm going clubbing, not getting married."

"It doesn't matter." Amara winked. "After the ritual, your clothes are coming off anyway."

Heat fanned Eilea's cheeks. "I'm trying not to think about that part," she lied. Actually, that was all she thought about.

Standing behind Eilea, Amara clutched her shoulders. "You're going to be my stepmom after this."

"I know." Eilea grimaced. "Weird. I think of you more like a sister."

Amara clutched her heart. "Really?"

Turning to her, Eilea clasped her hand, worried she'd offended her. "But I can be your stepmom if you'd like."

Amara shook her head. "Sister is fine. I'm so happy you're mating with my fathers."

"Me, too," she said, pleased that her new stepdaughter liked her. Hopefully her mates' sons would, too.

Amara searched her eyes. "You ready?"

She released a slow shaky breath. "As I'll ever be."

They turned at a knock on the door. Her jaw dropped when Nakomi popped her head in.

"What are you doing here?" Amara asked.

As regal as a queen, wearing a beautiful long gown of emerald green with gold trim, Nakomi shut the door. She carried a woven bag and set it on the floor at her feet. "I've come to wish the bride good luck, if I may."

Eilea forced a smile. "Of course." Hopefully the shifter didn't decide to curse her instead.

Clasping her hands in front of her, Nakomi's features softened. "I'm not judging you, but I wanted to share with you a little trick I learned from my Ethiopian auntie."

"Oh? What is it?"

"When it is time to drink," Nakomi continued, "mix your blood in the cup and have them drink it. It will have the same effect as them taking your virginity."

"Okay...?" She couldn't help but sound skeptical after everything Nakomi had put her through. Maybe the shifter was just trying to sabotage their wedding.

"I know it works," she said, lilting humor in her voice, "because my mates and I couldn't wait until the ceremony."

"Thanks," Eilea said, not bothering to hide her skepticism.

Nakomi made a face, like she'd just sucked on a sour lemon. "I have also come to apologize for misjudging you. I realize now not all humans are the same."

Was she for real? She shared a questioning look with Amara, who shrugged, a faint smile tugging at her lips. Eilea tried to determine if she saw deception in Nakomi's eyes. She hadn't sensed any malice in her words. Could the African shifter be sincere? Nakomi had made her life hell, but no use holding onto a grudge. Katarina had held onto a grudge, and look where that had gotten her.

She took Nakomi's outstretched hand. "Apology accepted." They shook.

Nakomi wouldn't meet Eilea's gaze as she picked up the canvas bag at her feet. "I've brought you wedding gifts. A habesha dress from Ethiopia and matching wolf jewelry in silver." She pulled a bundle wrapped in tissue paper out of the bag.

Eilea unfolded it and gasped when she saw the shimmery royal fabric bordered with silver trim. "Oh, it's too beautiful." She tried to hand it back. "I can't accept this."

Nakomi backed up. "You can, and you will. My mates would've died without you. Our entire tribe would've perished."

Eilea said, with a glance at Amara, "I had a lot of help."

Nakomi pulled out another wrapped bundle and handed it to Amara. "These gifts will never be enough to repay you for your kindness and bravery, but please accept them."

Amara took her package with a squeal, ripping it open like a kid on Christmas. "Eilea!" She held up the shimmery orange dress with gold trim. "They have little wolves stitched into the fabric."

Eilea examined her gown again. Sure enough, the silver trim had been stitched in the form of wolves, joined head to tail and circling the bottom of the gown, the sleeves, and neckline.

"It would make a perfect ritual dress," Amara said.

"It would," Eilea admitted. It sure beat the hell out of her cocktail dress.

Amara set down her package and latched onto Eilea's zipper. "Help me change her."

Together they helped Eilea into her new dress. Nakomi accessorized the outfit with silver wolf earrings and a wolf necklace.

"Now you look like a bride," Nakomi said with a smile.

Amara clasped her hands together. "A fairytale bride."

Turning in front of the mirror, Eilea admired her new dress, thinking she looked like an African princess. Granted, her neck wasn't as impossibly long as Nakomi's, but her grandmother had said she had pretty eyes. They stood out better with her hair pulled back, and her earrings caught the flecks of silver in them. When Nakomi put a silver clip with blue flowers in her hair, her look was complete.

"Thank you, Nakomi."

"It is my pleasure."

When Nakomi unexpectedly hugged her, Eilea hugged her back.

"Ready?" Amara asked.

Eilea admired her reflection one more time. "I hope so."

UNCLE JOE WAS WAITING in the hall for her, hands clasped behind his back. He looked so handsome in his tuxedo, exactly like she remembered her father, with the exception of the graying hair cropped close. He smiled, his eyes lighting up and crinkling in the corners.

"You look beautiful, niece," he said as he took her arm.

She sucked in a shaky breath, smoothing trembling hands down her sides. "Thanks."

When he walked her to the auditorium and stopped at the door, she froze when she heard four familiar howls.

"They're ready for you," he said with a wink.

She didn't know why she'd been expecting the traditional wedding song. Nothing was traditional about marrying four men at once. Hell, it wasn't even a wedding. It was bonding, which her mates had told her was like a wedding, only better.

Her knees wobbled when he opened the door, revealing a crowd of people gathered at the bottom of the auditorium. Tor stood on a dais, dressed in a colorful robe and clutching what appeared to be a scroll. His brothers and sons stood around him. In front of the dais stood her mates, looking longingly at her.

She swallowed nervously, focusing instead on Amara, Annie, Mihaela, and Tatiana, who came to greet her. Amara and Mihaela wore colorful robes similar to Tor's, but Annie and Tatiana had on white gowns. White represented their virginity, and she felt self-conscious that she wasn't wearing that color as well. Uncle Joe joined Tor and the other men on the dais.

What the hell was she doing, marrying four men and moving to a foreign country? She didn't even speak Romanian. She had to have lost her mind.

Giggling, the women placed flower petals in her hair, then laid a trail of petals on the floor for her to follow.

Focusing on putting one foot in front of the other, she couldn't bring herself to look up at her mates for some reason. Walking and breathing had become hard enough.

Once she reached her mates, she bit her lip, giving Amara a pleading look as she backed away, sandwiching her between Marius and Geri. What the fuck had she been thinking? She didn't even speak Romanian.

"Hey." Geri entwined his fingers through hers. His smile was dazzling. "It will be okay. Promise."

Nodding, she released the breath she hadn't realized she'd been holding.

Marius took her other hand. "You look beautiful."

"Thanks." She managed a tremulous smile, then felt hands on her shoulders. She cast a furtive glance at her two large alphas. This was it. No turning back. She was trapped in a stud sandwich.

Tor began. "Brothers and sisters, we are gathered here today to witness the bonding of sister Eilea Johnson with brothers Boris, Jovan, Geri, and Marius Lupescu."

Skoll handed Tor a familiar looking silver goblet inscribed with images of wolves. It looked exactly like the goblet she'd drunk from when she'd turned. Leaving the dais, Tor held the goblet in both hands, Skoll following him with a long blade. The hairs on her neck stood on end.

Boris rumbled in her ear, "Relax, Eilea. We will keep you safe."

She absently nodded. Skoll pricked the thumbs of each of her men, then dipped their thumbs in the goblet. When he came to her, she held out her thumb and closed her eyes. He obviously knew Nakomi's little trick. Why was she acting like such a baby? She'd closed a demonic portal, for Ancients' sake.

"Ouch!" She instinctively jerked her thumb back.

Tor held out his hand with raised eyebrows. She let him dip her thumb in the cool liquid, then silently berated herself for causing a scene.

After swirling the blood and wine, Tor handed the goblet to Boris. "Repeat after me," he said. "We take the blood of Eilea, binding our souls to hers. We vow our love, honor, loyalty, and protection to our mate from now until eternity."

Each one repeated Tor's words and took a sip of the wine.

After Marius was finished, he handed the goblet to her, an anxious look in his silver-touched eyes.

Clasping the goblet like a lifeline, she looked into the swirling liquid, knowing this was a turning point. A fork in the road. She'd downed a similar drink once before in hopes of saving her mates. Now all danger had passed except one, the risk she took in committing herself to four virile, possessive shifters.

"Repeat after me," Tor said to her. "I, Eilea, take the blood of my protectors, binding our hearts and souls as one. I vow my love, honor, and loyalty to my mates, my protectors, from now until eternity."

She numbly repeated the words, heart hammering in her ears. Though her mates said not a word, their expressions said everything. They looked at her like men longing for the chance to be happy, to be loved. Who was she to deny them?

Tilting the goblet to her lips, she drank every last drop. The taste of her mates' blood mixed with the sweet wine wasn't bad at all. In fact, she swore she felt a jolt of energy pass through her. Handing the empty cup to Skoll, she wiped her mouth and smiled.

You did it! Geri's voice echoed in her head.

I did! Her hand flew to her throat. *Omigod! I can hear you in my head.*

When she heard all four of her mates howling in her head, fear transformed into pure happiness and she laughed with joy.

Chapter Twenty-One

EILEA GNAWED ON HER lip as the guests filed out of the auditorium.

Boris scratched his head, looking at a large bed covered with white sheets. She hadn't even noticed it before.

Marius flushed. "This is usually the part of the ceremony where we take your blood."

Leaning up on her toes, she kissed his red cheek. "But you already took it."

"That's okay." Jovan flopped on the bed, patting the space beside him. The thick pole jutting from between his legs made his colorful robe look like a circus tent. "We can still pretend."

She frowned. *I'd rather not pretend. I'd rather you take me for who I am.*

We do, they said in her head.

Oops. She hadn't realized until it was too late that she'd projected her thought.

Geri stroked her lower lip. *I love you for exactly who you are, Eilea, incredible witch doctor and my mate.* Then he tugged her toward the bed.

She'd never felt more awkward in her life than when she sat between Jovan and Geri. She'd never had sex with more than one man at a time before. How would they do this? Take turns? All at once? "This is strange, having sex here."

"This is how it's done," Geri answered. "All packs take their mate's vir... uh, make love to their mates in the ritual room right after the bonding."

There it was again, the issue with her virginity.

Then we shift and run through the forest for the first time as a pack, Boris said in her head.

She hit the side of her head, like she was trying to drain water out of her ears. "Hearing you in here is weird."

"Would you rather we spoke normally?" Jovan asked, tickling her palm with his finger.

"For now. This will take some getting used to." She hugged herself, feeling self-conscious. "What do we do in the forest?"

Jovan shrugged. "Play, hunt, bond."

Bond? Her mind raced with possibilities. "We don't have doggie sex, do we?"

They chuckled.

Boris gestured toward the bed. "We prefer it this way."

She released a shuddering breath. "Good."

Marius grabbed a bottle of wine and filled the ritual goblet. "Here." He held the drink out to her. "You need to relax."

"Thanks." She greedily drank, then burped and laughed. She fell back on the bed, looking up at Geri as he moved over her.

"Feeling better?" he asked, stroking her thigh.

She nodded, feeling less anxious.

He gently massaged her leg. When she felt a hand on her shoulder, she looked up at Marius.

"Let me rub out the tension," he said.

"Okay." Her veins were turning to liquid sludge. She wasn't much of a drinker. Maybe she shouldn't have had so much wine.

She groaned when Marius pulled back her hair and kneaded her neck, working out each knot. Her shoes fell off, and Jovan and Boris each grabbed a foot. Soon she was getting the most relaxing body massage she'd ever had. She relaxed, her bones turning to putty as they worked their magic.

"There's no rush on this, Eilea," Boris said as he worked a knot out of the sole of her foot. "If you're not feeling comfortable, we can wait."

Marius nibbled on her ear. "Do you want to wait?"

She looked at him. "Do you?"

"It doesn't matter what we want," Jovan said.

"Of course it does."

"We've wanted you for over a year," Boris said.

She batted her lashes. "Then take me."

THROWING HER HANDS over her head, she heaved a sigh as they stripped off her gown. She laughed when Jovan became frustrated with all the knots. Luckily, Marius had more patience and eventually figured them out. After she'd been stripped down to her bra and panties, she felt self-conscious again.

She flinched when Marius traced the thin scar across her back.

Eilea, he asked in her head, *what's this?*

She pretended the souvenir she'd received the night the drunk driver had taken her family meant nothing. "It's an old scar," she said, still feeling weird speaking to them telepathically.

"Why did you wince when he touched it?" Jovan said.

"I don't know. I just do." She jerked away when Marius touched it again. "Could you leave it alone?"

Does it hurt? Marius asked.

Fuck. Why did they have to bring this up now? The last thing she wanted to think about on her wedding night was that bleak part of her past. "No," she snapped. "I just don't like anyone touching it."

I'm sorry, Marius said. *It must have hurt when it happened.*

She spun on him, her inner-wolf growling. "Why do we have to do this now? It's a painful memory. I don't want to talk about it."

"Okay." Marius held out his hands n apologetically. "I'm sorry we brought it up."

No longer in the mood, Eilea snatched up her gown, tears welling when she tried and failed to figure out the many folds.

"Eilea. Look at me." Jovan clutched her shoulders desperately. "We're sorry. It wasn't our intention to upset you." The others voiced their agreement.

"Amara told us about the accident." Marius stood beside his brother, gently stroking her shoulder. "We know your emotional burden. We only wanted to help you carry it."

Marius's eyes were so large and luminous, her heart nearly broke. She wiped her eyes. "It is a heavy burden," she finally admitted, "and thank you for wanting to share it. Maybe one day...." Her anger quickly dissipated when she realized she was truly blessed to have mates who cared so much about her.

When Marius wrapped his strong arms around her, she buried her head in his shoulder, letting tears fall while she clung to his neck like a lifeline.

Her other mates closed in, taking turns holding her and surrounding her with a cocoon of love. She'd never felt safer or more cared for.

One day she would tell them all about her dark past, but their bonding night wasn't the right time. She wiped away the last of her tears and smiled. "Are we going to enjoy our wedding night or what?"

Boris said, "I'm more than ready to enjoy this night with you, lubirea mea."

When he slid a finger under her bra strap, she backed away, wagging a finger. "You're not taking off any more of my clothes until I get to take off yours."

Boris frowned down at his robe. "Our attire is simple, Eilea."

She ran her hands down his broad chest, loving how solid he felt under the thin fabric.

"There's a clasp in the back," he said to her, reaching behind him.

Ducking under his arm, she smacked his hand. "Don't tell me how to undress you. I made it through med school. I think I can handle this."

She unfastened his robe and pulled it down over a broad back and a perfectly round ass. There was nothing under that robe.

She walked around him, admiring the massive erection that jutted toward her like a heat-seeking missile. Flattening her hand on his chest, she slid it along a line of pale hair down to his naval. "You have a beautiful body."

He slid a bra strap over her shoulder and brushed his fingertips across the swell of her breast, his eyes turning from blue to silver. "Let us see the rest of you," he said in a deep protector baritone.

She swayed toward him like a reed in the wind, fighting the urge to obey. "Not yet," she teased before moving to Jovan.

He stood stoically while she unfastened him, his mouth hitching up in an impish grin when his robe fell to the floor, his glorious pink torpedo jutting toward her, head glistening with moisture.

He breathed in harshly when she dragged her finger across the wet slit, rubbing the moisture down the length of his cock.

I'm going to shove it down your throat.

She was unable to hide her smile. *Are you? I'm sorry, but you'll have to wait your turn.*

When he lunged for her, she skipped away, whistling an innocent tune.

Leaning up to kiss Geri, she groaned into his mouth when he returned the kiss urgently, sweeping her into his arms. When he deepened the kiss, fucking her mouth with languid strokes of his tongue, she fumbled with the clasp and pulled his robe down. He wasn't as tall or broad-shouldered as his brothers, but what he lacked in size, he certainly made up for with passion. After removing the robe, she clasped the hard globes of his ass, pressing his thick length into her thigh. Chest heaving, she finally came up for air when he squeezed her tit, trying to pull her bra down.

She went to Marius, gingerly removing his clothing, suspecting he preferred gentle lovemaking to rough, dirty sex. They shared a deep, sweet kiss.

Strong arms wrapped around her waist, and a stiff cock jutted into her backside. She tilted her head back and looked into Boris's glowing eyes.

"It's time," he said, taking her breast in a bruising grip.

Jovan wedged himself between her and Marius. Jerking the fabric off her breast, he pinched her nipple hard, stretching it until she cried out. Then he led her to the bed, eyes gleaming.

Holy shit! She was about to get royally fucked.

Falling onto the bed, Jovan released her hand, choosing instead to drag her by her panties. She quickly found herself on her knees over Jovan's erection. He ripped off her bra, then nudged her face toward his groin. She had no idea why she was letting him dominate her, but his control made her pussy weep.

Boris slid off her panties and stroked her slit with a thick finger.

When Jovan nudged her closer to his dick, she took him in her mouth, relishing the salty taste of his pre-cum, slurping halfway down, then back up. She longed to suck him to the root, but he was so big.

Jovan fell back with a groan when she sucked him again and again, going a little deeper each time. Boris continued to stroke her weeping pussy, making her swell with need.

Shoving her ass toward him, she was hoping he'd take the hint and fuck her.

Marius moved in and drew tight circles around her swollen button. She thought she'd come undone. Geri laid down on her other side and teased her nipples with wet fingers.

Holy fuck, this was amazing.

When Jovan put pressure on the back of her head, she realized she'd stopped sucking. She took him in again, trying to focus while her mates toyed with her. With Jovan's dick buried in her throat, she cried out when Boris inserted a finger into her weeping channel, tunneling into her slowly. She wanted him to pull out and fuck her with his glorious cock instead. Then she remembered she could think to him.

Not your finger, she begged. *Please fuck me.*

As you wish, lubirea mea, Boris answered with a low growl.

He slid into her one glorious inch at a time. He was so very big, filling and stretching her until her sheath felt like a rubber band about to snap. When he rammed those last few inches into her, she jerked forward, taking Jovan deeper and nearly gagging when his cockhead tickled her tonsils.

Relaxing her throat, she sucked him deeper, impressed when she almost made it to the root. He growled his approval.

Focusing on Jovan while straining for that climax turned out to be easier than she thought. Boris's deep thrusts made her want to suck Jovan harder, faster. They found their rhythm, Boris fucking her until her pussy swelled to agonizingly delightful proportions.

Euphoria rushed over her like a tsunami. She slurped Jovan's cock, stilling when he roared and pulsed in her mouth. She was barely aware of swallowing when her orgasm reached a new peak. She surrendered to it while holding Jovan in her mouth. Her mates continued to play with her breasts and swollen nub, bringing her pleasure to new heights.

Boris swore when he burst. She relished the glorious feeling of his cockhead pounding her sweet spot. Releasing Jovan's shaft, she whimpered, jerking against Boris as another climax built.

Throwing her head back, she begged, "Please don't stop. I'm going to come again."

When he slid out with a teasing chuckle, she turned to him, growling and snapping. She sighed in relief when Marius entered her, pounding her until they were both singing their releases.

After Marius withdrew, she slumped on the mattress, spent and sated. She smiled at Marius when he wiped her with a towel. Groaning, she threw an arm across her eyes. The alcohol had made her dizzy and tired.

When she felt hands on her knees, she looked up. Geri was positioned between her legs, giving her an expectant smile.

Spreading her legs wide, she held out her arms to him. "Come here, my love."

He sank into her embrace, thrusting into her slippery sheath.

"Forgive me," he said, brushing a strand of hair out of her eyes. "I wanted you all to myself."

Warmth flooded her as she took his face in her hands and kissed him. He rocked into her slowly, making her gasp with need each time he withdrew. She lifted her legs higher, taking him deeper, alternating between kissing his neck and biting his shoulder. She loved the look of pure bliss on his face. If she could bottle and save this memory, she would, replaying it in her mind over and over. This man had come to mean so much to her.

She smoothed her hands down his shoulders, loving the contrast of his pale skin against hers, a perfect blend of coral and ebony, daylight blending with night. She also loved that their difference in skin color meant nothing to them.

What are you thinking, my love? He asked as he moved inside her.

She sighed, her pleasure building.

I'm thinking how perfectly we fit together, she answered. *And how I want to bottle this moment and save it forever.*

His lips melded into hers as easily as the blending of their bodies. *You have me forever, lubirea mea.*

The orgasm that claimed her was a gentle rolling wave. She called out his name while riding out the convulsions, digging into his tight ass with her fingers, urging him deeper. He came almost as quietly as she had.

I love you, Eilea.

I love you, too, she said without hesitation. She should've been alarmed that she'd fallen in love so easily, but she was too drunk and sated to care. This man had sacrificed everything for her and their family, surrendering his soul to the abyss to save them. How could she not love him?

She snuggled against him when he rolled over and took her with him. When Marius laid behind her, rubbing her shoulders and kissing her neck, she realized she could definitely get used to this. She no longer worried about having to move to Romania. She'd follow these shifters to the moon.

NEVER HAD EILEA FELT more alive. Howling at the moon, she ran with her mates through the silver-lined darkness, jumping over logs and rocks and tumbling playfully with her pack. Her tail was in constant movement until they reached the small stream. They nuzzled each other and lapped up cool water.

Geri raised his snout with a low growl.

What is it? Jovan asked.

I smell something strange. Something dark.

Jovan turned up his nose. *I smell it, too.*

Let's get Eilea home, Boris thought. *We will come back and investigate.*

When they jumped over the stream, she prepared to follow but a strange cry caught her attention.

She pricked her ears. *Did you hear that?*

Her mates immediately rejoined her, their lips pulled back as they snarled at something upwind.

Geri whimpered, flattening his ears against his skull. *I knew I smelled something rotten.*

Another strange cry rent the air.

Boris and Jovan shifted from wolves to protectors.

Clenching his hands into fists, Boris scented the air. *What the hell is that?*

Marius pressed against Eilea.

Geri's snout wrinkled. *It smells like a human corpse.*

Whatever it is, it's not dead, Eilea thought. *I can hear it crying.*

Boris's eyes glowed like twin suns. *Stay here, Eilea.* He nodded to Geri. *We'll check it out.*

"Help me!" a voice cried.

It's an injured human! Eilea leapt ahead of her mates, running toward the sound.

Eilea, get back here! Boris boomed, but she refused to stop. Just because she was a shifter didn't mean she should forsake her oath and deny care to the sick. And it sure as hell didn't mean she was beholden to her mates. They'd learn soon enough she followed no man's orders.

Stop! Jovan hollered.

And she did, but not because he'd told her to. She'd nearly barreled head first into the vilest creature she'd ever seen.

Howling, she retreated, slipping on what she thought was moss but turned out to be a trail of green ooze. What the hell was that thing?

The creature crouched on its haunches, one eye socket an empty bloody cavity and the other attached to an eye that dangled by its nose. Its claws resembled a badger's, bones like daggers protruded from its spine, and it was naked, dirty, and stunk to high heaven.

When she barked at it, it flinched, curling inward.

Get away from it! Jovan roared, jumping between her and the creature.

Shielding its grotesque face with its hands, the beast whimpered.

It's injured, she thought. *I need to help it.*

No! Boris boomed. *You will not touch it.*

It smells familiar, Marius thought.

Geri pulled back his lips in a snarl. *It's the quallu.*

Jimmy? Eilea let out a low whine. *No. That thing doesn't look like Jimmy.*

The creature let out a pitiful wail, sobbing into his hands.

Eilea's heart gave a tug. *I have to heal him.*

No, Eilea. Scowling at her, Boris pointed in the other direction. *Marius and Jovan will take you home. Do not disobey me.*

She stiffened, indignation flooding through her. *Now you listen here, you big beast. I'm a goddamn doctor, and you will not prevent me from healing the sick.*

We will take care of him, he said. *Now go.*

By taking care of him, you mean snapping his neck? Boris's eyes shifted from blue to white, and he released a deep groan. *You have a lot to learn about our kind, Eilea. Protectors make the final decision when it comes to the pack's safety.*

Not anymore, she huffed, slipping between Jovan's legs and leaping toward the pitiful creature.

No! Jovan hollered, grabbing her tail.

She yelped when he tugged her too hard, looking back at him with a snarl.

An ominous howl filled her eardrums, and the creature knocked her to the ground so hard, her head spun. He sank his teeth into her neck before she could react.

What the hell, dude? I was trying to help you.

Jovan kicked the beast off her. Squealing, it flew through the air.

Eilea looked up in time to see Jovan and Boris rip the beast to shreds, popping off his head and all four limbs.

She tried to sit up, but she was paralyzed by a burning pain. Had that fucker had rabies?

She shifted into her human skin, clutching her neck as blood flowed.

Geri shifted and dropped down beside her. "Eilea!"

Ouch. He was too loud, sounding like a thousand cymbals banging in her ears. "Keep your voice down," she tried to tell him, but all that came out was a howl.

What the fuck?

"Get Amara," Jovan boomed. "Hurry!"

She heard the shuffle of paws before Jovan fell beside her, rattling the ground with his heavy protector frame.

"Stay with us, Eilea," Jovan cried.

Why was he crying?

She curled into herself, unable to bear the liquid fire burning through her. She'd never felt such agonizing pain. Holding her hand against the wound, she tried to summon her healing spell, but she couldn't remember it.

JOVAN PRESSED HIS RABID mate against a tree, pinning her arms with one hand and holding tightly to her jowls with the other. She howled and thrashed, trying to rip open his arms with her sharp claws.

"I don't know how much longer we can hold her," Boris grunted, trying to hold down her legs. "She's so strong."

"Do not let go, Boris!" Jovan roared, narrowly dodging the venom that dripped from his mate's fangs. "Do you hear me? We're not losing her."

Geri and Marius ran back, panting.

Amara's coming! Geri pointed to the headlights flickering in the distance.

Jovan howled. "Thank the Ancients."

"How did she get here so fast?" Boris asked.

She saw the attack in a vision, Geri answered.

Time seemed to slow to a crawl as their daughter and her mates sprinted up the incline.

"Fathers!" she cried. "I'm coming."

"Amara, wait." Hakon dug his fingers into her arm.

Jovan said, "I will not let her hurt our daughter. Hurry, before it's too late!"

Hakon refused to release her. "Are you prepared to kill Eilea if she tries to harm Amara?"

"It won't come to that, Hakon," Boris snapped.

No, it wouldn't, Jovan thought. He wouldn't let Eilea kill his daughter, but if Eilea died, he wouldn't let her go into the afterworld alone.

"Please let her help." Boris grunted when Eilea thrashed like a fish out of water, kicking him in the shin. "Please."

Holding tight to Amara, Hakon moved forward, guarding her while she placed a hand on Eilea's arm.

Eilea let out an ear-splitting howl, chest heaving, and fought Amara's touch. Amara closed her eyes, shoulders relaxing as she focused on Eilea.

Eilea's breathing slowed, and her crooked snout and dagger-like claws retracted. After she morphed back into a human, she fell into Jovan's arms, blinking at him in a daze.

"Jovan?" she asked. "What happened?"

"You were turned into a werewolf," Jovan said, the fear in his heart replaced with a dull, heavy ache.

Her mouth fell open. "I was?" She wiped moisture from his eye. "Were you crying?"

Suddenly too choked up to answer, he handed her to Boris and mouthed his thanks to Amara. Then he turned on his heel and stormed away.

"Jovan, wait!" Eilea called, but he refused to turn back.

He was too distraught and angry to talk. He'd almost lost his mate, letting her slip between his legs like a fool. His delayed reaction could've cost Eilea her life. What kind of protector was he?

EILEA FOLLOWED HER mates back to the house, tail tucked between her legs. Why had Jovan left her?

As soon as they reached the house, she shifted and let Marius help her into the shower. She washed off dried blood and the foul smell of the creature that'd attacked her. At least she knew Jimmy's fate. He'd obviously been bitten by a werewolf and turned into the human equivalent. She remembered seeing his severed body parts strewn across the forest floor. He'd been a quallu, but she wouldn't wish that kind of death on anyone.

After she showered, she gladly took a glass of wine from Marius, thanking him with a kiss, grateful when he didn't scold her for putting her life in danger. She probably deserved a scolding, though. Thrust into their magical world, she thought she could live by human rules. Nope. That was a hard lesson to learn. And a painful one. Next time her protectors told her to stand back, she sure as hell was going to listen.

She sat at a table with Marius, sipping her wine in silence, the unspoken words between them as thick as soup.

"Where are the others?" she asked.

"Boris and Geri went back to clean up the mess, and Jovan is outside."

She looked out the window, seeing only the silhouettes of tall pines illuminated by the faint light of the moon. "I'm going to find Jovan," she said, touching his soft cheek. "I'll be right back."

He grabbed her hand and sighed. "We almost lost you, lubirea mea."

She hung her head. "I know, and it won't happen again. I've learned my lesson."

"Good."

She gave him a kiss, then put on a jacket and went outside.

Jovan sat on the porch steps in human form, staring into an empty beer bottle. He wore tight jeans that clung to a round ass, making her lady parts spring to life. His wrinkled flannel shirt was only buttoned at the bottom, as if clothes had been an afterthought.

She sat beside him, trying not to feel hurt when he turned away. "Jovan, I'm sorry I didn't listen." She waited for him to answer, her heart plummeting when he simply stared at the waxing moon overhead. Taking a chance, she settled a hand on his forearm. "Jovan, please."

He tossed the empty bottle in the bushes. "I didn't reach Katarina in time." Staring straight ahead, his voice was devoid of emotion. "That's why she died."

"Her death was not your fault." She squeezed his arm, feeling ten shades of dog shit for refusing to heed her protectors' warnings. "She knew better than to leave the safety of the reservation."

He turned on her with such a harsh look, a lesser woman would've cowered. "What's the difference between what she did and what you did? You almost died, Eilea, and it would've been my fault." Shaking her off, he stood and moved to the end of the porch.

Following his retreat, she refused to give up. She would not end their honeymoon night with her mate resenting her. "But you saved me. You held me down until Amara healed me."

"Amara might not be there for you next time." He gazed at the sky, mumbling something about hard-headed females under his breath. "We're not trying to dominate you, Eilea. We just want to keep you safe."

She leaned into him. "I know that now."

A mixture of emotions crossed his features. His shoulders caving inward, as if he'd finally given up carrying the weight of the world. "Do you?"

"Yes, Jovan. I swear. I won't ignore your warnings again. Thank you for saving me."

He smiled. "You don't need to thank me for doing my job."

"Yes, I do." She feathered a soft kiss across his lips.

He responded with a groan, deepening the kiss and dragging her against his hard planes.

"Make love to me," she said.

"Here?"

"Yes, please." She ripped his shirt open and dragged her nails down his exposed skin.

"I don't think I can be gentle."

His ominous warning turned the slow drip in her underwear to a steady stream. "I don't want you to be."

He tore off her clothes, and she gasped when he exposed her breasts to the elements, nipples hardening to twin pebbles. When a shiver wracked her, he pushed her against the wall, covering her with his heat.

After hastily pulling his erection out, he hoisted her in his arms, and she wrapped her legs around his waist. He kissed her roughly, chafing her exposed nipples with the hair on his chest.

Probing her pussy with a thick finger, he let out a deep, sinister chuckle. "You're so wet, lubirea mea."

She cupped his cheeks in her hands. "Better for you to fuck me with, my big bad wolf."

He took her up against the wall with no preliminaries. She gasped at the jarring pain, clinging to him as he fucked her into oblivion.

She cried out his name when she came, driven into multiple orgasms by the frenzy by his passion. "Jovan!" she screamed. "Oh, please, oh, please." She didn't know why she was begging or what she wanted. She only knew this was so intense, she never wanted it to end.

He panted into her mouth while he burst inside her, throbbing so hard, she didn't know if the pulses were coming from her or him.

She was abruptly aware of her bare toes, that she was cold, and she shivered again. He kissed her more tenderly, then carried her into the house with her still impaled on his cock. He laid her on the bed and tenderly made love to her. Soon his brothers joined them, and they fucked well into the morning.

Epilogue

EILEA DRAGGED HERSELF into the kitchen, with Jovan, who'd been her assistant for the day, following her.

"Dinner's ready," Marius said, setting a platter of barbeque on the table.

"Thank the Ancients. I'm famished." Marius knew how much she missed her uncle's cooking. Lately he'd been recreating her favorite recipes, including his cornbread and pulled pork.

She and her mates sat around the table and ate. Boris glanced at the four empty seats at the opposite end of the long table. His sons had been coming in later and later each night, and some nights not coming home at all. They spent too much time at the pub, drowning their sorrows. Tatiana still refused to commit to a bonding date.

"Have a busy day today?" Marius asked as he poured her a glass of wine.

She added a generous amount of butter and honey to her cornbread. "Mended two broken bones and delivered a baby." She clasped Marius's hand. "Have I told you lately how much I love you?"

He chuckled. "Every day, and I never tire of it. I love you more than life, Eilea. I thank the Ancients every day for you."

"We all do," her other mates chimed in unison.

She looked at them from under her lashes. With the exception of her brooding stepsons, and the occasional sneers from her mates' former in-laws, life in Romania had been idyllic. "Do you?"

"Da." Geri set down his utensils, giving her a look so intense, it made her gooseflesh rise. "They couldn't have matched us with a more perfect mate."

"Ditto. Perfect mates in the kitchen"—she gave them a sideways smile—"and in bed."

They gazed at her like she was a choice cut of prime beef. She gulped her wine, not caring that it went to her head. Her mates were in a kinky sex kind of mood. Hopefully they'd break out the handcuffs and blindfold. She loved playing the game where she guessed who was fucking her. If she got it right, she was rewarded with an intense orgasm. If she got it wrong, she was punished with a lot more spanking, teasing, and delayed climax. Honestly, she preferred to be wrong most of the time.

After dinner, they sat around the fireplace, ignoring the television that hadn't been turned on in weeks.

"Come sit." Boris patted his lap. "Tell us about this baby."

She sat on his lap, grinding her bottom into his growing erection. "He was her third, so it was easy."

Boris arched an eyebrow. "For you or for her?"

"For both of us." She laughed. "But not for her mates. They were nervous wrecks."

Marius held up a hand. "I was nervous when our sons were born."

"Were you?" She wasn't shocked. Marius was the most sensitive of her mates.

"Da. I've been worried about those boys ever since. They languish, waiting for their mate."

She nodded in sympathy, regretting going down that rabbit hole. Their boys had been a source of consternation lately, snapping at each other over the slightest things. Eilea knew their edges would soften as soon as they bonded with Tatiana.

"Give Tatiana some time," she said. "She'll come around."

"I hope so," Geri said, dragging a hand through his hair.

A strange feeling came over her. Gripping her gut, she looked between her legs. What the hell was that?

Boris tensed under her. "What is it?"

Panic made her heart flutter. "I felt the oddest sensation, like a flower blooming inside me."

He stared at her a long moment, a tic in his jaw. "Eilea"—he enunciated each word—"your womb is ready."

Realization dawned. Holy fuck! "Is it?"

He inclined his head toward the bedroom. "If you want, we can make a child."

She looked at her mates, who were staring at her with a deer-in-the-headlights expression.

"N-Now?" she stammered.

"Da. I'm not sure when or if we'll have another chance."

Grabbing his hand, she placed it on her womb. "And you want this?"

He settled his other hand over hers, squeezing. "For you to have our son? Nothing would make me happier but know that it would be unfair to bring an only shifter into the world. Are you prepared to give him a pack of brothers and a sister?"

Her breath caught in her throat. One son for each of them, plus a girl. Five kids. Five beautiful bi-racial American/Romanian wolf shifters. Was that what she wanted? She thought back to her sad childhood, her lonely bedroom, evenings spent alone while her grandmother slept in her chair. Losing her brother and parents had been the most miserable experience of her life. Now she had the chance at another family, a big one, a house full of playful, happy children, and she knew without a doubt that was exactly what she wanted.

"Yes. Yes," she cried. "I want this. *All* of this."

Her mates howled their joy.

A wolfish smile split Boris's face. "Then you shall have it."

THE END

Dear readers, I hope you are enjoying my Amaroki as much as I love writing about them. If you could, please leave a review where you purchased this book. Your reviews help other readers find my books, so indie authors like me can keep writing. I don't care if it's short and simple. All that matters is that you leave a review. Thanks so much!

In the meantime, enjoy a sample from my completed fun and naughty PNR series, Eternally Yours. Book one, Divine and Dateless, won the eFestival of Words Best Romance. Book two won the Coffee Time Romance Book of the Year. I promise plenty of panty-melting fun.

Be looking for Annie's story, Fighting for Her Wolves in June, 2019. Please subscribe to my newsletter at www.tarawest.com for updates. My newsletter subscribers get free downloads of a selection of my books.

Books by Tara West

Eternally Yours
Divine and Dateless
Damned and Desirable
Damned and Desperate
Demonic and Deserted
Dead and Delicious
Something More Series
Say When
Say Yes
Say Forever
Say Please
Say You Want Me
Say You Love Me
Say You Need Me
Dawn of the Dragon Queen Saga
Dragon Song
Dragon Storm
Whispers Series
Sophie's Secret
Don't Tell Mother
Krysta's Curse
Visions of the Witch
Sophie's Secret Crush
Witch Blood
Witch Hunt
Keepers of the Stones
Witch Flame, Prelude

Curse of the Ice Dragon, Book One
Spirit of the Sea Witch, Book Two
Scorn of the Sky Goddess, Book Three
Hungry for Her Wolves Series
Hungry for Her Wolves, Book One
Longing for Her Wolves, Book Two
Desperate for Her Wolves, Book Three

About Tara West

Tara West writes books about dragons, witches, and handsome heroes while eating chocolate, lots and lots of chocolate. She's willing to share her dragons, witches, and heroes. Keep your hands off her chocolate. A former high school English teacher, Tara is now a full-time writer and graphic artist. She enjoys spending time with her family, interacting with her fans, and fishing the Texas coast.

Awards include: Dragon Song, Grave Ellis 2015 Readers Choice Award, Favorite Fantasy Romance

Divine and Dateless, 2015 eFestival of Words, Best Romance

Damned and Desirable, 2014 Coffee Time Romance Book of the Year

Sophie's Secret, selected by The Duff and Paranormal V Activity movies and Wattpad recommended reading lists

Curse of the Ice Dragon, Best Action/Adventure 2013 eFestival of Words

Hang out with her on her Facebook fan page at: https://www.facebook.com/tarawestauthor

Or check out her website: www.tarawest.com

She loves to hear from her readers at: tara@tarawest.com

Made in the USA
Monee, IL
01 May 2021